praise for
the proper care and
maintenance of friendship

"[A] life-affirming novel...A happy reminder that life is all about taking risks." —*Publishers Weekly*

"This well-written contemporary buddy book contains plenty of depth...the premise of friends knowing you at times better than you want to admit makes for a strong tale." —*Midwest Book Review*

"Quirky, original, and startlingly refreshing, this is a novel about friends. It's a novel about risks. And it's a novel about dreams, what we thought they were and what we discover them to be... [Higgins is] gifted and talented...Great novel. Great reading. Great characters and plot." —TheReviewBroads.com

"Ms. Higgins has a sure-to-be hit on her hands in this, her first foray into mainstream women's literature. The first thing that was apparent to me was her astonishing story-telling capability, the second was her capacity to pull some deep emotions from me while reading...a heart-wrenching tale that will affect even the most stoic readers...a gracefully flowing narrative that will transport her readers from the most exotic of locations to the mundane of everyday life...an inspiring, heartwarming, and very emotional read." —GoodReads.com

One good friend
deserves another

ALSO BY LISA VERGE HIGGINS

The Proper Care and Maintenance of Friendship

One good friend deserves another

LISA VERGE HIGGINS

five
spot

NEW YORK BOSTON

Copyright © 2012 by Lisa Verge Higgins

5 Spot
Hachette Book Group
237 Park Avenue
New York, NY 10017

www.5-spot.com

Printed in the United States of America

RRD-C

First Edition: June 2012
10 9 8 7 6 5 4 3 2 1

5 Spot is an imprint of Grand Central Publishing.
The 5 Spot name and logo are trademarks of Hachette Book Group, Inc.

The publisher is not responsible for websites (or their content) that are not owned by the publisher.

Library of Congress Cataloging-in-Publication Data

Higgins, Lisa Verge.
One good friend deserves another / Lisa Verge Higgins—1st ed.
p. cm.

ISBN 978-1-4555-0030-7

1. Female friendship—Fiction. I. Title.
PS3558.I3576O54 2012
813'.54—dc23
2011029516

To Caitlin, Molly, and Maeve,
who fill my life with joy.

One good friend

deserves another

chapter one

There you are." Kelly burst through the door. "Come on, Dhara. We have to get you out of here."

With a ringing of bangles, Dhara Pitalia turned to face one of her oldest and dearest friends. Kelly stopped before her, weaving on heels much higher than the little redhead was used to wearing. Her face, reflected in the dozens of mirrors in the vanity room, was tight with concern.

Dhara bowed her head, feeling the slow sinking of her hopes. She supposed she deserved being ambushed in the hotel bathroom like this. She'd just assumed that Kelly would have the good sense not to pin her down today. Not while two hundred and thirty-one members of the Pitalia and Bohara clans celebrated her engagement in the banquet room down the hall.

"I meant to tell you earlier, Kelly." Dhara plucked at the folds of her sari. "I really did."

"Oh, God." Kelly clutched Dhara's hand, crushing a stack of rings. "We couldn't believe it when we got the invite. We thought it was a joke. Then Wendy called the hotel and found out it *wasn't*."

"His name," Dhara said softly, "is Sudesh Bohara."

"I know. I read the placard in the hotel lobby just like everyone else." Kelly let go of Dhara's hand and wobbled on her heels to the door. "We can't believe you're being forced into marriage."

Dhara flinched and swayed back against the countertop. She understood Kelly's concern, she really did. Wendy, Kelly, and Marta were part of that other world, the American world, the one she'd had one foot firmly planted in her whole life. This was why she'd dodged their emails, texts, and phone calls all week. To explain to them the painful route her heart had taken to get her here—wrapped in a silk sari, draped in gold jewelry, and about to perform an ancient Hindu engagement ceremony—would take more than a few minutes locked in a hotel bathroom.

"Sudesh," Dhara said, his name strange on her lips, "is the son of one of my father's business associates."

"I know. I spoke to your cousin Ravi. He told me you met him only last week."

Dhara had met Sudesh ten days ago. She'd been seated on a couch in a pink sari in the lobby of this very hotel. She'd watched him discreetly while their parents worked out the details of the arrangement.

She tried to gauge the kind of man he was by the way he folded his hands.

"I want to hear the whole barbaric story, in gritty detail, over a rum and coke," Kelly said. "But first, we have to get you out of here."

"But it's almost time for the Ganesh *pooja*."

"It's all planned. Marta is keeping an eye on the hallway so we don't attract any attention." Kelly squinted out the crack of the door. "She says it's clear."

"After the *pooja* will be the exchange of rings."

"Then we better move fast. Wendy is already waiting in front of the hotel with the car running."

"If I leave before the ring ceremony, my parents will be publicly humiliated."

Kelly crossed the room in three quick steps. She stood so close that Dhara could smell cardamom and cloves on her breath.

"You know I adore your parents. You know I would never do anything to hurt them. But better they be humiliated now, than you spend the rest of your life sleeping with someone you don't love."

Dhara squeezed the counter until the edge bit into her palms. This was sweet, really it was. Her three best friends in the world, so concerned about her, had made arrangements to sweep her past hundreds of relatives into Wendy's Benz. Once there, Dhara supposed Wendy would deliver her to Kelly's nubby couch, where they would hide her from an army of Pitalias until she came to her senses and put a stop to the marriage whose future date would soon be determined by an Indian astrologer.

"Kelly," she said, her voice shaky. "Tell Wendy to park the car and come back to the party."

"Is there somewhere else you'd rather go?"

"Back to the hall, where all of my aunts are practicing their dance moves."

"Wendy said you'd resist." Kelly swiveled on a heel and began to pace. "She said this was a foolish idea. She said you're too attached to your family to play the runaway bride. But I remember that weekend, Dhara. I remember what you promised yourself."

Dhara's will withered. "That weekend" was such a defining moment in their friendship that all of them referred to it by no other name. It had been senior year, and the four of them had huddled together in their shared apartment—reeling from their own individual crises—resolutely making rules to forever protect their broken hearts.

Today, she broke Rule Number One.

Dhara took a deep breath and then gripped Kelly's arms to try to calm her. "I've warned you about the masala chai. How many cups have you had?"

"You're changing the subject."

"I am, because I know you don't want to hear what I have to say." She leaned in close enough for the jewel of her *maang tikka* to brush Kelly's forehead. "I'm not being forced into this. I'm marrying Sudesh Bohara willingly."

In the silence that followed, Dhara could hear the muffled sounds of her own engagement party drifting in from the hall—the Hindi chattering of her aunts and the shouts of her cousins as the DJ played the theme song of the latest Bollywood movie. Beyond that door lay the force of Indian custom, three thousand years of ancestral tradition. Inside this room, she faced the force of one determined Vassar girl.

"I don't understand." Kelly's face paled under her freckles. "Did you fall for him? Head over heels? So quickly?"

Dhara mustered a smile. Dear, romantic Kelly. While Dhara was in medical school, Kelly had teased her for not even noticing the fine young doctors Dhara spent her days with. Kelly knew better than anyone that she just wasn't the type to be swept off her feet. But Dhara supposed any explanation would make more sense than the idea that she might put her whole romantic future into the hands of her religious, tradition-bound parents.

"You swore you'd never let your parents choose your husband," Kelly said. "We were sitting in the Shakespeare Garden. You'd just dragged me to see that Karan Johar movie about the same thing. And now, all of a sudden..." Kelly's throat worked as she struggled to understand. "Admit it. This looks like some crazy kind of rebound."

Under eighteen feet of pleated sari, Dhara tensed. She dug her fingernails into Kelly's upper arms, willing her not to bring this up. "It's not a rebound. We've been apart for over a year."

"A year is nothing. If you include the decade you two knew each other as friends, then you were together practically forever."

Air hitched in Dhara's chest. Little thick bubbles of it, clogging the bronchi, making it impossible to inhale.

"I just can't come up with any other reason you'd do this. It must have something to do with Cole."

And at the sound of his name, Dhara's heart did a painful little roll. The cardiologist in her noted the arrhythmia, probably caused by a premature ventricular contraction overriding the sinoatrial node and compensated by a powerful subsequent contraction.

But the woman in her felt something different: a rushing ache, a yawning sense of loss.

Kelly said, "It's all right, Dhara. We all know you still love him."

⌒⌒

Kelly caught the flash of pain in her friend's kohl-rimmed eyes and found the proof she'd been searching for. Dhara was making the mistake of a lifetime. If there was one fundamental truth in the world, it was that Dhara Pitalia and Cole Jackson were truly, madly, deeply in love. When two people are in love, nothing should stand between them and happily ever after.

Kelly needed to believe that. With a fresh shiver of nerves, she thought of the hotel key card hidden deep in her purse. She needed to believe in a perfect world, today more than ever.

"Kelly, Kelly, you are so very sweet," Dhara murmured. "You're my fierce protector, come to save me."

"One word, and we're out that door."

Kelly didn't like the look on Dhara's face. Her friend was smiling. The trail of tiny jewels arching above her brows glittered in the fluorescent lights. But her friend's eyes were dry, and the expression in them apologetic.

"You must think I've gone utterly mad." Dhara lifted a length of coral chiffon, shot through with gold thread. "Here I am, dressed up like a village bride."

"Stop. I've seen you in saris before." Kelly had spent a good number of college vacations with the Pitalia clan, when she didn't have enough money for a bus ride back to Massachusetts. She'd attended family events dressed up in Dhara's saris, playfully sporting a *bindi* though she was an unmarried woman. "You look as glamorous as Vasundhara Das in *Monsoon Wedding*. As glamorous as you looked at our senior formal."

Kelly knew the memory would hit its mark. She suppressed a stab of guilt. It was her job to make Dhara see sense by any means. That's what friends did for each other. That's what they'd promised, ever since that weekend.

"Oh, Kelly, I know you believe that Cole and I belong together. A year and a half ago, I was so blind with love that I would have agreed with you."

"Then don't let your parents get in the way of your happiness."

"It's not about my parents. It hasn't been for a long time." Dhara worried her hands in the folds of her sari. "Think about it. When I finally brought Cole home to my family, I was thirty-five years old."

"Practically dead."

"You know that's ancient for an unmarried woman in my family. You know my sisters all married before me. I could have brought home a Punjabi Sikh from Kashmir, and my parents would have showered him with flower petals. By the time I worked up the courage to introduce Cole, they welcomed him."

Kelly shook her head. That piece of information never did fit in. For so many years, Dhara had resisted Cole precisely because she was afraid that her family would not accept a laid-back, Ultimate-Frisbee-playing boy from Oregon as a potential husband.

"If that were true," Kelly murmured, "we'd be celebrating your engagement to Cole right now."

"It's not that simple. Life is never that simple."

"It can be." Kelly thought of the key card again. "It *must* be. One phone call to Cole and you know he'll come. He'll sweep you right away from here. It'll be like the ending of that Mani Ratnam movie—"

"Kelly." Dhara ran a finger across her brow, wincing as if she had a headache. "Cole asked me to marry him last year."

Kelly started.

"I should have told you. I should have told *all* of you." Her chest rose and fell on a sigh. "I didn't, for a lot of really good reasons. But mostly because when he asked me to marry him, I said no."

Kelly stood numb, the words bouncing off her, as incomprehensible as the Hindi growing louder from the other side of the door. It wasn't true. It couldn't be true. She felt like she'd been caught by the crosscurrents at the Isle of Shoals in Gloucester Bay—a stretch of dangerous water her father never taught her how to navigate. She leaned forward, full of questions. But Dhara held up the flat of her palm, her bracelets jangling.

"I have to go now. They're looking for me."

Kelly recognized the voice of Dhara's mother, rising in alarm in the hallway.

"Be happy for me, Kelly." Dhara touched her arm. "Trust me. I know what I'm doing."

"Are you all right, Kelly?"

Kelly glanced up. In the mirror she watched Wendy Wainwright poke her head around the door and then sweep into the vanity room. Kelly suddenly realized that she hadn't moved from this spot since she'd heard the jingle of Dhara's ankle bells fade down the hall.

"Dhara's gone, Wendy." Kelly bent over the sink so she could dodge Wendy's eyes. "Somebody should go after her. We can't let her walk out on an intervention."

"Yes, we can. This was a very bad, very ill-timed idea." Wendy twisted Kelly's hair in one hand and lifted it off the back of her neck. "Promise me you won't pull this in September at my wedding."

"Why would I? You love your fiancé. You guys have been together so long it's like you're already married."

"Still. The extent to which you guys are willing to meddle makes me nervous."

"But Dhara and Cole belong together. I know it."

"You're working yourself up. And the air-conditioning in this place stinks. Come on, run some cold water over your wrists. Just try to breathe."

Kelly bent more deeply over the sink. Nothing made sense anymore. Her thoughts circled and short-circuited one another like a jury-rigged motherboard. She was the wrong friend to send on this job. She understood patterns, logic, and flowcharts. Amid the complications of human relations, she was a lumbering dolt.

Above all came this thought: If such a couple as Dhara

and Cole couldn't make it, then what possible hope did *she* have, with the mercurial man who'd just swept back into her life?

"Are you coming, Kelly?"

Wendy let go of Kelly's hair. As she twisted her string of pearls, Wendy waited for an answer to a question Kelly hadn't heard.

"Ahh ..."

"No way, Kell," Wendy interjected. "We might not approve of this engagement, but it'd be disrespectful to leave before the ceremony. Afterward, you can tell me and Marta exactly what happened." A line appeared between Wendy's brows. "In the meantime, we have to get back to the hall."

Kelly realized she'd been asked to join the party again. She also realized, as a redhead with a frightening tendency to faint in the heat, that she had a legitimate excuse to delay.

"It's like Bombay in that hall." Kelly flattened the wet palms of her hands against her cheeks. "You and Marta go on ahead. I've got to cool off. I'll catch up later."

Wendy's gaze narrowed, but then she nodded and headed out. As soon as the ladies' room door squealed shut, Kelly slipped into the other room and made a beeline to a stall. She locked the door and leaned up against it. Blindly she tucked her hand in the pocket of her purse and clutched the hotel key card so hard that the edges dug into her palm.

She was free now. Free to dance with Dhara's flirtatious cousin Ravi, free to stuff herself with tandoori chicken, free to join in the line dance from last week's showing of *My Name Is Khan* at the Bombay Cinema.

Free to go to *him*.

She squeezed her eyes shut. Her rational mind—the one that served her so well in the IT department where she worked—was screaming. She knew she shouldn't do this here, not now. It was dangerous. It was too soon to take the risk. If Wendy, Marta, or Dhara caught her with him, the intervention to follow wouldn't be a gentle version of lock-the-bride-in-the-bathroom. It'd be a full-blown screaming match that wouldn't end well.

Trey.

The edges of the card cut more deeply into her hand. Who was she kidding? She'd known she would go to him. She'd known the minute he'd slipped the key card in her pocket.

Kelly tucked her clutch under her arm and exited the bathroom. As she passed by the open doors of the banquet room, still throbbing with music, she caught a glimpse of Marta and Wendy but she didn't pause. She reached the main lobby and walked to the bank of elevators, pressed the UP button, and darted inside the first open one. The last thing Kelly saw as the elevator doors closed was the young clerk behind the reservation counter bobbing to the Bolly-wood beat.

The eighth floor was blessedly empty. She slipped down a corridor and found the room. She ran the card through the slot and watched the light turn green. Just then, the door opened under her hand.

There he was, his brown eyes bright with mischief.

Tall, mussed, and shirtless.

And once again she was struck by the fact that she, little Kelly Palazzo from the North Shore, who spent every summer of her teenage years in rubber boots on a fish-stinking trawler, was an object of affection for this Princeton-educated scion of an old family whose smile stole her capacity to breathe.

Trey hauled her into his arms. "What took you so long?"

"Sorry I was delayed." Kelly dug her fingers into his shoulders. He smelled like clean, powdered starch. "I couldn't get away from your sister."

⌒

"Where's Kelly?"

Wendy glanced around the hotel lobby, now swarming with guests saying good-bye. Mrs. Pitalia beamed beside her daughter. Even Mr. Pitalia—normally a quiet man who preferred the comfort of his own den—stood with his hands clasped behind his back, rocking, a beatific smile on his face. In this swirling, chaotic crowd of mostly dark-haired Pitalias and Boharas, redheaded Kelly should be easy to spot.

"I haven't seen her since she disappeared into the ladies' room with Dhara." Marta scrolled through her email as she slipped a wireless headset in her ear. "Maybe she left without us."

"She wouldn't have gone without telling me." Wendy worried her pearls with her fingers. "She never got a chance to tell us what happened in there."

"Poor kid. With this mess with Dhara and Cole, I guess she figures she lost her matchmaker magic." Marta dropped her phone into her purse and glanced up the street in search of a cab. "Hey, maybe she just bumped into Ravi—he's an engineer, right? They're probably so absorbed talking about the latest *Star Trek* movie that they forgot there was a party. Here's your car."

Wendy turned to see the sleek white Benz pull up in front of the hotel. She took the keys from the valet and slipped a bill into his hand. "Marta, you know I would drive you both—"

"Don't be silly. No sane woman would drive into Manhattan during rush hour." Marta tilted her head so one oversize gold hoop gleamed on her cheek. She gave Wendy a sly smile, showing off white teeth against bright red lipstick. "Unless, of course, you're determined to miss that appointment with the wedding planner?"

Wendy's stomach did one of those funny little drops, like it did sometimes on Parker's sailboat when they ventured into rougher seas. It was silly to worry about a meeting that would revolve around world-rocking issues like whether to fill the table vases with river stones or glass beads. Silly to worry about it, even though tonight she was determined to confront her mother about her sister Birdie.

The sight of a familiar silhouette saved her from responding. "Ah, here's my brother."

Marta lit up. "Trey! Where have you been hiding?"

"Dancing with one of Dhara's gorgeous cousins." Trey sauntered over and leaned down for Marta's airy, double-cheek kiss. "Missed you, Marta. We could have shown them how it's done."

"Oh, how sweet, you," Marta said, and then gave him a playful slap that would probably leave a mark. "It's *such* a pity you're a player."

Trey's smile widened as he rubbed his cheek. "Know a hot Latino who can settle me down?"

"Latin*a*, baby, *Latina*." Marta gave him a wicked smile. "Unless there's something you want to get out of the closet . . . ?"

"You know me better, *chica*."

Wendy resisted the urge to roll her eyes. Since the ugliness with Kelly all those years ago, she'd spent most of her adult life keeping her older brother, Jeremiah "Trey" Warner Wainwright III, clear of her friends. The patter that sounded so banal to her seemed to work wonders with an alarmingly wide range of intelligent women. Even worldly-wise Marta came to life in Trey's presence, but Wendy knew Marta understood his type.

"Come on, Trey." Wendy swung around to the driver's side. "Bitsy's waiting for us at the club, and I'd like to get there before her third gin and tonic. You'll take care of Kelly, Marta?"

"Don't you worry. I'll find our disillusioned friend and share a cab with her back to the city." Marta gave her a sassy wink. "Have fun picking out wedding favors."

Marta headed back into the hotel as Trey slipped into the car. He flung the jacket of his Savile Row suit in the backseat.

Wendy slipped the car into gear and said, "Next time, I'm making you take the train."

"What?"

She reached over and tugged the Egyptian cotton of his Oxford shirt. "Your shirt is buttoned wrong."

"The dance floor was packed. I unbuttoned to cool off."

"You *stink* of sex."

"That's sweat." He gripped his collar and buried his face in the cloth.

"Trey, I asked you to meet me here for *convenience*. So I wouldn't spend two and a half hours trying to fetch you out of the bowels of Manhattan. I did *not* ask you here so you could cause trouble at Dhara's engagement party." Wendy felt her temper rising. "And just because your driver's license is suspended doesn't mean I have to be responsible for driving you upstate every weekend."

"Relax, relax!"

"Just convince me," she said, as she turned into traffic, "that you didn't hook up with any of Dhara's cousins."

"Hey, I don't 'hook up' with your friends anymore." He fumbled with the buttons. "Ancient friggin' history, Wendy."

Wendy's jaw tightened. He was right, of course. The thing with Kelly was a long time ago. And he'd made his apologies back then, as best he could after the emotional damage was done. But Trey's screwups were frequent and had a very predictable cycle: he'd do something stupid and then spend an inordinate amount of time flailing about, looking for ways to patch things up.

Problem was, a fragile woman's heart just couldn't be made new again.

"So," Trey said, settling back in the leather seat, "it's finally getting to you."

"What?"

"You know, Bitsy's plan to make your wedding the Event of the Millennium."

Wendy's grip tightened on the steering wheel. She would have closed her eyes, if she weren't weaving through rush-hour traffic. "Mom's heart is in the right place," she said. "But you'd think, if you hired a Manhattan wedding planner to coordinate an event, that the wedding planner would make most of these decisions *for* us."

"As if Bitsy would let that happen."

"Dhara got engaged only a week ago," she said, "yet her parents managed to throw together a party for two hundred relatives."

"Balloons, Wendy. There were balloons."

"They called a relative who manages the hotel, and they had a hall. They called another family friend who catered the food. They hired a DJ who was a member of the family. Voilà, a party."

"Right, I can just see Bitsy eating lamb curry with a plastic spork."

"No sixteen-piece band, no harpist at the cocktail party, no—"

"My dear," he said, imitating their mother right down to the cadence of her speech, "that's just the way things are *done*."

Yes, Wendy thought, that was the way things were done with the Parkers and the Wainwrights and the Livingstons of Westchester County, that's the way it had been done for generations, and so that was the way it was going to be done now and for all generations going forward, like a succession of rogue waves battering each bewildered young couple.

Poor little rich girl.

Wendy cleared her throat to cover up a humorless laugh. Poor little Wendy with her rich-girl problems. What she really needed was perspective: There were much worse wedding situations than hers. Dhara, for example. Agreeing, for reasons Wendy still couldn't fathom, to marry an utter stranger.

Wendy wasn't marrying a stranger. She was the luckiest woman in the world. In three months, she'd be married to Parker Pryce-Weston.

An hour later, when she pulled up the long drive to the Briarcliff Country Club, she glimpsed Parker leaning against one of the Corinthian columns that flanked the entrance. His blond hair made him instantly recognizable, bleached a shade short of white by weekends spent sailing the Long Island Sound. The moment the Benz rounded the long, curved driveway, a sexy Mario Lopez dimple deepened in his cheek.

She stepped out of the car and tossed the keys to the valet. Trey vaulted up the steps. "Hey, bro. Get in any sailing today?"

"Nah. Worked all day."

"Parker Senior's a taskmaster, eh?"

"Hey, at least I'm not in the mailroom anymore."

"Yeah, I hear you. Listen, I've got to shower and change." Trey tripped backward toward the door. "See you later for a drink?"

"Count on it."

Parker watched Wendy come up the stairs. He held his drink with cocksure preppy confidence. He gave her that sideways little smile that always made her feel like he knew what she was thinking, and knew better than to ask.

"Hey, you," she said, raising her face for a kiss.

"Hey, beautiful."

He tasted like breath mints and lime. His hand stretched across the small of her back, comfortably familiar.

"You shouldn't let Trey bait you," he murmured. "You know it only pisses you off."

"I believe that's his mission in life." She noticed that the sunburn on his forehead and forearms was just starting to darken. "I suppose they're waiting for me?"

"Bitsy just ordered number three." He guided her toward the doors. "Sorry I missed Dhara's party. I was looking forward to watching her aunt Indira rocking on the dance floor."

Wendy smiled. Parker had attended a party Dhara's family had thrown after Dhara finished her medical residency. Inspired by the family's exuberance on the dance floor, he'd stripped off his tie with admirable abandon and joined them. It had been one of their first dates.

"It was fantastically chaotic," she admitted, as she stepped into the high-ceilinged lobby, where natural light spread down from a skylight in the cupola. "And, as unbelievable as this sounds, the marriage really *has* been arranged by her parents."

Then Wendy stiffened as she saw a tennis foursome blocking the path between the lobby and the yellow parlor. As they turned with pleasant smiles, she braced herself for the battering of small talk, curious questions, and embarrassing advice that her and Parker's presence always seemed to elicit.

But then Parker—perceptive Parker—gently took her arm and propelled her forward, smiling at everyone but not slowing their pace, nodding and making excuses until they'd passed through the gauntlet.

"You know," he said, his voice rippling with amusement once they were out of earshot. "You and I could always just skip out of here and get married on the sly." He leaned into her. "We'd tell them we were going out on a date. No one would know we were missing for days."

"Yes, but as soon as we got back, my mother would continue with the wedding plans as if nothing had occurred."

"Your mother is a force of nature. But you'll sail through the storm."

"Well, brace yourself tonight." Wendy heard her mother's voice, drifting from the open doors of the yellow parlor. "I'm going to talk about Birdie."

"Right now?" Parker stopped a few paces from the door and gave her an odd look. "Sure you want to do that?"

"I can't put it off much longer or the seating arrangements will be written in stone. I'm just glad you're here—"

"*Here* are the lovebirds."

Wendy started. Bitsy appeared at the door of the parlor, striding forcefully toward them.

"We've been waiting for you, my dear." Bitsy brushed her smooth cheek against Wendy's. Her hair, a mix of blond and white, was drawn back in a sleek ponytail. "Traffic bad?"

"Terrible." Wendy loosened her grip on Parker's arm and gave him a *here we go* look. "We sat on the Whitestone Bridge for half an hour."

Her mother's gaze lingered for a moment on Wendy's right ear, and Wendy realized she'd forgotten to remove the pewter stud in her cartilage piercing. It was only the second piercing in that ear, the other four having closed up long ago. Her mother liked to call that piercing Wendy's "last little eccentricity." Wendy remembered well her mother's reaction when she came home with it.

Honestly, my dear, I'm a little relieved. Every Livingston has an eccentricity. At least you didn't run off to join a polygamous cult in Utah like your cousin Beth.

Bitsy raised a brow but said nothing aloud. Instead, she led Wendy into the parlor. "You remember Terry, of course?"

Wendy thrust her hand at the wedding planner. "Terry, so good of you to make the trip up here again."

"There is *so* much to be done." Terry slipped her reading glasses onto her nose as she settled down to consult her binder. "If you all don't mind, I'd like to skip the pleasantries for now and get right down to work."

Bitsy gave Wendy a wide-eyed look. *You know how these New Yorkers are.* "Very well then. Wendy, Terry was just showing me some fabulous ideas for the wedding favors..."

Wendy sat with her eyes glazing over as Terry flipped through a book of suggestions, elaborating on each one. Wendy couldn't help compare these engraved silver vases and cigar holders with the handcuffs she'd received at an artist friend's wedding last year, held in the basement of an East Village pub. The dress code for the ceremony was leather. The guest book was black canvas stretched across the back wall, finger-painted in red.

Nope, no painted miniatures of copulating stick figures for her wedding. It would probably be Tuscan candy dishes, if her mother's keen attention was any indication. They all talked about the candy dishes for a good fifteen minutes, until Parker finally quipped that they should definitely do the pottery—but keep it far from Uncle Tad. Everyone laughed, because Uncle Tad was a notorious imbiber and was best remembered for breaking a seventeenth-century Chinese vase at the Livingston-Randall wedding thirteen years ago.

Wendy joined the laughter, because if she smiled along with everyone else, then the first issue of the evening would finally be resolved.

Her mother moved quickly to another topic—what to do with the children invited to the wedding. Wendy's smile froze. She and her mother had already "discussed" this issue, and Wendy had made her intentions quite clear. Many of her and Parker's friends had beaten them to the altar, and several already had babies and toddlers. Wendy wanted *all* of them there, milling about in their joyous chaos, just like the swarm of dark-haired young Pitalias and Boharas at Dhara's engagement party, racing around the hotel ballroom like pods of mackerel, weaving and changing direction in silvery unison.

Parker squeezed her hand. She jumped a little and realized she must have grunted.

"Mother," she said, feeling like an actress who'd just been prompted for her line. "As we discussed, we can ask the club for the use of one of the parlors. We can hire a few babysitters, have some games. The children can join us for the meal. It's as simple as that."

"I suppose that would work." Bitsy gave her a high-browed look. "If you continue to insist, that is."

"I *do* insist."

There, she'd violated the unwritten WASP code of expressing strong feelings, and in the parlor, there descended a moment of acute discomfort. The wedding planner must have sensed the sudden stillness, for she lifted her face from the ink-splattered page of her planning book and her gaze traveled between the two women, her pen poised above the page.

Well, my little Birdie, Wendy thought, it's now or never.

"While we're on the subject," Wendy said, corralling her courage, "there's something else—"

"Excuse me, ladies."

Parker squeezed her hand painfully. Startled, she glanced at him as he rose from the chair.

"I'm going to leave you to your plotting and scheming." He gestured vaguely to the parlor door and beyond, to the smoking room. "My future brother-in-law is saving me a stool at the bar."

Before Wendy could react, Parker dropped a quick kiss on her head and strode toward the door. She sat stunned, watching him leave the room. Then, ignoring her mother's elevated brows and the planner's curious look, Wendy stood up to follow him.

She ran into him just outside the door.

"I've been thinking about this, Wendy," Parker said, shoving his hands into his pockets. "And I disagree with you about Birdie."

She shook her head, not understanding. Parker knew how much this meant to her. She could do without the sex-toy wedding favors, the black strobe lights, and the techno-punk band.

But there was no way she was getting married without Birdie.

"Your sister," he said, "just doesn't belong at our wedding."

⌒

Marta ushered Kelly into the cab and then squeezed in after her, addressing the cabbie before Kelly could.

"Take the Fifty-ninth Street Bridge," Marta said, pressing the screen on the back of the seat to mute the voice urging her to buckle up. "Then go to Fifty-sixth and Eighth."

"No, no, your apartment is closer." Kelly sat in the corner of the cab, her hands white on her clutch. "Have him drop you off at Tudor City first."

"I'm not going home yet." Marta slipped her oversize bag off her lap and let it jangle on the seat between them. "I'm visiting Carlos at the restaurant, so it just makes sense to drop you off first."

It was a little white lie, but it worked, and Marta watched Kelly succumb to the edgy silence in which Marta had found her, toying with the ribbon of a balloon in the corner of the ballroom. Kelly had been flushed and sweaty. Marta had done a quick scan of the hall, hoping some hunky Bohara might be responsible for Kelly's disheveled state, but Kelly was most definitely alone.

Marta nudged her shoulder, trying physically to knock her out of her mood. "Stop thinking about Dhara, Kelly. We'll drag her out for lunch next week." *If I can squeeze that in, with that IPO looming.* "We'll slip some gin into her ginger ale, and she'll spill the whole story. We've got some time. The wedding date isn't set yet. Her sister said something about the astrologer looking at dates in the fall, so the family can fly over some relatives from India."

Kelly glanced at her, blankly, and it was as if the girl were waking from a deep sleep.

"Isn't it weird, though, how happy she seemed?" Marta glanced out the window. Under the elevated railway, the storefronts changed from Hindu newsstands to Greek diners to Spanish bodegas. "Maybe Dhara knows something we don't. In some ways, this arranged marriage idea is smart. It's efficient. You make the decision, and boom, it's done."

Kelly blew out an exasperated sigh. "Marta, she's not shopping for the perfect sweater. She's choosing her *husband.*

And you don't agree to an arranged marriage because you're thirty-seven and you think it's time."

"We've all got biological clocks, and they're tick-tick-ticking."

"You marry for love. Period."

At the look on her friend's determined face, Marta felt a familiar stab of worry. It was charming, in a way, that a woman Kelly's age could still believe in something as slippery and romantic as true love. The problem was that the belief seemed to keep Kelly from getting involved with *anyone*. Kelly—always waiting for the Big Thing—might miss the love boat altogether if she didn't open herself up to possibilities.

"Hey," Marta said, "what ever happened to that guy you work with, the one who keeps bugging you to go out for coffee?"

Kelly frowned. "Lee?"

"Yeah, that Chinese guy, the one with the fabulous hair."

"Marta," Kelly said, in full you've-got-to-be-kidding-me mode, "I *work* with him every day."

"I know. That's the point." Sometimes trying to get Kelly to pick up on social cues was like trying to explain intellectual property law to a thirteen-year-old hacker. "I mean, he's a computer genius too. That raises the chances that he'll have a collection of Lego action figures like yours, you know what I'm saying?"

"He's a *Star Trek: The Next Generation* fan."

"Yeah?"

"I'm a fan of the original series." She stared at Marta, waiting for her to make some connection. "Oil . . . water?"

"Oh, please."

"Hey, in the geek world, this stuff matters."

"C'mon, Kelly. Take Lee up on that invitation. For me, okay? Believe me, you never know what can happen over coffee."

It was over a cup of sweet, foamy *café Cubano* that Marta had first met Carlos. He'd been serving it to her, all six-foot-three-inches of him, while she was dining with clients at a chic little restaurant in the Village. The look he gave her with those black eyes was hotter than the sweet espresso. Her thighs had reacted instantly, going quivery and warm—oh, she'd been working so hard, and it had been so very *long* since she'd had a sweaty bout of sex—but she'd promised the girls and swore to herself to guard her heart carefully and never to get involved in meaningless and unhealthy hookups with baristas, waiters, and struggling actors.

And anything with Carlos would have been meaningless, because she'd already passed the point in her Life Plan—first written when she was nine years old—when it was time to find an appropriate husband. For a law associate on her last chance for partnership in a white-shoe law firm, waiters were definitely *not* husband material.

It was a week later, when Carlos served her another *café Cubano*—this time buck naked among the sweaty sheets of her king-size bed—when he boasted he was about to quit waiting tables at Cuba Libre to open a restaurant of his own. Wrapped in satin sheets, Marta had felt a moment of triumphant relief. Now she didn't have to put on the mantilla and slink off to confess to the girls that she'd sheepishly slept with a hot waiter. She could tell them she'd started a *relationship* with an *entrepreneur.*

"So?" Marta prompted, digging an elbow into Kelly's arm. "Are you going to take Lee up on the coffee date or what?"

"No promises, Marta." Kelly gazed at the Manhattan skyline as the cab rumbled over the Fifty-ninth Street Bridge. "He's just...Lee Zhao. There's nothing there."

"Sometimes with guys, it's a slow burn, you know what I'm saying? You never know, really, until you give them a try."

Kelly turned sullen eyes upon her. "Is that what it is for you and Carlos? You guys have been living together for what—a year and a half?"

"Sixteen months," she corrected. "Why? You going all Catholic on me?"

Instantly, an image rose in Marta's mind of her grandmother grasping the large gold medallion of the *Sagrado Corazón*, praying loudly to a legion of saints for intercession in the matter of her thirty-seven-year-old unmarried granddaughter, living in sin in Manhattan.

"Marta, don't you think something should have happened by now? Like meeting his mother in Miami?"

Marta stifled the urge to swear in Spanish. She was tired of having to explain that she worked at least sixty-five-hour weeks at Sachs, Offsyn & Reed. Her ambitious, sexy, entrepreneur boyfriend also spent seventy-hour weeks at his restaurant. By living together, they had a chance to see each other for a few hours before they both fell, exhausted, into bed. A trip to Miami to meet Carlos's family? Not so easy to arrange around the time bombs of her corporate calendar and Carlos's need to be on-site, all the time.

And as of two weeks ago, all those long hours had finally paid off. She and the girls had celebrated with mojitos in Carlos's trendy new restaurant, Café Havana. She was the granddaughter of Puerto Rican immigrants only a step out of the barrio—and now she was also a junior partner.

Junior partner!

Partner!

Sometimes, when she was in her office at night, breathing in the scent of paper and ink and Pine-Sol as the janitor cleaned the floors, she would listen to the thrumming hum of her laptop and the high-pitched whine of the fluorescent lights and just gaze out her tenth-floor window. She'd sit there taking in the long canyon view of Midtown—so very, very far from Washington Heights—and she'd feel such a thundering rush of glee that she'd leap up out of her chair and do a Sacred Heart basketball team victory dance all around the empty office.

"Marta, what are you grinning about?"

"It's your fault." Marta glanced at Kelly, knowing her face was hopelessly bright. "Now you've got me thinking about Carlos."

Carlos, whose sweet patience with her crazy schedule she would reward in abundance tonight. For now that she'd made partner—*mission accomplished*—she could turn her full attention to the next goal in her Life Plan.

Marriage.

After seeing Kelly off, Marta directed the cab driver to

go back across town to her Tudor City condo. She checked her phone but saw no message from him yet. Sometimes it took him hours to text her because he was so crazed in the kitchen. He was usually home by eleven on Sunday evenings, and it was barely seven thirty, which would give her time to prepare for his arrival. A leopard-print thong, she mused, and five-inch red stilettos. He always liked her to keep those on.

Once inside her apartment, she reflexively flipped the switch just inside the door, but the light didn't go on. She frowned up at the fixture, remembering that she'd asked Carlos to fix it.

Then she heard his laugh.

She glanced down the narrow hallway and saw the blue light spilling into the hall from the bedroom door, partially ajar. His wallet and keys lay on the hall table, and his cell phone blinked with notice of her text message. He must have come home early to do some work on his computer, she thought. She hoped nothing had gone wrong at the restaurant.

She went a little weak behind the knees. He was home already. They had a whole Sunday night—hours and *hours* of time. It seemed like months since they'd shared anything more than a quickie. With a growing sense of mischief, she shrugged off her suit jacket and laid it on the floor to muffle the sound of her purse as she set it on top. Flicking at the buttons of her crisp tailored blouse, she tiptoed down the hallway.

Then she heard a voice.

Marta froze. Her instincts bristled to high alert. All kinds of scenarios flooded her mind. She heard the voice again and realized that it sounded tinny, distorted, like it was coming through a speaker. Her relief was swift, but tinged with yet another suspicion. Carlos was video chatting. With a woman.

A cold, prickling sensation flooded her. Marta muffled her footsteps as she drew near enough to see him through the crack in the door. He was sitting at the desk with his back toward her. His laptop lay open. On the screen bobbed the image of a young girl, chattering in Cuban-tinged Spanish. Then the girl opened her mouth to display a missing front tooth.

The relief whistled out of her. She really was a distrustful little jerk. Here was poor Carlos, catching a moment to chat with his nieces and nephews in Miami, while she snuck around suspecting he was masturbating to the sight of that busty, twenty-two-year-old Staten Island waitress he'd recently hired.

Then a new face loomed into view. Marta pressed her palm hard against the doorframe. This was a young woman, with a shock of glossy black hair and the full, dewy skin of a girl not yet out of her twenties. The woman's eyes arced with humor as she gazed into the camera.

"See? Now you have to come home, *mi amor*." The woman pulled the child away from the camera and set her snugly on her lap. "You made a promise. And a father never goes back on his promises."

⌒ that weekend

Dhara waved good-bye to her parents, her smile fading as the car rumbled away from the Terrace Apartments. She slipped into building number nine and climbed the stairs to the shared living area.

They were all there, waiting for her, gathered around a coffee table littered with Chinese food containers. Kelly sat cross-legged, ignoring the three sheets of paper on her lap. Wendy stabbed at her lo mein with disinterest. Marta perched on the couch clutching a paper bag that bore the logo of the local pharmacy. Dhara felt a tremor of dread for Marta, for what she knew was inside.

Dhara kicked off her shoes; they all turned to her with stricken eyes.

Marta was the first to speak, skillfully cutting off any chance for Dhara to ask probing questions. "Dhara, that guy your parents brought with them today. He's not—"

"Yes, he is." Dhara sank into the chair with a broken spring. "You just met my potential bridegroom."

Wendy froze with her chopsticks in midair. "But your parents aren't—"

"Yes, they are. They can't wait to make arrangements for the wedding. Apparently, our astrological charts are well matched."

Dhara drew her knees in tight. Her parents had taken her by surprise, arriving for a visit with a young stranger in tow. At the sight of him, her stomach had dropped. Her mother had filled the sudden silence with chatter. Sanjay was in his second year of medical school, her mother said. He had an opportunity to take the weekend off. Surely Dhara would enjoy talking to someone who'd made it through the first difficult year, a boy she must remember from her cousin's wedding last summer.

Their eyes had brimmed with hope.

"Dhara!" Kelly leaned forward, her gaze incredulous. "You're not considering this, are you?"

She laid her cheek against her knees. The knocking noise of her parents' eleven-year-old Hyundai still rattled in her mind. Faded ink stained her mother's elegant fingers, a reminder of the part-time job her mother had taken in a dentist's office just to help pay Dhara's way through college. Now Dhara was about to graduate, and the time had come. In a moment alone, her mother had bubbled over with talk of silk saris and jeweled bangles and all the wonderful chaos of a Hindu wedding.

Dhara wanted all that. She really did. She would marry, someday. She'd just imagined that she'd marry a man she *loved*.

"My sister wants to marry," Dhara explained, "and it's tradition that I marry first. I told my mother I'm not ready. I told them to let her jump the queue."

Wendy exchanged looks with the girls and said, "But that means they'll try again soon."

"Yes."

"That's medieval," Marta added. "No offense, Dhara."

"None taken. The tradition is older than that, actually. But, right now, it's feeling pretty archaic to me, too."

"This sucks." Kelly hugged her own arms, though the room wasn't the least bit cold. "There should be rules about all of this."

"Yeah," Marta said. "And rule number one is a no-brainer: choose your own man."

An image rose in Dhara's mind of Cole, sprawled in a chair across from her at the library, absently thumbing the cleft in his chin. Cole, with his long hair combed back, tamed at the nape of his neck with a rawhide tie. Breathlessly beautiful Cole. Forbidden Cole.

Dhara's heart tightened. She loved her parents. She adored her whole sprawling family. She respected the Hindu traditions.

But in this, she was wholly American.

She would choose her *own* husband.

chapter two

From the moment Dhara was old enough to walk about town unattended, she and her girlfriends would spill out of Our Lady Queen of Martyrs and wander the sprawling business district, squealing over wedding saris displayed in the various shops. Gazing into the windows of the beauty salons, they argued over the henna designs, hair extensions, and head pendants draped over Styrofoam wig models, planning their own glorious weddings.

And now, as Dhara stepped out of the taxi in front of the Mysore Sari Emporium—one of the biggest sari shops in Jackson Heights—she realized that even thirty-seven-year-old cardiologists could still experience girlish thrills.

She slung her purse over her shoulder and pushed into the store, clanging the bells hung on a string. The place smelled of tandoori smoke from the next-door restaurant. She toed off her low-heeled shoes and lined them up on the shoe shelf, craning her neck in search of her mother.

The shop was the old-fashioned kind, a little taste of old Delhi in Queens. The store had no tables, only miles of shelves and cabinets along the walls. The cabinets with the most expensive saris were locked with tasseled keys. As she shuffled her way up the aisle toward a cluster of familiar figures, she noted with amusement that her mother had brought Dhara's aunts along on the hunt for the perfect wedding sari.

"Nisha, stop making the salesman pull the gold silks." Dhara's mother elbowed her younger sister as the salesman left to fetch more saris. "You know Dhara will wear red to the wedding."

"But she looks so *darling* in gold!" Nisha, the youngest of Dhara's aunts, looked like a Bollywood star just stepped off the screen, in a brilliant, turquoise sari. "And she won't need a sari just for her wedding, Roopa. She'll need one for the *Sangeet Sandhya,* and for the Mehndi ceremony and for after the wedding, when they come back to visit you as a couple."

Indira, Dhara's older aunt, gripped the price end of a sari and leaned into Dhara's mother. "Sixty-three per yard, Roopa, for this scratchy thing." Indira always looked as if she'd just taken a bite of a lemon. "Now the saris in Jhalini's shop—"

"Jhalani's shop doesn't have silks from Rajasthan," her mother countered, "nor Banaras brocades." Her mother turned as Dhara danced up behind her. "Ah, Dhara! You're finally here."

"So sorry—emergency at the hospital." Dhara folded into her mother's embrace, breathing in the scent of incense her mother burned every night in the hopes of a smooth wedding. "I see that you brought reinforcements."

"We wouldn't miss this for the world, darling. We've been waiting for it for a very long time." Nisha took Dhara's face in her hands and then frowned. "You look so tired! You need to get more sleep, to look your best for your new husband. A little kohl might help—"

"Leave the girl alone, Nisha," Indira said, pushing her aside. "She's a doctor. She has more important things to think about." Indira gave her a dry peck on the cheek and then whispered in her ear. "Talk some sense into your mother, Dhara. This place is—"

"Indira-*didi*." Her mother's voice was a warning. "You did not have to come."

"Of course I did. Do you think I let them do to you what these thieves did to me? Embroidering in silver rather than gold, and—"

"Oh, look, Roopa!" Nisha intercepted the returning salesman and pulled a length of muted gold silk from his arms. "Can you not see your daughter circling the sacred fires in this?"

"Nisha, really"—her mother gestured to a pile of red silks on the mattress—"it's red she's wearing. I don't know what you're thinking."

Dhara met Nisha's teasing gaze and suppressed a smile. Her mother and Nisha were often at loggerheads. Nisha was the kind of woman who shocked distant relatives by opting for cocktail dresses rather than saris at family events. During last year's *Diwali* celebration, instead of bringing *Kaju Pista* rolls as she was bidden, Nisha showed up at the house with a box of cannolis.

Dhara let the argument flow right over her. Once she'd made the decision to agree to an arranged marriage, it had been a relief to cede the details to her ecstatic and enthusiastic family.

"Have a seat, Dhara," her mother ordered, pulling at the various reds on the mattress. "Let us show you what we've found."

Dhara lowered herself to the padded white ticking. She probably should have worn jeans instead of coming directly from the hospital in her straight black skirt, but she hadn't expected this place to be quite so old-fashioned. As she curled her legs to one side, she soon forgot any discomfort in the thrill of the moment—the unaccustomed luxury of having a salesman unfurl bolt after bolt of silky fabric on the cotton batting, a scarlet-and-gold rainbow of texture and hue.

As she watched her mother and aunts rooting through the piles of cloth, Dhara suddenly remembered one of the first family gatherings to which she'd invited Cole. He'd stood in the doorway of her kitchen running a nervous hand over a head freshly shorn of its usual mop of curls. He watched her mother and aunts arguing as they chopped a mountain of vegetables.

"Now I know where the image of the goddess Kali comes from," he'd whispered. He pointed to an idol of the goddess sitting on a shelf nearby, waving her multiple arms—half raised in blessing and the other half gripping swords.

Dhara smiled at the memory, a smile that softened almost as quickly as it came, doused, as usual, by sorrow.

"You like, Dhara?"

Dhara blinked up at her mother. Her mother leaned in, displaying a length of silk over her arm. Dhara gave herself a quick internal shake. It was best not to remember Cole. Especially the better days, before it all went so very wrong.

She ran her fingers over the smooth silk. She placed her other hand beneath the cloth to gauge the transparency. The fabric was cloud-soft, so deep a red it was almost plum, and slipped across her fingers like water. "Oh, it's gorgeous, Mum."

With a flip of her arm, her mother draped the fabric over Dhara's shoulder. Dhara's aunts approached on either side, peering down at her, blocking out the harsh fluorescent light.

"Too dark." Nisha wrinkled her nose, and her nose-stud winked. "It makes her look old."

Dhara laughed. "Thanks, Aunt Nisha."

"Dhara, you're a young girl getting married. You should look your age!"

Dhara resisted the urge to remind her that she was a doctor who'd spent the morning administering stress tests, studying imaging data, and discussing a particularly critical patient's situation with a cardiothoracic surgeon. Or that her youngest sister had jumped the queue years ago, much to her mother's dismay, and all but one of her buddies from high school had long circled the sacred fires.

"I think it makes her look lovely," her mother said, squinting. "We could order a border, embroidered in gold."

"Well, have her try it on then!" Indira said. "You won't know until you see how it drapes."

Her mother and Indira headed toward the mirrors at the back of the store. Aunt Nisha held out her hand to help Dhara up from the mattress. Her kohl-rimmed eyes were bright with mischief. "You know, you don't have to listen to your mother," she murmured, drawing her so close that Dhara could smell the musky perfume her aunt favored. "You can wear any color you like. You're more modern than any of us."

"Nisha, you'd have me in some horrendous pouf of white satin if you had your way. I really do like the red."

"I've got your best interests in mind." Nisha led her leisurely toward the back of the store. "I think that it might be better to appear on your wedding day...less traditional than most Indian brides."

Dhara felt a little frisson. Among her high school friends, it was frequently whispered that it fell to your mother's sisters to fill you in on the pleasure-secrets of the wedding night—whether you wanted to hear them or not. Dhara hoped Nisha had the good sense to spare this thirty-seven-year-old such a ridiculous conversation, but the look on Nisha's face suggested there were other secrets dancing on her tongue.

"I probably shouldn't be telling you this." Nisha rolled a wrist dismissively toward her sisters. "Your fiancé seems to admire American girls. He had at least one girl with whom he was quite serious."

Dhara resisted the urge to block her own ears. "In that case," she said tightly, "Sudesh and I are very much alike, aren't we?"

"Yes, that's true." Nisha leaned in, to speak in a whisper. "And that's exactly why you might want to break from tradition. Show him you're not bound to it. That you're Indian, but modern too, a little bit of both."

Dhara stared blindly ahead while Nisha spoke like a little devil on her right shoulder. She didn't need to know this. She didn't want to know anything more about Sudesh Bohara than that he was Hindu of the Vaishya caste and the Khandewal subcaste, and that his family originated in Ajmer. That he was from a good family, a distant cousin of one of her father's business associates. That he was a vegetarian, who didn't smoke or drink.

And that he was a man with very kind eyes.

"Don't be nervous, Dhara, it's just a suggestion." Nisha pressed close and gave Dhara's arm a little squeeze. "A suggestion from a married aunt to her most favorite niece."

The question rose to her lips before she could stop it. "What happened to Sudesh's girlfriend?"

"Oh, he broke it off not long after the engagement." Nisha raised her brows. "One can only imagine what he discovered to make him forgo a wedding night."

Nisha should have just poured ice water down Dhara's back. Her words had the same effect.

"Nisha," her mother said. "Stop talking mischief to my daughter. Come, Dhara, let's get this on you." Her mother clicked her tongue at Dhara's skirt and shell. "You should have brought a petticoat and a *choli*. I guess we'll just have to make do."

In sudden numbness, Dhara gave herself up to them.

Dhara's mother found the plain end of the sari and started tucking the edge into the waistband of her skirt. With deft hands she folded the fabric into pleats, tucked it to just one side of her navel, then brought the rest of the fabric around her back and draped it over her shoulder.

Dhara stood with her arms raised, aware only of the pulling and the tugging, of the vague murmur of Hindi, all the while struggling to ignore Nisha's revelation. It wasn't her business that Sudesh had had a serious failed relationship. It wasn't her business to wonder if Sudesh still loved this other woman—if Sudesh had resorted to an arranged marriage only because of family pressure—if Sudesh, like herself, still found himself needled by memory.

But the knowledge raised an inevitable question: Would Sudesh think differently of her if he knew that she'd had a relationship with an American farm boy of no caste? A relationship that was, in every physical way, a true marriage.

Dhara squeezed her eyes shut. She wished she could take back the last few minutes. In an arranged marriage, the relationship started on the wedding night. It would be a relationship based on mutual respect, mutual goals, and a determination to make things work. She didn't *want* to know anything about Sudesh other than his basic goodness.

She had known everything about Cole. And that had only brought her pain.

"*It's a game.*"

Cole's voice echoed in Dhara's head, clear as the memory.

She'd been sitting with her girlfriends in the lecture hall, clutching a cup of strong black coffee. In her other hand, she'd held a cardboard square upon which Cole had drawn a grid. In each square was a photo, apparently copied from the freshman register. She'd recognized Cole's photo in the center free space.

She'd held the card, not understanding why he'd given this to her. She could have blamed it on the hour. What had possessed her to take Art History 101, which was offered only at 8:30 in the morning? She'd never make it to class on time. The room was always dim, to better see the slides on the overhead projector, and the professor tended to drone. To make it worse, the class had been full of pretentious upperclassmen adding insights from their last trip to the Uffizi. She'd found it odd that the card was full of pictures of all those first-row show-offs.

But it hadn't been just the hour that made her slow-witted. Her brain had stopped working the minute the wild-haired, lanky Cole Jackson had swung his long legs off the top of the next row of seats and then leaned down to whisper in her ear.

"It's like Bingo," he'd murmured. He'd smelled of meadow grass, and sunlight, and sleep-tousled man. "When one of them talks, you cross off his picture."

Just then, one of the preppy boys in the front row had asked another question. Marta had made a muted yip as she'd crossed his face off her card.

Only then had Dhara understood. Cole had made up the game to amuse them through the sleep-inducing class.

He'd called it Asshole Bingo.

Now Dhara made a sudden choking noise, a bubble of reflexive laughter. Her breath came out with a little hitch. The memory was like a swift blow to the solar plexus, and she stood dazed, trying to breathe.

"Dhara, what's the matter?" Aunt Nisha gave her a puzzled look, her dark eyes intent. "Are you all right?"

Suddenly, three women gathered and peered into her face. Her heart palpitated oddly. She looked away to hide her expression—and instead caught her own reflection in the three-way mirror.

She stared at that woman swathed in plum-colored fabric. She searched the reflection for the free-spirited girl who had dared to fall in love with the Frisbee-wielding American son of a single mother and bring him home to her tradition-bound parents. But all she could see was the pure Indian in her, the Hindu (religion), Vaishya (caste), Khandewal (sub-caste), Pitalia (clan), from Jaipur by way of Dholagarh. All dressed up like a village bride.

"I need some air."

She yanked at the pleats at her waistband. She tugged at the fabric with strangely fumbling fingers. Her mother and aunts cried out and tried to stop her, their hands everywhere at once. She wrenched and pulled, panic rising.

Every jerk only bound her more firmly amid eighteen feet of Rajasthani silk.

chapter three

I t was a rainy Friday night, and Kelly clutched the DVD of *What's Your Raashee?*, a lushly filmed love story from Bollywood director Ashutosh Gowariker. Dhara's aunt Nisha had recommended the movie at the engagement party last week, and Kelly had spent three lunch hours searching for the DVD among the dusty boxes of several downtown street vendors. She'd squealed when she found it—which upped the price a few bucks—but Kelly didn't care. Juicy, romantic stories were her favorite rainy-night date. So she'd put on her softest pajamas, popped the movie in, and settled on her couch with a box of tissues and a bowl of microwave popcorn.

Suddenly, the door buzzer sounded.

Kelly froze, a fistful of popcorn halfway to her mouth. She stared across the room at the intercom. There was only one person who would arrive at her apartment building without warning this late at night.

She jumped off the couch, upsetting the bowl. A warm flush prickled over every last freckle. She thrust her fingers into her unwashed, humidity-frizzed hair and frantically tumbled it on top of her head as she glanced around the living area of the one-bedroom apartment. She noticed the torn window shade she'd been meaning to replace, and the cat box in the corner that needed cleaning. She wondered if she had any eggs in the fridge or coffee in the cabinet. Then she gave up on her hopelessly wild hair, ran her palms down her pajama bottoms, and scolded herself for not taking a shower when she'd come home from work.

The buzzer went off again.

Shoving her hair behind each ear, she hurried to the intercom and pressed the button, tensely balancing on her toes. "Yes?"

"Kelly?"

The voice gave her pause. "Who's this?"

"It's Cole."

Kelly stared at the slats of the intercom, not understanding. She thought he'd said "Cole," not "Trey." She must have heard wrong. She pressed the button harder. "*Who* is this?"

"It's me, Kelly. It's Cole."

She knew that voice, though she hadn't heard it in a long time. Disappointment dropped her to the soles of her feet.

"Kelly, you there?"

She fumbled with the button. "Yeah, yeah, I'm here."

She pressed her head against the wall and berated herself for her raised hopes. She had her own damn self to blame. Trey had promised he'd call the next time he had a chance to come over—and he hadn't called tonight. She really shouldn't have jumped to conclusions. Look what she was becoming—*exactly* what she'd sworn not to be: pitiful Pavlov's dog, salivating at the sound of the buzzer.

"Hey, Kelly, it's friggin' pouring out here. Can I come up?"

Kelly shook herself to her senses. "Of course." She pressed the button to buzz the building door open. She wondered what Cole was doing here at ten o'clock on a Friday night when she hadn't heard from him in months. After he and Dhara had broken up, Kelly had expected him to call her to commiserate about the state of the relationship and, perhaps, ask for her help to patch things up. But Cole had mumbled through every phone call Kelly had made to him, and so, after a while, she'd stopped calling.

When he tapped at the door, she unbolted and unchained it, pulling it open to peer at him from around the edge.

She started to say *hello stranger,* but the words died in her throat.

Cole had been raised as a vegetarian on an organic farm in Oregon. He'd always been long-muscled and whip-lean, the kind of guy who could wolf down prodigious amounts of food and not develop a fatty bulge. But she'd never seen him so thin that his clavicle pushed against the wet cotton of his soaked shirt, his skin so pale that she could see the bones in his wrist where he braced himself against the door.

"Hey, Kelly." His eyes were lost in shadows. "Can I come in?"

She swung the door wide, and he stumbled over the threshold. He looped an arm around her neck, almost taking her down with him. Kelly seized his wrist and steadied him as she caught a blast of his breath. "What the hell, Cole—you're drunk!"

"I had a few with the guys."

"A few what? A few gallons?" Stumbling under his weight, she kicked the door closed behind her and then led him teetering toward the sofa. "It's only ten o'clock."

"Started after the markets closed," he muttered, pushing aside the popcorn bowl and tumbling onto the couch. "No big deal."

Kelly took a good, long look at him. His once sunbleached brown hair, chopped short years ago in deference to Wall Street conformity, had grown dark and far out of its cut. It curled against his neck and stuck up at odd angles from his head. His face was sharp-edged at the cheekbones and chin, and his green irises showed eerily bright against the bloodshot whites.

Kelly didn't always pick up on what the girls called normal social cues, but she didn't need a neon sign to know that the drunk keeling over on her couch was in the midst of dealing with—or *not* dealing with—some serious issues. After Dhara's sudden engagement last week, she had a pretty good idea what those issues were.

Poor Cole. She dropped to one knee to pull his size ten shoes from his feet. "Jeez, you're as wet as if you were out in a nor'easter." She tipped the two-hundred-dollar Johnston & Murphy shoe to dump the water onto the carpet. "I didn't think it was raining that hard."

"I walked. From Mondo's."

Kelly frowned. The name was familiar. It was the kind of place that showed up on Page Six of the *New York Post*. "Isn't that place on Houston Street?"

"I needed the air."

For forty, fifty blocks? She tossed the shoes toward the door. "Why didn't you just take a cab?"

"Tapped out." He blindly yanked at his pants pockets, pulling out the white cotton insides. "Totally tapped out."

His argyle socks sagged with moisture. She pulled them off and dropped them into a soggy pile. His feet were icy to the touch. "You should have gone straight home. Your apartment is much closer to that bar. One phone call, and I would have caught the subway over. You *know* that."

"Can't go home." He let his head fall onto the back of the couch, his Adam's apple jutting. "I've been evicted."

Yeah, right, Kelly thought. Evicted from the relationship with Dhara for sure, but certainly not from his apartment. This was just his puckish sense of humor. Cole swam in cash from working as a trader on Wall Street.

"Stop with the fish tales," she said, determined to take care of first things first. "You need to get out of these clothes."

Cole laughed, a phlegmy laugh that threatened to turn into a cough. "I knew I came to the right place."

"Shut up." She stood up and headed to her bedroom. "I think I have a pair of pajamas that'll fit you. I don't want your wet butt staining my yard-sale couch."

She returned a few minutes later with a towel and an old pair of drawstring pajama bottoms. She flung them both in his general direction. He struggled to pull the damp button-down shirt over his head and then fumbled with his belt. To give him privacy, she went into the kitchen to clean the dishes in the sink and put on a pot of water to boil. She heard him stumbling around, drying himself, kicking off his pants, swearing as he tripped back onto the couch while pulling the pajamas up over his legs.

When she turned around, he was shirtless, wearing a pair of white cotton pajama bottoms speckled with little red hearts, which ended just below his knees. She thrust a glass of water in his hands and held out a couple of pills. "Take both of these and drink all the water."

"Tell me they're quaaludes."

"Vitamin B$_{12}$ and some aspirin. You'll thank me in the morning."

"Okay, Mom."

"Don't be a wiseass." She tugged a *Star Trek* throw blanket off the back of the couch and then tossed it across his chest. He pulled it over him while he slugged back the pills. "Now, are you going to tell me what's going on?"

"I told you," he said, shrugging one bony shoulder. "I was evicted."

"Cole—"

"Came back last night to find the locks changed," he continued, lifting the glass, "and a sheriff's posting on the door."

Kelly fell silent. The Ramen noodles she'd eaten for dinner shifted. He couldn't possibly be telling the truth. If he were, he wouldn't be so frustratingly calm. Cole knew what it meant. Evictions happened to people like his mother, a feckless ex-debutante who, along with her organic garden, cultivated marijuana on the side to help pay the heating bill. Evictions happened to men like her father, fishermen in

Gloucester, whose income rose and fell on seasonal stocks of flounder.

She said, "It must be a mistake."

"No mistake. I was legally warned." He looked beyond her, toward the kitchen. "You wouldn't happen to have a beer, would you?"

"No."

"Vodka? Whiskey?"

"You've had enough, don't you think?"

"No." Then he closed his eyes and rested his head on the back of the couch. "It's never enough."

Kelly sank onto the couch next to him, giving up all expectation of a cozy night watching a Bollywood movie. A boatload of real drama had just arrived on her doorstep. "You want to tell me how you got to this point?"

He made an ugly sound, a bitter little laugh. "Like you don't know."

"No, Cole. I don't."

He turned his head, opening his eyes into slits, and she could see the effort he was making to focus on her face.

"Dhara's been tight as a clam." She curled her legs up under her. "I had no *idea* your situation was so serious. At her engagement party last week, I confronted her, but she didn't say a word about you." Well, Kelly thought, except for that unbelievable tidbit that Cole had asked her to marry him and she'd said no. "She certainly didn't say anything about an eviction."

Cole went unnaturally still. His pupils constricted, making his striking eyes all the more green. He looked like he'd just received a fierce right hook and was struggling to regain some sort of equilibrium.

"Hey." She pushed the hopeless frizz of her hair out of her eyes and leaned into him. "Are you okay?"

His lips moved, but no sound came out. He had the distressed, tight-faced look of a landlubber on his first deep-ocean voyage. She glanced at the *Star Trek* throw blanket, an old present from the girls, already so thin from age that she feared the threadbare split by Spock's face would rip entirely if she washed it any more. She cast a swift glance toward the sink, wondering if she had enough time to fetch a bucket from under the counter before he hurled.

He tried to say something, but it came out garbled. Then he visibly took hold of himself.

"En...engagement?"

Kelly sucked in a long, slow breath. She covered her mouth with her hand. She'd just assumed he knew...assumed it was the news of the engagement that sent him on this bender. But now, thinking about it, Kelly wondered whom he would have heard the news from. After the breakup, he'd isolated himself. If he wasn't talking to *her*, then he wasn't talking to any of the girls.

She was such an idiot.

"I'm so sorry, Cole." She spoke through her fingers. "I just...I just assumed the news of the engagement is what brought you to my apartment after so much time."

Cole planted his elbows on his knees and then sank his head in his hands. She reached over and rubbed his back. She could feel the nubs of his vertebrae against her palm.

"When?" His voice had gone raw and husky. "When did this happen?"

"The engagement party was last Friday. It's...it's an arranged marriage."

"Arranged."

"We tried an intervention," she said in a rush. "I mean, this was the one thing she swore she would never do. I still don't understand it. None of us do. We keep calling her, trying to get her to talk. But she just keeps stubbornly insisting that this is what she wants. It's exasperating."

"Man," he said, lifting his head, his elbows splayed on either side as he stretched back against the couch. "This is just fucking perfect. You sure you don't have any scotch?"

"No."

"Wine?"

"Cole—"

"Arsenic?"

Kelly squeezed his knee. "All I've got is tea," she said, as the sound of a screaming kettle came from the kitchen. "Tea and a whole lot of time."

When she returned five minutes later carrying two mugs of steaming chamomile, Cole looked, if possible, more haggard than before. The news had sobered him up. He barely acknowledged her return when she slid the mug across the coffee table toward him. He stared into the steam as if he could read his future in the milky fluid.

"Why don't we start," she said, sinking onto the couch beside him, "with the eviction."

"It's what usually happens when you don't pay rent."

"Okay." She sipped the tea tentatively, a bit too weak. "Why would you ever forget to pay your rent on that fabulous two-bedroom with the fantastic view over the East River?"

"Because, when you lose your job, you don't have any money."

She tightened her grip on the warm cup. He'd been a trader on Wall Street since he'd earned his MBA, moving up the ranks by flipping from one bank to another, amassing an impressive portfolio of private and institutional clients, as well as a nice little fund of his own.

Kelly began to realize just how much Dhara was keeping from all of them. "For Pete's sake, Cole, when did you lose your job?"

"Last June."

She stilled a moment. Last June was a year ago, much longer than she expected. But she supposed it took a whole year to put an eviction proceeding into effect. Her mind raced in sudden calculation. If he lost his job last June, that was about three months after Dhara broke up with him.

"Is that why you've been dodging my calls for so long?" Kelly wondered how much deeper the story went. "Hell, Cole, if it weren't for you, I'd still be wearing those ratty cheap sneakers from freshman year. Why didn't you tell me?"

"Because I could handle it." He paused. "I thought I could handle it."

"What about your savings?"

He made a short, humorless laugh. "Nothing that could hold that apartment for a year."

"But—"

"I'd made some bad trades. A couple of big ones. You know, the higher up you get in this business, the bigger the risks. The bigger the failures too. No one outside the business really *gets* that."

Kelly drew back, stung by his frustration.

"And there was this guy on my floor. Gunning for me." Annoyance roughened his voice. "He kept shorting me, whenever he could, like he was trying to prove something to his boss." Cole began tapping his foot, his knee working up and down. "That, coupled with a few bad trades, and my boss started to listen to him. He told me I was risking a date with the SEC."

Kelly took another sip of tea to hide her surprise. She and the girls never really understood what Cole did. Trading derivatives. Putting short-term bets on volatile stocks. Working overseas currencies in his favor. It was part of what impressed them all at Vassar. He'd started e-trading when he was barely sixteen, using an account he'd opened in his mother's name. He'd developed a statistical system that worked a half-percentage more than any others he knew of, trading on daily fluctuations in commodity prices first, and, later, on blue-chip stocks, and then still later on some new-fangled thing called electronically traded funds. He'd made enough to pay for his tuition while still managing to financially support from afar his mother's ever-languishing organic farm. It was this genius that got him an acceptance into Vassar, despite a spotty educational history.

" . . . the next thing I know, I'm facing disciplinary action.

Got all the white-shoes frowning down at me. Do you know how much money I made those guys over the years? They said if I left the firm willingly, they'd let it all slide. No reporting, no blot on my record. And no job."

And all Kelly heard was *disciplinary action,* and she wondered if that was what sent Dhara away. Dhara was as by-the-book as the day was long. She once raked over the coals a whole room of medical students for playing pranks with the dissection corpses. But surely Dhara would have given Cole every last chance to prove his innocence to her.

Unless he couldn't.

She watched him now as he chewed on a hangnail, staring blankly at her coffee table. She felt a swell of compassion. She always knew how out of place he felt in his Wall Street firm, a farmer's son who'd tripped into a fancy school but never really felt as if he fit in. She herself had always felt like a fish out of water, having spent summers working the lines with her father in Gloucester Bay until no amount of lemon could wash the smell of brine out of her hair.

But *cheating?* It just didn't feel right.

"I shouldn't have said all that," he muttered, using his cup to rub the watery ring it had made on the table. "It's . . . more complicated. I'd appreciate it if you'd keep this between us. I'd rather not let everyone know what a fuckup I've been."

Kelly's swelling compassion then spread to Dhara, who'd clearly insisted on protecting Cole—even when he was wrong—even against the friends who loved them both.

"My lips," she promised, "are sealed."

"I could use a place to stay too." He talked more to himself than to her. "I need to get the ground back under my feet. I can day-trade still. I've got a few clients. I might get a few more, if I make some calls."

"Sounds like a plan."

"It won't take long," he added. "Once I've got a cushion in the bank, I'll find my own place."

It took a full minute for Kelly to realize that he was asking to stay here, in her apartment, for an extended and open-ended period of time.

"Oh!" she said. "Oh."

Cole couldn't possibly stay *here*. Trey had been coming over, spending whole glorious weekends between her faded sheets. It was all going so well, so swimmingly, so *perfectly*. From that moment Trey had stood outside her office building, leaning up against a signpost with a long-delayed apology on his lips—to the wild tear-off-his-clothes, grinding-naked-on-the-hotel-room-floor of last Friday's hookup, she'd been living in a hypersexualized bubble of dreamy wonder. It couldn't stop.

She didn't want it to stop.

"I'd appreciate it," Cole said, his gaze on his hands, "if you kept this quiet. You know. From the girls."

But Cole—Cole!—here!—of all people! In college, Cole had been the one who'd delivered the bad news to her about Trey. Cole had overheard Trey bragging in the cafeteria, outlining to the rugby team his strategy for bagging a redhead. And when she—lost in a sensual haze—had refused to believe him, Cole had dragged her to the computer to show her a chat site for pickup artists where Trey had discussed, in intimate detail, the techniques he'd used to lure the cute virgin off the barstool and into his bed.

"Kelly?" Cole turned to her, his eyes hooded. "You can say no, you know. I'm getting used to hearing that."

She froze with her teacup halfway to her lips. Cole looked at her with bloodshot eyes. And she was reminded that it was Cole who'd first recognized her as a kindred spirit freshman year—two working-class kids in a sea of preppy, trust-fund babies. It was Cole who'd offered her cash to tutor him in Physics. She didn't figure out until years later that the trading wiz didn't really need the tutoring. It was Cole who paid for her plane ticket to Aruba during spring break, claiming he had plenty of frequent-flier miles, just so she could join everyone on one last college fling. And it was Cole who'd fronted her the first and last month's rent on her very first New York City apartment, more money than she'd ever had in her bank account at any one time.

Kelly scraped her cup across the coffee table. "Of course you can stay." She pressed her cheek against Cole's shoulder. "Stay as long as you need to."

She closed her eyes. A complication was inevitable, she supposed. Her relationship with Trey was clandestine, crazy, impossible, and breathlessly romantic. Something that good couldn't possibly come easy. Just like in a Bollywood movie.

But she would find a way.

She *would*.

If she had to move mountains, she would keep Cole and Trey apart.

~~~~ chapter four

Wendy ascended the wide central stairs inside the Haight-Livingston Museum, the clatter of her heels echoing off the frescoed ceiling. Clutching her coffee, she breathed in the morning hush. She'd spent the weekend negotiating seating arrangements for the wedding and now felt like she'd just emerged, blinking, from some wartime bunker.

At the top of the stairs, she came to an abrupt halt. Thick wires snaked along the floor of the Greek and Roman gallery. With growing unease, she followed the path of the extension cords around the bases of the marble statues to where they converged, at a ladder on the far side of the room.

There, in a little oasis of shadow, stood another perfect form, this one warm-blooded—Gabriel Teixeira.

She suppressed an inner groan as she crossed the room, gingerly stepping over the wires. She'd completely forgotten that a major distraction would be working just outside her office today. A temporary amnesia, she figured, brought on by the quarrel she'd had with Parker and the stress of holding the pin in the Birdie grenade.

She summoned her best brisk professional voice. "Good morning, Mr. Teixeira."

Gabriel poked his head down from the ceiling. He was Brazilian. She'd gleaned that information from his slight accent and the few references he'd made to São Paolo. A Portuguese background would explain the Castilian broadness of his forehead and the sharp cut of his jaw. But those exotic, slanting cheekbones, the slight flattening to the bridge of his nose, and the tilt to the corners of his eyes... well, those she couldn't place. Native American of some sort, she'd thought. Maybe Guarani.

She took a long, controlled breath. Exotic-looking men had always been her undoing. A series of boyfriends paraded through her mind from the Czech sculptor at Vassar to the Jamaican potter who liked to get dirty to the Greek miniaturist with a secret stash of porn. Thankfully, her awakening libido settled right back down.

Too late. Gabriel had caught her staring.

He gripped the edge of the open ceiling. With a knowing smile, he glanced down at her through the space between his broad chest and impressive biceps. "Two weeks we've been working together. When are you going to call me Gabe?"

"It's an old habit. I'd probably develop a tic if I tried to break it." Humor, she decided, was the best way to diffuse workplace sexual tension. "It was beaten into me by tough old ladies who wore their glasses on chains at Miss Porter's School for Girls."

"Those nuns can be brutal." He reached deep into the

ceiling, blindly searching for something. "They bruised my knuckles but good."

Wendy didn't bother correcting his assumption that Miss Porter's was a Catholic school, and not the most ultra-exclusive private boarding school on the Eastern seaboard. In her youth, she could have used the influence of nuns.

"So," she said, pointedly glancing at the dust-encrusted wires he tugged from the ceiling, "looks like dirty work today."

"Getting rid of the old wiring." He held up a ceramic end, turning it over as if he were examining some artifact he'd pulled out of an archeological dig. "Knob and tube. Ancient circuitry. Probably been here since this museum was converted from gaslight."

"Please tell me," she said, thinking of the museum's lean liability policy, "that they're not a fire hazard."

"No." He started coiling the old wire around his arm and shoulder. "They've been replaced. I'm just stripping out the old stuff."

"Which—let me guess—will take the whole day."

"Oh, yeah." He grinned, a flash of even white teeth. "I'll be interrupting your electrical service, scratching around the ceiling, churning up some dust, and overall making a complete nuisance of myself."

He looked down at her with a half smile. Wendy tried mightily to return it. Gabriel's increasingly distracting presence was starting to affect her stress levels. Until his arrival, this museum was her only oasis. Her mother owned her nights and her weekends. And the only things that distinguished a five-star general from Bitsy-on-a-mission were fatigues, hand grenades, and a pith helmet.

Above all, roiling in the back of her mind was that uncomfortable dispute with Parker.

"You know," Gabriel said, shrugging his shoulder to nudge the gathering coil more firmly against his neck. "I can't let you get away with this 'Mr. Teixeira' stuff much longer. When you call me that, it reminds me of the owners of the coffee plantations in the Paraíba Valley, where I grew up. They were 'senhora' this and 'senhor' that and padded their names with that of their four grandparents." He lowered his voice in rumbling mockery. "Gabriel de Bragança e Ligne de Sousa Teixeira."

"Please don't make me call you Mr. de Bragança e Ligne de Sousa Teixeira. Not before my second cup of coffee."

"Sure." Dust motes drifted to the floor as he continued to pull the wire from the ceiling. "As long as I don't have to call you Helen Vivien Livingston Wainwright."

She pinked up, then found interest in the drops of coffee that had slipped onto the lid of her cup. She wondered when he'd figure out that one of her last names was also on the museum. It was an embarrassing truth that one of her ancestors had donated this house and all its contents to the county, and that her mother, because of her birth, was one of the lifetime trustees.

"Ah," she said wryly. "My dirty secret is out. I really should scrap that nameplate."

"I thought I was in the wrong office. I went looking for you this morning to warn you I'd be shutting down the electricity. The security guard set me straight. Such a big name for a little blonde."

Wendy coughed to cover the sound of her indrawn breath. She had been called many things in her life—athletic, healthy, and big-boned. They were all euphemisms for her essentially tall, show-horse figure. She managed through biweekly tennis games to keep herself lean. But no one had ever called her a *little blonde*.

"But what I've been trying to figure out," he persisted, "is why everyone here calls you Wendy."

"It's a family thing. None of us go by our real names."

A rumble of laughter echoed in the exposed rafters. "Aliases?"

"Self-preservation. Imagine facing your schoolmates with a name like Jeremiah Warner Livingston Wainwright the Third."

Gabriel paused as the wire snagged. "Really?"

"We call him Trey. In other ways though, the names just get silly." Her mind ran over the sweeping cast of characters in her extended family. "My mother is Elizabeth—but we call her Bitsy. I've got an Aunt Oatsie," she added, "a sister Birdie, and a Cousin Boop."

"You're making this up."

"There's a reason why half my relatives are in therapy."

She didn't mention that she and her relatives were all descended from robber barons and governors, and the family tree bent under the weight of senators, shipping magnates, and even one vice president. Since one achingly painful incident in college, she made a point to keep that information under wraps—particularly around eligible men.

"But Wendy is not an unusual name," he persisted. "It's from *Peter Pan*."

"Yes, that's right."

Her father had called her Wendy for the way she controlled her stuffed animals in the storylines she set up for them. *Off to Neverland again,* he'd say, coming into her nursery to find her in the middle of some complicated plot twist. He sometimes called her brother Peter Pan, but for a completely different reason.

Then her gaze drifted to Gabriel's toolbox where she spied a tattered copy of William Faulkner's *The Sound and the Fury*, the bookmark a little deeper into the story than it had been last week, when she'd first noticed it. Curious. He was a reader, this electrician. And *The Sound and the Fury* was one of her favorite books.

She felt a tingle of curiosity. A sure indication that it was time to move on.

"Well," Wendy said brightly, turning toward her office, "if you're going to be working here all day, I'd better close the gallery."

"Don't."

Her shoes scraped against the floor as she halted abruptly.

"The kids like it so much." He jerked his chin toward the statues. "They get an art and anatomy lesson, all in one."

She glanced around the room and remembered last week's group from the local all-girls private high school, who'd stepped into the gallery squealing in a pitch high enough to break glass. But as assistant curator, she had liability issues to consider. "They'll have to be satisfied with the view from the hallway. I have no choice but to close this gallery. The dust—"

"I'll keep it contained."

"—and the wires. They pose a hazard."

"I've taped the wires down good." He popped his head down for a moment, scanned the room, and then—shockingly—blatantly—her bare legs. "And I don't think any ten-year-olds will be wearing shoes like that."

Wendy's arches prickled. She'd worn strappy red sandals, a bit higher in the heel than usual, but she'd been in that kind of mood this morning. The I've-been-worn-down-by-my-fiancé-and-my-mother-so-I'm-going-to-wear-red-heels-and-pretend-I've-got-it-all-under-control kind of mood. It clearly wasn't working. Because when Gabriel's gaze slipped back up her body, his leisurely perusal felt like a feather tickling her inner thigh.

She took a swift sip of her skinny latte. She really should eat a healthier breakfast, even if it meant not losing the last six pounds before the wedding.

Honestly, she knew exactly what was going on here. She'd known since the first day she'd laid eyes on this broad-shouldered, narrow-hipped hunk of man. She was all too clear about the fundamentals of sexual engagement. She'd been an anthropology major, after all. She'd written her thesis on the courting rituals of the Wodaabe tribe of Cameroon.

Here's the thing with Gabriel Teixeira: Gabriel was a handsome man waltzing into her life in the vulnerable months before she married. It was no surprise that she would simply and strongly *respond*. Her thoroughly physiological reaction to Gabriel's knee-melting gaze was an evolutionary impulse. It was her body urging her to take in a variety of genetic material before settling down with one mate.

You know, like a bonobo.

And there it was, categorized and labeled. Now she could put it firmly behind glass.

"I have no choice," she said, swiveling on one of her slim red heels. "I'll call downstairs and see about closing the gallery."

"Wendy, hold on." He climbed down the ladder, bracing the enormous coil of wire against his shoulder. "I almost forgot. I found something this morning that I want to show you."

He let the coil slide off his shoulder to fall in a cracking heap on the floor, raising a puff of dust. Then he pinched something off the pile of flotsam near the bottom of the ladder and straightened to hold it out toward her.

She approached, drawn by the sight of a pair of grime-encrusted spectacles. She noted the small circular lenses and the delicate, blue-steel wires. "They look very old," she murmured. "Turn of the twentieth century, maybe."

"I found them sitting inside the ceiling on a beam. Probably been there for a hundred years."

He turned them over in his hands, examining them with the kind of respect she was used to seeing in white-gloved experts of primitive art.

"Can you see some poor worker," he said, "finishing the ceiling and then, when it's all closed up, patting his pockets for his glasses?"

"He must have been frantic." She reached out to wipe some grime from the lenses. "They were expensive in those days."

She'd leaned in too close. Gabriel was a good head taller than her, so different from Parker, who topped her by only a few inches. More than that, she felt the warmth of him, and his scent of dust and burned wire and an honest man's labor, and, strangely, the faintest aroma of resin, a perfume that teased the corners of her memory.

She noticed his paint-flecked knuckles and abruptly understood.

She blurted, "You paint."

She saw the surprise flicker in his eyes. Saw, too, the darkness of emerging stubble on his cheek, a prickly little line of it following his jaw.

"I do paint." His voice was a rumble. "Not houses. Canvases."

"Of course."

She took a step back and felt herself blushing. Not a swift pink tinge to her cheeks, but a full-blown flush rising up from the collar of her silk blouse, the kind of embarrassed glow that would make the skin of her chest, exposed beneath a few open buttons, a complete patchwork of blotches.

"I'm working on a large canvas now." He returned the dusty eyeglasses to the top of a pile of flotsam by the foot of the ladder and then reached for a rag in his toolbox to wipe the grime from his hands. "In a month, I'm going to have a booth at the Hudson Valley Art Fair."

Thoroughly unnerved, Wendy thought of the Brazilian artists she knew. She thought of the brilliant colors and the textured street scenes of Sérgio Telles and the Picasso-like nudes of Ismael Nery and the way Antônio Garcia Bento painted water. She thought of the lovely woodscape by Batista da Costa acquired by her Soho art gallery, the one she'd repeatedly failed to sell and so had finally, guiltily, bought for herself.

Gabriel was an *artist*. A *Brazilian* artist. Showing up in her gallery like the ghost of Christmas Past.

"You should come by the fair," he said. "I'd love to show you my work."

Wendy stilled the reflex to say *yes*. She loved discovering new artists, loved the juxtaposition between who they seemed to be and what subjects they chose to draw. But she had to decline. This offer went beyond a friendly exchange between a contractor and his client. She'd heard this approach a dozen times while she'd worked for the art gallery, spoken from the mouths of so many bohemian artists, unshaven, unwashed, eyeing her three-hundred-dollar shoes and hoping for more than just a showing. It wasn't quite *"come up and see my etchings,"* but often the sentiment was the same.

And in that moment, Parker materialized beside her. Not kind-but-stubborn Parker, holding firm against the idea of Birdie at the wedding, but possessive Parker. She imagined him slipping an arm around her shoulder and giving Gabe the eye before deftly changing the subject to sports.

"My weekends are pretty busy these days," she said, granting Gabe a noncommittal smile, "but I'll certainly try to drop by."

And then, to save them both from any more awkwardness, she switched her coffee to her right hand. With her left hand, she tucked her hair behind her ear and let her fingers linger, wishing for the first time that she'd opted for a garish two-carat Harry Winston engagement ring, rather than the discreet topaz heirloom Parker had inherited from his great-grandmother.

Certainly Gabriel would understand this gesture, this international sign language for *I'm already taken.*

He greeted the exaggerated motion with a brief curiosity, and then, as his gaze fell upon the ring, the expression in his eyes shifted.

"I understand about busy weekends." He tossed the rag with careless aim toward his toolbox. "So hard to fit everything in, especially if you have family."

"Every Saturday with my mother," Wendy said, "and every Sunday with my sister."

"Me, I spend all my time with my son."

My son.

The information sank in, like a flint skipping across water and then diving beneath the surface to drift, in a rocking motion, to the bottom.

"Just so we're clear," he said, thrusting out his hand. "You'll be calling me Gabe from now on, yes?"

She hesitated. His expression was open, regretful. A teasing smile twitched at the corner of his lips. This situation could have been awkward, if Gabriel had had the usual contractor swagger or if she'd been forced to verbally turn him down. She shouldn't worry about ceding him this one small request. She was not, after all, one of the American Woodland Indians, reluctant to reveal her own name lest she lose a piece of her soul.

"Of course." She took his hand in hers. "Gabe."

He had a working man's hand, callused and thick-knuckled, still rough with the grit of the ceiling. Holding it, she understood three things in swift succession. In a few weeks, Gabriel would be finished updating the electricity in the museum. In three months, she would be wearing a sixteen-thousand-dollar designer wedding gown on the grounds of the Briarcliff Country Club, taking Parker Pryce-Weston as her lawfully wedded husband. And right now, there was absolutely no harm in gorging herself on the glorious sight of Gabriel Teixeira—and his strangely haunting, beautiful puzzle of face.

His lips curved as he read her mind. "My grandmother was Japanese. People always wonder."

Caught again.

"I'm *pardo*. Mixed blood." He shrugged. "In Brazil, it's very common."

"You have most unusual features."

"And you," he said, his gaze roaming, "have the most incredible skin. Almost translucent. I'd don't think I could ever...."

Paint it.

In the trailing silence, she heard what he didn't speak. Her heart did a little flutter. An image bloomed in her mind of Gabe behind an easel, and her reclining on a sun-drenched couch, naked.

Then she felt a tingling between their palms. A strange sort of prickly static, concentrated, like the electric charge she'd gathered as a child shuffling in her socks across the Aubusson rug in the parlor. It grew in intensity until it was pinpoint-painful, until she felt the heat crackle between their skins.

She pulled her hand away, like a little girl afraid of the spark.

chapter five

Marta called the pity party, and Kelly was the first to arrive. The pint-size redhead wandered into the hip East Village bar like a lost soul. Catching sight of Marta alone at the far table, Kelly launched herself across the room as fast as her gladiator sandals could take her and dragged Marta off her chair to envelop her in a hug.

Marta braced herself as her circulation was cut off at the waist. She was a good half foot taller than Kelly, but Kelly was squeezing for the kill. Marta tried very hard to blink back the tears that prickled behind her eyes. If she started crying now, it would be a hell of a watery night.

Kelly pulled away long enough to take Marta's face in her hands. "I'm so, *so* sorry."

Marta gave a casual shrug, the airy response she gave to anyone who asked her about the breakup with Carlos, because it was always easier to pretend it didn't hurt so much than admit she was cut full through.

"Drinks are on me tonight," Marta said, as the waitress approached. "Are you having your usual sticky poison?"

"Absolutely."

"A rum and coke," Marta said to the waitress, and then she tilted her own pomegranate Cosmo. "And another one of these for me."

"This whole thing just doesn't compute." Kelly heaved her messenger bag over her head and slung it across the back of the chair. "The last time we talked, I thought you and Carlos were completely mind-melded."

"I know."

"When you called me with bad news, I thought you were going to tell me you were *engaged.*"

"I know. Your voice hit dolphin pitch. I had to tell you quick, before you woke up the neighborhood dogs."

"Listen, I can be dense about these things." Kelly gathered the swirl of her floral skirt and hiked herself on the chair. "But you were talking in the cab when we left Dhara's engagement party like all that was left to do was finalize the design of the rings."

Marta lifted the rim of the glass to her lips to hide an involuntary spasm. She knew Kelly meant well. Kelly was just being Kelly. The girl honestly didn't understand that reiterating Marta's own idiocy might not be the best way to soothe an already battered heart.

"Apparently," Marta said, "I can throw together a twenty-million-dollar IPO, but I'm not so good at reading men."

"I can't believe he's been living with you while he has a wife in Miami."

"With three kids." Marta tapped her glass back down on the table. A boy and two girls. Their school photos, tucked in his wallet. "The oldest is maybe five. She just lost a front tooth."

"He's one hell of a son of a bitch."

"To both women involved."

Then a purse landed with a clank on the tiny table, and Dhara came up behind it, looking disheveled and heavy-eyed. "Please solemnly swear that this is not some lame ploy to get me to another intervention."

"*Chica,* I honestly wish it were."

Dhara visibly deflated. She sank into her chair, covering her cheeks with both hands. She stared at Marta with widening eyes.

Marta swept her fresh Cosmo off the tray as the waitress approached. "You'd best get the doctor here a ginger ale," Marta said to the waitress. "For her, that's the hard stuff."

"I'm going to need something stronger."

"Whoa, we're cutting loose. Make it an ice tea," Marta corrected. "But *not* the Long Island type."

"Yes, yes. Sweetened. With a lemon." Dhara ran her hands down her face and then let them drop onto the table. "I'm an ass. I should have known you wouldn't joke about this. How long?"

"I kicked him out the night of your engagement party. I haven't seen him since." She tightened her grip around the stem of her glass, remembering how she'd tossed the pictures of his children at him, ashamed at the tears on her face. "So, which one of you won the pool?"

Kelly's brow furrowed. "What pool?"

"The betting pool." Marta tried that casual shrug again. "Over how long this thing with Carlos would last."

"Oh, Marta, you must really be hurting to suggest something like that." Dhara shook her head. "You know that all of us were hoping that Carlos was the one."

Marta's throat constricted even more. She'd thought Carlos was the one too. She'd even brought him home to her family last January for El Dia de Reyes, the feast of the three kings. Must have been fifty people in her mother's cape house, twenty-one of them children. He'd played dominos with her father. He'd dissected every dish, asking her mother how she made the meat and plantain *pasteles,* sniffing the *sofrito* that flavored the rice dish her aunt made with pigeon peas. He'd even chased around her three bratty nephews, the ones Marta referred to as Pedro Stop, Sanchez Put-That-Down, and Alejandro Don't-Hit-Your-Brother.

It was the only time, she now realized, that he'd ever met her family.

"Tell me he's out of the apartment." Dhara dragged her purse off the table, dropping it with a clank to the floor by her feet. "Tell me you launched all his stuff out the fifth-floor window."

Marta thought of the echoing spaces she'd confronted when she'd come home from work last night—the stretch of her closet, the two gaping drawers, and the pot-rack devoid of copper-bottomed saucepans. It had been days since she'd thrown him out, but she couldn't seem to get the smell of his aftershave out of her towels. "His dry cleaning showed up on my door this morning. But from what I hear," she said wryly, "the Salvation Army is always in need of Egyptian cotton shirts."

"Sure you don't want to take a scalpel to them? I have a supply."

"Tempting."

"And if you see him again, I could teach you how to make two small incisions on either side of his scrotum—"

"If I ever got that close, it wouldn't be the scrotum I'd cut."

"How could he keep a secret like that for so very long?" Kelly said, looking genuinely uncomfortable. "I mean, eventually, isn't it going to come out anyway?"

"Kelly, here's something I have to face." Marta searched for courage in the rosy depths of her drink. "I'm no better than those well-meaning women who marry door-to-door salesmen only to discover—to their surprise—that those long trips the guy makes? Well, they are to one of his other four wives."

Dhara made a muffled noise. "Marta, don't do this to yourself."

"Think about it. If I hadn't made Carlos sign those loan papers, I'd be like some Florida granny who'd had her fortune siphoned off in marshland real-estate scams."

"No," Dhara insisted. "No."

"Did you know that there's a new reality show called *Who the Hell Did I Marry?* Can't you just see me on it?" She morphed her voice into the drawling lilt of last night's televised victim. "'Sixteen months I lived with him, and all that time I thought it was *charming* that he was so *affectionate* over the phone with his 'nieces' and 'nephews.'"

"Clearly," Dhara said, "he was very good at compartmentalizing."

"Yeah, like the wives of those serial killers." Kelly leaned

over the table. "They never seem to notice the human re-
mains in their freezers, you know? You're lucky Carlos didn't
go all Sweeney Todd on you—"

"All right, that's it." Wendy waltzed into the conversation,
holding a drink in each hand. "You are all hereby banned
from late-night TV."

Marta met Wendy's wryly amused gaze, her heart swelling
in gratitude that Wendy had made the long trip from
Westchester to this East Village bar. After Marta had first absorbed the shock of Carlos's betrayal, it was Wendy she'd
called first. It was Wendy she'd kept abreast of all the devel-
opments in their sad detail.

Once a freshman roommate, always a freshman roommate.

Wendy scraped a highball glass across the table. "I asked
the bartender for a good postbreakup drink," she said,
swinging into the chair next to Kelly. "He called it a *Bastardo.*"

"Perfect." Marta shoved her Cosmo aside, raised the *Bastardo,* and tipped it to each of them. "Cheers, ladies. Here's
to saying good-bye to one no-good cheating Cuban."

Dhara raised her ice tea. "Good riddance."

Kelly heaved her rum and coke in the air. "*Hasta la vista,*
baby."

Marta took a sip of the *Bastardo* and felt the bite of the
bitters all the way down her throat. The taste mixed really
well with the ashes of failure and the gall of being duped.

She'd had her fill of both. Last Sunday at her mother's
house, after confessing a modified version of the bad news

to her hovering gaggle of female relatives, she'd been smothered with clucking sympathy while cousins thrust their sticky babies into her lap, her aunt overfed her empanadas, and her mother casually discussed the nice young man who worked at the Home Depot. The growing miasma of unmet expectations threatened to suffocate her as she stared at the collage of pictures on her mother's refrigerator.

Pictures of other brides, other people's babies.

And now, among her friends, all she wanted to do was sink her head onto this sticky café table and collapse into a bubble of shame, remorse, and self-pity. These friends had followed her romantic misadventures with great compassion since that life-altering weekend in college. They knew better than anyone how important it was for her to keep her head on straight, to avoid getting swept away and making a dangerous misstep. She'd thought, after meeting Carlos, that she'd finally figured it all out.

But she'd come here not to wallow, but to understand. She filled her lungs with air and summoned the memory of Coach Sammon at the regional Catholic Sports League finals, rolling his wheelchair in front of the bench at halftime when they were down twelve points, his black hair standing up from clutching his head in frustration. He'd yelled at her—bruised, heaving, and achy—to get up off her sorry ass and stop acting like a sobbing little girl.

Start playing smart.

Playing smart. It worked for her in basketball. It worked for her in college. It worked for her in the law firm.

It must work for men.

Seizing her briefcase, she riffled through the pockets and pulled out a fresh yellow legal pad. "Now that you're all here," she said, slapping it on the table, "it's time to start the Marta Lauren Sanchez Arroyo love-life reclamation project."

"Uh-oh," Wendy said. "Deposition time."

"I need some help figuring out what went wrong so I can make sure I don't make the same mistake again."

Wendy arched a brow. "Can we start by trashing your infamous Life Plan?"

"My Life Plan is fine—it's my love life that is not. Now, I've been thinking it over, from the first time I met him, all the way to the moment he grabbed his Williams-Sonoma corkscrew and walked out my door." Marta rolled the pen between her fingers. It felt good, to pull back and think logically about things. She was good at picking details out of six hundred pages of documents. She was good at carrying through plans. "What were the signs I missed? There had to be a pattern of some sort. One thing I *do* know is that you girls never really liked him. And I, blinded by the Cuban god that was Carlos, just ignored everything you said."

The three women exchanged furtive glances.

"*Ay Dios mío*, be honest, please! How am I ever going to figure this out, if you all don't help me? I mean, c'mon, Carlos was *perfect*—he was smart, he was ambitious, and he was one of the hottest guys I'd ever had."

Six foot three, all lean muscle, and even now, after all that had happened, she found her body responding to the memory of him. She hated herself for thinking with her loins. She was smarter than this.

At least, she liked to think she was smarter than this.

"Honestly, Marta, we hardly knew him." Apparently, with the silent vote tallied, Wendy was chosen as the spokesperson. "I think I met him only three times."

"No, no, that's not right." Marta resisted the urge to pull out her BlackBerry and scroll through past appointments. "Off the top of my head, I can think of three times you all have met him just since the New Year's Eve party."

"At the New Year's Eve party," Wendy said, "he was working in the kitchen."

"And when I made partner—"

"Again," she interrupted, "he was working in the kitchen."

"And your engagement party."

"At my ridiculously large engagement party," Wendy added, with a roll of her eyes, "I was lucky to speak more than two words to anyone all evening."

"That's the only time I remember him too," Kelly added. "I mean, you talked a lot *about* him, Marta, and we made a lot of attempts to get together, but that's the first and last time I remember actually meeting him."

Marta looked at Dhara, waiting for her take on the subject.

"He was a very good-looking man," Dhara conceded, "and apparently he made a mean mojito. But frankly, Marta, he was no Tito."

The sound of Tito's name brought the old familiar pang. Her friends still adored him. Tito, with his easy ways, his laid-back attitude, his quick laugh. Years ago, when she was in law school, Dhara in medical school, and Kelly struggling at her first job, it was generous, dependable Tito who'd take them all out to a small Puerto Rican restaurant in Brooklyn, plying them with drinks and food, and showing them how to dance the merengue. He never had much money, but he spent it generously. Tito had adored her. Marta had adored him back.

Ah, mi bonita, you'll never marry a man like me.

"No, he was no Tito," Wendy agreed, slipping her hair behind one ear to expose a Tiffany knot earring. "And that's just the thing, Marta. You never talked about Carlos like you talked about Tito. You talked about Carlos in the same way you talked about the three-foot regional basketball trophy you helped bring to Sacred Heart."

Marta sputtered mid-sip.

"You asked for honesty." Wendy reached for her, her eyes soft. "Even if he was a trophy, even if you didn't really love Carlos, what he did was such a bastard move it would still break the strongest of hearts."

No. *No.* Marta dismissed Wendy's words. Wendy didn't know what she was talking about. Wendy had Parker, after all. Faithful, friendly Parker, who Wendy had known since they were kids. Parker would never get caught with another woman because he wouldn't dare—he'd be terrified Wendy would find out through their special telepathic twin language.

Marta shook herself. It was a jealous thought—unworthy of her. Leave it to her old roommate to cut to the heart of the matter with a cold, sharp cleaver. Marta had been so fixated on making partner this year that she'd barely noticed that Carlos had avoided contact with her friends and her family. She thought he was being accommodating. She thought he was being sweetly patient. The truth was that he was using her for free rent and quick sex. She'd been using him too. Their relationship, on both sides, had been based on convenience. He was as much her fuck-bunny as she was his.

"I'm just going to remind you," Wendy said, as she pulled the red stirrer out of her drink and made a little circle in the air, "that, just as you proved at Pete's Place on Founder's Day junior year, you still have the power to rise from this table, swish that lovely backside, and have half the men in this bar on their knees, remember?"

Marta doubted it. First of all, it'd be pretty hard to put on the confident act, when her ego was a quivering lump of jelly. But, more important, when she glanced toward the bar, to the eclectic collection of young couples, clusters of men just off from work, and a few hipsters from the neighborhood, what she noticed was that most of them were younger than she. Less the age of a thirty-seven-year-old partner in a law firm and more the age of Carlos's lovely wife.

Tick-tock. Tick-tock.

Just then, the tapas arrived, sparing her from further analysis. She slipped the unused pad of paper off the table, tucked it back into her briefcase, and felt grateful when the conversation shifted to another subject.

"All right, I have some news," Dhara said, spearing a tiny battered and fried squid—a *chopito*—with a toothpick. "It should cheer you all up immensely."

Kelly pulled away the shrimp she was about to pop in her mouth. "You've called off the wedding?"

"No," Dhara said, drawing out the word, "but I am having

coffee with Sudesh tomorrow. Just the two of us. No chaperones."

With her index finger, Wendy painted an invisible line in the air. "One point for the American side."

"Buy some stock in incense. Ever since I told my mother about the date, she's burning it to Ganesh twenty-four/seven."

"Hey," Marta said darkly, "do you want some advice on the dangers of getting involved with a man you hardly know?"

"In India," Dhara said gently, "the courtship starts *after* the wedding."

Kelly blurted, "When it's too late to do anything about it!"

"Here's the difference. I actually *do* know quite a bit about Sudesh. About his family and his commitment to this marriage." Dhara cast her gaze away from all of them. "But I've decided that all of you are right in one particular way. It can't hurt for us to start the conversation a little early."

"If you don't like him," Kelly asked, "will you stop the wedding?"

"Frankly, it's more likely after our talk that *he's* not going to like *me*."

Dhara started to say something more, then stopped. Biting her lip, she toyed with a tip of a toothpick stuck in the tapas on the tiny plate before her. Looking at Dhara's suddenly stricken face, Marta's heart turned over. She reached out to touch Dhara's arm, and with a sudden rattle of glasses and plates, Kelly and Wendy did the same.

What a jerk I am. Here Dhara was, holding back boatloads

of pain. *Real* pain. From a *real* relationship with Cole. Unlike herself, whining over some hot jerk who took advantage of her own ridiculous self-absorption.

"Hey, girl." Marta gave Dhara's sleeve a tug. "If it doesn't work out, it's you and me hitting the bar scene on Saturday nights, got it?"

"Unlikely." Dhara's shoulders rose and fell. "My mother will have me doing another Shiva fast, poring through on-line profiles of other prospects."

"Mine is on her knees at every eight a.m. Mass praying to the Holy Mother, but that's not going to keep me away from Nobu on a hot night."

"Oh, but you can't do that." Kelly talked around a mouth-ful. "That breaks the rules."

"She's right, Marta." Wendy tipped her martini at her. "You have to take a six-month hiatus after a serious relation-ship. It's the only way to avoid a rebound. So no dating, no looking. Got it?"

Marta felt a prickle of unease. Her biological clock was ticking at a beat much faster than the Spanish guitar music thrumming through the restaurant. Carlos's betrayal had been a serious setback to her Life Plan. She'd learned the hard way that any deviation was dangerous, any mistake could upend a lifetime of dreams. She did not realize how much she'd been counting on Carlos to be the one to com-plete the next step, until he walked out of her life.

Him and his thick black hair and his broad, strong shoul-ders and his fancy food processor.

The girls were watching her, chewing in silence, anticipating her response with expectant eyes. She felt a sharp pang of guilt. She didn't want to do this on the sly. But she couldn't let some dusty old dating rules—or Carlos's betrayal—put a stop to the plan now hatching in her heart.

"Oh, what fun is that?" Marta gestured to one of the dishes. "Pass me that chorizo, will you? Looks like it's the only real sausage I'll be getting for a good long time."

chapter six

The first time Dhara slipped on a pair of jeans, she'd been a private high school student changing out of her uniform in the stall of a movie theater bathroom. The jeans had been a pair of cast-offs from a schoolmate—contraband—and Dhara had breathlessly accepted them. She remembered marveling at the way the thick seam lifted and separated her buttocks. She remembered feeling a terrible half-angry, half-shameful thrill in bucking her parents' rules, along with a growing exhilaration that the prep-school boys at the nearby academy would now see what she'd been hiding under a shapeless plaid skirt.

Now, wearing a far-better fitting and more upscale pair of jeans, she felt some of the same sense of rebellion as she took the steps, two at a time, out of the subway stop at Houston Street, about to meet her fiancé on a date for the very first time.

She saw him before he saw her. He was leaning against the wall with one foot flat on the bricks behind him, so totally absorbed in his iPod that he was oblivious to the New York crowds passing by.

Sudesh was a good-looking man. Dhara had noticed that from the first. He had the sort of medium-roast complexion that held up well with age and a youthful leanness, probably due to the fact that his family raised him as a vegetarian. Her mother had eventually admitted that he was nearly forty. That explained the look in his eyes when he'd first met her—the patient but nervous gaze that, miraculously, remained above her neck rather than traveling with avidity over her ever-softening, thirty-seven-year-old figure.

She remembered being almost wearily grateful that he wasn't steeped in cheap cologne like the first man her mother had suggested, or laden with gold jewelry and a porn-star mustache like the second.

"Hey, Sudesh."

He glanced up. Behind the shade of her sunglasses, she watched his expression as he pulled out one earbud. She was suddenly, exquisitely, conscious of the slinkiness of her black tank top, the sleek fit of her jeans, and the careless way she'd clipped up her hair to get it off the back of her neck. Last time he'd seen her, she'd been swathed in an apricot sari.

He pushed away from the wall to greet her. She couldn't quite tell if the flicker in his eyes was his gaze slipping, lightning-quick, over her figure, or just a moment of sudden recognition. His gaze was difficult to read behind the glasses that made him look both scholarly and a little bit owlish.

Funny, the two times she'd seen him before today, he hadn't worn glasses.

"It's good to see you, Dhara. But please, call me Desh."

"Desh."

"That's what all my friends call me." He searched the side-walk behind her, his lips quirking into a smile. "What, no protective hordes?"

She let out her breath, not realizing until that moment she'd been holding it, nervous about his reaction to her appearance. "I shook them off in the subway. Though I wouldn't put it past my mother to send a spy or two."

"Ah, so you made the same mistake."

"Pardon?"

"I told my family over dinner last night that I'd be meeting you today."

"Oh, no."

"I'd never noticed before how the smell of incense can ruin a really good vegetable curry."

"Ah, yes," she murmured. "Guilt is a terrible seasoning. My mother is wearing out her knees praying to Ganesh."

"For my mother, every day, a havan to Lord Agni," he said, "to rid the evil spirits."

Dhara nodded in sympathy. Only an Indian mother could make her daughter feel guilty about having coffee in a public place with her own fiancé. First by dramatic and devout prayers, and second by a good hour and a half of strenuous and apparently logical arguments.

What for, Dhara? What good can come of it? You'll have plenty of time to get to know each other after the wedding is done.

And now, face-to-face with that man, Dhara wasn't en-tirely sure that her mother was wrong.

"Come on." He picked up a sports bag and something clanked within. "This place has the best iced masala chai."

She was surprised he remembered. She'd ordered one at the engagement party after the confrontation with Kelly, in the hope that the milky spiced tea would ease the twinge of a headache.

"After we order," he said, opening the door for her to a blast of air-conditioning, "I have a proposition for you."

Proposition.

Dhara gripped the strap of her purse as a whole fleet of possibilities rippled through her mind—a mélange of dark rooms, clean sheets, and sweaty skin. She dropped her gaze as she sidled by him, inadvertently brushing his arm as she entered the coffeehouse.

"Desh," she said, opting to sound casually blasé as she stopped before the counter. "I've already said yes, remember?"

He coughed a little laugh—a nervous hiccup of a sound—as he came up beside her. "I mean a *small* proposition," he corrected, as he pushed his glasses straight with his index finger. "I was just going to suggest that, after we get our drinks, we could go to that park over there."

With nervous relief, she glanced out the window to the green space across the street. "And?"

"They've got bocce courts."

"Bocce."

"Yes." He ordered a double-shot latte along with her iced chai. "I play it sometimes with a crowd of local guys. Have you ever played?"

"The closest I've ever gotten to sports is the StairMaster in the hospital gym, three times a week."

"It's simple. I'll teach you."

She paused, uncertain. A coffee date had a particular advantage. She could call an end to it whenever she wanted, just by rising and leaving. She'd even set up a plan. Marta was scheduled to call her at 6:05 p.m., pretending to be from the hospital, just in case Dhara needed an excuse to get away. The way Dhara figured it last night, while tossing sleepless in her bed, this date could go two ways. Desh could wave off her confession with an easy laugh...or he could break off the engagement, a seismic event whose reverberations would shudder all the way to Jackson Heights.

"Listen, Dhara," he said. "Why don't we pretend, just for a moment, that we're simply two people on a blind date, and thousands of Indian ancestors—and maybe my mother—aren't watching us right now."

Dhara loosened her grip on the strap of her purse. "Tell me, how do we do that?"

"Like this." Desh tucked the iPod in his pocket and thrust out his hand. "Hello, Dhara. I'm Desh Bohara. I'm a professor of philosophy at Hunter College."

She took his hand. It was smooth, and his grip firm, and the unfamiliar feel of it sent a little tremor through her. "A pleasure to meet you, Desh. I'm Dhara Pitalia, a cardiologist at New York Presbyterian Hospital."

"The pleasure is mine. See?" His teeth flashed. "That wasn't so bad."

"Actually," she said, dropping his hand, "aren't all blind dates awkward?"

"Absolutely. Which is why I figured," he said, as steamers

steamed and coffee grinders whirred, "that it would be a lot easier to talk while we played a game. Otherwise, it'll be the classic blind date." He tilted his head toward a table by the window. "You and me staring at each other across that rickety table, with nothing to distract us from the fact that in three months, we two strangers will be wed."

Wed.

Her knees went wobbly. Drawing in a slow breath, she flattened her hand against the counter for support, then turned her attention to the cup the barista was shoving across the table. She hadn't wanted to think about this—in fact, she'd trained her mind not to travel in that direction. It would be better if she *didn't* notice the gentle swell of Desh's biceps against the cotton of his shirt or the movement of his shoulders beneath the cloth. It was unnerving to be standing so close to a warm, breathing, vital man she hardly knew, and with whom, in less than three months, she'd be sharing a nuptial bed.

"Bocce," she muttered, with a swift nod. "Bocce it is."

Dhara followed Desh out of the coffee shop in a mutually awkward silence, clutching her drink as they strode through James J. Walker Park. She was grateful the day was warm but not oppressively humid. She welcomed the early-evening breeze that set the leaves rustling over their heads and went a little way toward cooling her skin. Maybe bocce was a good idea. Clearly, sitting across from him close enough to map the swoop of his cheekbone and the pronounced hollows underneath was not the best way for her to logically, and unemotionally, share her intimate secrets.

But then again, she was growing increasingly convinced that sharing her secrets might be the stupidest idea ever. For Desh continued to live up to her initial impression of him. He was a really nice guy.

As they approached a series of narrow courts, an older man sitting on a folding chair called out with familiarity. Desh waved and exchanged a few words with him as they passed by. Once on the empty court, Desh clanked his sports bag on the ground, crouched down, and unzipped it.

"Hey," she said, "did you just speak to that man in Italian?"

"Badly." Desh pulled out eight fist-size red and green balls and set them in lines. "I spent my junior year in Florence, but I learned all the Italian I know from him and his crazy Sicilian friends."

She glanced over her shoulder. "Is that why he's laughing?"

"Not entirely." He hid his face by peering deeper into the bag. "He's teasing me about you."

With sudden embarrassment, Dhara returned the grinning man's wave, then turned away as Desh launched into an explanation of the game. He tossed a small white ball—called the jack—down the length of the court. With brisk efficiency, he explained that the point of the game was to get as many balls close to the jack as possible. Each ball ahead of his was worth one point. They would play to sixteen.

Sixteen. Didn't seem so long. Maybe, just maybe, it was long enough for the inner traditional Dhara and the outer hypereducated Dhara to wrestle to some kind of hybrid

Indian-American solution. She wouldn't mind being unimpaled from this cultural fence.

"So," she said, lobbing the first ball toward the jack, frantically searching for a neutral topic of conversation. "My parents mentioned that you were a professor, but they didn't tell me you were a professor of philosophy."

"It's a dirty, dirty secret." He stepped up and weighed the ball in his hand. "Like my aunt Chunni's divorce, we don't discuss it in public."

"Let me guess: they wanted you to be an engineer."

"They'd have settled for a chemist, or even an accountant." He stepped forward, lobbing the ball in one smooth, effortless motion. "I told my father that the world needs only so many bridges."

"I took a philosophy course once." She didn't mention that she'd done it only because she needed to fulfill some humanity requirement in a schedule full of hard sciences. "Problems of Philosophy, it was called. If it weren't for Wendy, I'd have failed it altogether. So much talk, so much probing, and so few answers."

"There are no answers." He handed her a green ball, waving her to the head of the court. "Only questions. Three of them, if you go by classical Greek philosophy."

"There have to be more questions than that." Like *how did I get myself in this situation? Why the hell am I playing bocce? Does he really need to know the truth? And how can a man smell like both soap and saffron?*

"Three questions," he reiterated. "And they're deceptively simple. What is there? What should we do? And how can we know? Essentially, it's about the nature of being, the nature of ethics, and the nature of logic. And now," he said with a laugh, "I sound like I'm starting a lecture."

"Full confession." She gave him an apologetic little shrug. "Philosophy gives me a headache."

"Physics used to give me a headache. And I bet you aced it. There—you're a little short," he said, eyeing her throw. "Right now, what I'm studying has a lot to do with linguistics—what each language develops as their verb 'to be' says a lot about their philosophy." He got into position to lob another ball. "And if I go into this any deeper, you'll need a fresh chai."

"Linguistics... That explains why you know Italian?"

"And Hindi and Urdu. I tried a little German. Frankly, I thought I was going to be a language major in college, but though I enjoy parsing out foreign grammar, I can't get my tongue around the Italian r's." He handed her another ball after his fell too long. "Why did you become a cardiologist?"

The question vaulted Dhara right back to her youth when she visited her uncle the pediatrician. Unlike her siblings, who screamed whenever they passed through his door, Dhara had adored him and all the shining implements of his office—the stethoscope, the stainless-steel tools, the measurements cleanly marked on charts, and even—though she winced when she got them—the sharp efficiency of the vaccinations. Medical school had always been a certainty.

"My uncle Japa inspired me," she mused. "But choosing to become a cardiologist, that was a process."

"A difficult one, I imagine."

"Not really. The heart is the body's motor—the source of all power. While I was in school, I just became fascinated with it. It's vital to all life, yet so fragile. It's amazing how easily some crossed electrical signals can make it erratic, how human behavior like smoking, drinking, and diet can so thoroughly affect it in the long-term." She lobbed her last ball, a little farther than the others. "Heart muscle cells are the only cells in the body that can't regenerate."

"That is," he said, tilting his head thoughtfully, "philosophically perfect."

"I suppose. What it really means is that you have to take *special* care of your heart. Once part of it dies, it's gone forever."

A shadow passed over her. She shook the shadow away as Desh led her to the end of the court to count points.

"I do know," Desh said, "that your family is very proud of your accomplishments."

"Ah, my family." Dhara focused on the pattern of balls by the jack. "I feel guilty sometimes the way I strung them along all those years. Had they any idea that it would take me so long to be certified, to have a real position... well, they probably would have nipped the idea of medical school in the bud while I was still in college."

"No, they wouldn't." Desh put up the score—two points to zero—on the battered scoreboard screwed into the cement wall. "I watched them during the engagement party. They dote on you."

Dhara felt a little bubble of warmth. Her parents had doted on Desh too, squiring him around to all her crazy relatives. And Desh had gone right with the flow, even greeting her grandmother by bending down and touching the old woman's feet without hesitation and with great reverence. Desh made it all so effortless. There was no awkwardness. No strained smile. No panicked looks from across the room, amid milling crowds of curious aunts.

Stop.

"It's one of the many reasons," Desh said, crouching down to line the balls up in the dirt as they reached the end of the court, "why I agreed to this arrangement. You can tell a lot about a woman from the way her family behaves around her."

He unfolded himself from the ground and looked at her. Behind the rim of his glasses, she met his soft brown eyes. Steady, honest eyes. And Dhara felt a little shiv of guilt slide between her ribs.

Dishonesty. That's what had killed her relationship with Cole. The lies he kept from her, the truth he was unwilling to confess. That was the reason she had to confess to Desh the one secret that concerned him, before he made the irrevocable step of tracing the vermilion upon the part in her hair.

She took a deep, shaky breath. "You seem like a very sweet man, Desh."

He froze for a moment. "Now I know I'm in trouble."

"I'm sorry?"

"I always hope for *dashing* or *romantic*. I'd even settle for *interesting*."

"Desh—"

"*Distinguished* even." He tried a casual shrug. "Maybe *rugged*."

"There's nothing wrong with *sweet*." She swept up a ball, weighing it in her hand. "Not many men are sweet."

"You are trying to be kind." He stepped back, ceding the space so she could throw. "But I suspect you called me because you are having second thoughts about this arrangement."

The guilt shiv slid a little deeper. Why did she think she could hide her motives? Desh understood how out-of-the-ordinary this unchaperoned date really was, in Indian eyes.

"Dhara, let me tell you something." He traced patterns in the dirt with his feet. "I'm thirty-nine years old. I've been a full professor for three years now. You've probably heard that this is not my first serious relationship."

Dhara remembered her aunt Nisha's secretive little whisper about the American girl Desh chose not to marry.

"It's a difficult thing, for someone without an Indian background, to understand my situation." He squinted as he gazed to the end of the court. "My brothers have their own families, their own houses, but I am the youngest and the last. I will take care of my parents in a house we will share. Perhaps you can imagine that this has been an issue with the women I've brought home to meet my family."

Dhara could almost hear Marta clacking her fingernails, in her post-Tito-breakup era, over a man she'd once met. Mama's boy, Marta had called him—a man in his thirties who still lived with his mother.

But in a traditional Indian family, a mother-in-law ruled

the house and expected to rule the bride. Dhara adored Desh's mom, a dumpling of a woman who'd hugged her so enthusiastically at the engagement party. His mother was round and energetic and bursting with good humor—a dream of a future mother-in-law.

"And so," he continued, gesturing for her to go ahead and toss the ball, "I finally decided that it was time to stop trying to fit square pegs into round holes. I needed an Indian bride who would understand my family obligations."

An Indian bride. A soft, malleable virgin, who'd submit without question to the will of her husband.

Dhara lobbed the ball blindly. It fell considerably short of the jack.

There would never be an easy way to say this.

"I had a serious boyfriend also." She spoke softly, backing up off the court. "And he was so *not* Indian. He was raised by a single mother, with no other family at all. His life was as unfettered as mine was grounded." She watched as Desh idly picked up a ball but made no attempt to take his position or lob it down the court. "I think that was part of the appeal. I never knew what he would do next. Just being around him was..."

Intoxicating.

She was talking too much. Telling too much. And yet, not telling enough.

"I know how this ends." Desh rolled the ball from one hand and then, thoughtfully, to the other. "You couldn't take him home."

"On the contrary. I *did* take him home." She backed up

and felt the bite of the concrete divider against her hip. Blindly, she reached for her iced chai sitting on the flat top. "And my wonderful parents swallowed their many reservations, and they welcomed him. With open arms."

His knuckles went white around the ball. "You loved this man."

She felt a surge of feeling, a sudden rush of emotions, tangled up and so complicated. She remembered one fall afternoon sitting under the huge sycamore outside the Vassar Library, trying to read Milton while Cole lay with his head in her lap, a Frisbee on his stomach, grinning up at her.

"It was a very long courtship. I resisted getting involved." She took a swift sip of her drink, trying to swallow the lump rising in her throat. "But in our thirties, in everything but name, he was my husband."

There. It was spoken. She tilted her chin, but she couldn't muster the courage to look him in the eye. She felt ashamed, and yet at the same time, strangely defiant—the same mix of tugging emotions that had kept her unnerved, uncertain, and in a terrible flux for too many days. The fact that the moment ticked away in an increasingly tense silence told her that Desh wasn't about to gently laugh this off, as one deep part of her had secretly hoped.

Already, she was thinking forward to the inevitable confrontation with her mother when she would have to explain why, suddenly, the Bohara family had backed out of the engagement. A result that became increasingly more certain as she listened to the clack of bocce balls being thrown in other courts, the creak of a branch swaying in the wind, and the chatter of two mothers pushing carriages across the paths. Dhara suspected Desh would be circumspect no matter what. He was a kind man. But she couldn't—wouldn't—tell her mother the truth. It would hurt her too deeply.

Then Desh moved, ambling across the court toward her, finally resting a safe distance away against the divider. "Now," he said, "I understand why you called me today."

She was doing the right thing. Yes, she was. If he couldn't accept this truth, it was best she know now. Even if it did kill the marriage agreement, her family's bubbling happiness, and her plans for the future. She would be free.

To do what, she couldn't even fathom.

"Now it's my turn," he said, "to tell you why I agreed to come today." He leaned back against the divider, rubbing the sand from his hands with more concentration than the task required.

"Last summer," he began, "my parents and I traveled to Ajmer. My father has some distant relatives in a little village outside the city."

Her mind tripped over itself, seeking secret meaning in what was a common thing—an Indian family returning to their birth village to strengthen ties with the distant relatives.

"One afternoon, they took me to the house of a family I had never met before. My father gave me no warning." A muscle flexed in his cheek as he scraped his hands on the divider behind him, bracing himself. "There was a young girl in the family. She was wrapped up in a pink sari. She wouldn't look at me. It was then that I realized that my parents had brought me there to look her over. As a potential bride."

Dhara began to understand. Many Indian-American men went back to their home villages to search for a bride of the appropriate caste and clan. It was a venerated cultural tradition, as old as time.

"The poor girl was maybe fifteen, not a day older." Desh made a strange sound, somewhere between incredulity and frustration. "She didn't speak a word of English. And she was trembling like a bird. I would have married that girl and brought her back here," Desh said, "if what I wanted above all was a virgin bride."

Dhara lifted her gaze and found Desh looking straight at her.

"I did not choose that Ajmer bride, Dhara." His gaze traveled with slow intent from her hairline, across her cheek, and to her lips, where she could feel the heat warming her skin. "I chose you."

H e's a predator, Kelly," Marta said. "You have to be especially careful. You're more vulnerable than most women."

Kelly shared a glance with Dhara and Wendy, silently wondering if they, too, sensed the irony in the statement. Marta hadn't wanted to talk about her situation all month. They were trying to honor her wishes. But Marta, with feigned disinterest, had just pulled a box out of her pharmacy bag.

It was a home pregnancy test.

"You don't have a bullshit detector." Marta unfolded the instructions with deliberate calm. "If you did, you would have known that Trey wanted nothing more from you last night than a hookup."

Kelly flinched. Her heart still didn't believe that. Cole had delivered the bad news earlier today. She hadn't believed him. Even when Marta backed him up by saying she'd witnessed Cole throwing a punch at Trey in the cafeteria, Kelly had just figured Cole must have overreacted to some casual remark.

But on her lap lay the truth. Three pages printed from pickupartists.com, where TreyW300 spilled all the gritty details of his amorous adventures with an easy redhead, posted only hours after he rolled his warm body out of their bed.

"He's my brother but he's still an asshole, Kelly." Wendy struggled with her anger. "When I see him again, I'm going to rip him a new one. But, God, I just wish you'd waited for us before leaving with him."

Kelly plucked at the papers, grappling with the knowledge that she'd brought this upon herself. Last night as she'd nursed a rum and coke at the bar, cooling her heels until her friends came, she'd glanced up and glimpsed a dream. She knew who was sauntering toward her, though she'd missed the rugby game that afternoon. She'd seen photos of him in silver filigreed frames on the grand piano in Wendy's home. The living, breathing version far overwhelmed the image in her fantasies. She kept blinking, not believing that tall, ruddy-cheeked Trey Wainwright, still in his grass-stained rugby shirt, was approaching her with interest in his whiskey-brown eyes.

He'd slipped his elbows on the bar and given her a look that could melt bones.

Beautiful redhead, tell me you're free tonight.

"Well, I've got another rule," Marta added grimly. "Don't get involved with a guy until he gets the thumbs-up from your friends."

Kelly knew Marta was right. Trey was a thousand miles out of her league. But last night a descendant of vice presidents and shipping magnates had swung his arm around her shoulders as he led her out into the spring night. Last night, Trey Wainwright had tugged her into his room in the Alumnae House and gently stripped off her clothing. He'd traced her cheek like she was something as delicate and precious as the china that filled the breakfront in the Wainwright parlor. He kissed her like he loved her, all the more ardently when she whispered that this was her first time.

And for one brief moment, Kelly forgot that she was the infamous Gloucester orphan, the two-day-old infant abandoned on the firehouse steps.

"Yeah, and I've got another rule." Marta pulled a stick out of the box. "No more one-night stands for you, Kelly. And no more mistakes for me either."

chapter seven

Lee Zhao leaned against the opening to Kelly's cubicle, rubbing his eyes as he talked about last weekend's Comic-Con convention. "It was awesome," he said. "I think the only time I slept was on the plane."

Kelly scooted to the edge of her seat, noticing his rumpled shirt and the creases in his khaki pants. "Did you just get back from San Diego?"

"This morning. My suitcase is stashed under my desk."

"Don't worry, the boss-man is waist-deep in router issues." Min Jee, Kelly's cubicle mate, chewed her gum noisily as she hiked her thigh-high boots onto the desk. "Did you and Jack wear the costumes?"

"Oh, yeah. During the *Star Trek* presentation. The whole convention floor was rigged up to look like the inside of the *Starship Enterprise*."

Kelly suppressed a sigh. She'd always wanted to attend the convention, but student loan payments still sucked up a good part of her disposable income. So she got what thrills she could following bootleg cell-phone videos, Twitter feeds, and Lee's stories.

Lee cocked his head at her. "You know that I met Moto Hagio?"

She sucked in a breath. "The Japanese manga artist who created *shojo*?"

"The very one."

"Yeah, but did Jack get to meet that babe from the vampire show?" Min Jee tugged on the blue ends of her choppy hair. "He told me he was going to hunt her down and offer himself up as a sacrifice."

"He wants to tell that story himself." Lee shoved his hands in his pockets and rocked in place. "If you're interested, Jack and I are going out for coffee in a few minutes to try to power-caffeinate ourselves through the rest of the day. Want to join us?"

"Oh, man, I'm so going." Min Jee dropped her feet off the desk and started shutting windows on her computer. "I'm so sick of beta-testing this network software that I'm going to scream if I have to firewall another fake workstation. Can we make it lunch? As long as it's not that burrito place."

"Lunch would be okay. What about you, Kelly?" Lee did another toe-to-heel rock. "We've got a whole bag of swag to share."

She hesitated, plucking at the edges of her lightweight cotton sweater. She'd really love to have lunch with Lee and Jack. But over the past few weeks, it was becoming increasingly apparent that Lee was interested in sharing more than just TV obsessions with her. Even Min Jee sensed it, for her gum chewing had slowed to a contemplative pace.

Then a bouquet of pink roses appeared, handed to her

from over the edge of her cubicle. Startled, she grabbed them and looked beyond to the man thrusting them at her.

"Hey, darling. Surprise."

Kelly blinked. Trey stood before her, his hair haloed by fluorescent lights, and it was such an unexpected sight that for a moment she wondered if Lee Zhao had somehow stolen from Comic-Con a life-size cardboard cutout of the actor Robert Pattinson, who Trey somewhat resembled. But this handsome hunk draped his arms over the edge of the partition, smiling as if his arrival in her office was an every-day event, rather than a first-time-ever.

Then Kelly noticed that Min Jee had stopped chewing her gum entirely, and Lee Zhao was frozen in place.

"Hey, Trey." She pressed her face into the flowers, smelling nothing in her confusion. "These are just lovely."

"I knew you'd like them."

She placed them on her lap and then checked the pencil-roll of her hair, tucking in some wayward strands. "Um . . . this is such a surprise. What are you doing here?"

"Rescuing you from this maze." He rolled his eyes at the room and its seemingly endless rows of boxy cubicles. "I've blown out of the office for the day. It's sunny, it's warm, and it's too nice to work. Come have lunch with me."

Sharp little prickles danced all over her skin. She became exquisitely aware of her naked thighs under her breezy, cotton sundress. She hadn't been alone with Trey in two full weeks. Trey had bunked in Parker's spare bedroom since coming back from London six months ago, with the intent of taking over Parker's lease after Wendy's wedding. The chance of running into Wendy prevented Kelly from going to that sweet sixteenth-floor apartment. Now Cole's presence on her couch prevented Trey from coming to her.

"Don't be rude, Kelly, introduce us to your friend." Min Jee leaped up and thrust out her hand, black fingernail polish and all. "I'm Min Jee, Kelly's lunchtime mah-Jongg partner and fellow C++ programming geek."

"Whoa, Mingee, nice eyebrow stud." Trey grinned as he shook her hand. "I'm Trey Wainwright. Kelly's boyfriend."

Trey slid his gaze toward her with lazy confidence, and a smile that said *I'm not telling them anything that ain't so.* Min Jee's eyes nearly popped out of their black-lined sockets. With his usual good manners, Trey turned to introduce himself to Lee Zhao, who looked like he'd eaten a bad burrito. Lee shook Trey's hand, mumbled some excuse, and shuffled off the field of battle.

Kelly said, "I'd better find a vase for these." She swept the flowers off her lap, crinkling the cellophane. "Trey, why don't you follow me? I'll show you the lunch room."

Kelly exited her cubicle and brushed by him. The friction churned up a whole shower of sparks. His broadening smile told her he'd felt them too, as he fell into pace beside her.

Trey leaned close. "Mad at me?"

"Furious." She meant to sound angry, but the word came out husky instead. Her palms had begun to sweat on the cellophane, but her body was buzzing with excitement. "You didn't call me first."

"We don't have to hide from anybody here."

Kelly wasn't so sure of that. She'd left her desk only to

avoid Min Jee eavesdropping on their conversation, but as she paraded through her workplace carrying a dozen roses with a handsome guy trailing behind, she began to realize the full impact of her decision. As she passed each cubicle, she heard the squeal of chairs against carpet protectors, the clack of a dropped mouse, and the deep-breathed rise of her coworkers from their seats. It was like she were some sort of self-propelling, super conducting magnet, strong enough to pull geeks free from their computers and alert them to a shocking new social paradigm.

"Without my approval," Kelly said, heaving a shaky breath, "you've just made a public quantum leap with our relationship."

"Yes," he murmured, all sexy vibrato. "Yes, I have."

It was impossible to be mad at him, not while the fragrance of a dozen roses billowed around her. The last time she'd received flowers, they were daisies from her prom date, who'd picked them from her own front yard. She'd been wearing a borrowed dress made of cheap rayon. She'd pinned one of the daisies on her bodice to hide a stain.

She swept into the lunchroom, a sprawling room littered with game tables, Foosball, a Nerf basketball net, and a small putting green. Trey paused a few steps into it.

"Whoa."

Kelly waltzed to the sink. A foursome in the middle of a mah-Jongg game—the office's latest obsession—stopped clicking tiles long enough to stare. Kelly waved and then shielded her face with the door of the upper cabinets, where she searched for a vase.

Trey leaned a hip against the counter. "Is this place for real?"

"It's under construction. We've been lobbying for some old-fashioned arcade games, but can't budge the higher-ups."

"No, I mean, seriously. We get memos if we're caught playing computer solitaire. You've got a Ping-Pong table."

"Tournament starts next week. Min Jee's the reigning champion."

"How many piercings does she have?"

"It depends if you count all of them," Kelly said, "or just the ones you can see."

But Trey wasn't paying attention. Two guys from system administration were leaving the lunchroom; one had a blue Mohawk, the other, a leather fetish that revealed itself in vests and chaps. Trey gave them a friendly head bob, and as soon as they left the room, he spoke out of the corner of his mouth. "This place is like that cantina from the *Star Wars* movie."

"The Mos Eisley Cantina on Tatooine." On their last date, she'd made Trey sit through the original three of the series. "Ten geek points to you, big boy."

"How do you get anything done? I'd be playing Foosball all day."

"Discipline." She pulled a dusty acrylic vase from the back of a middle shelf. "Programmers work long hours. We catch inspiration where we can. And, for starters, we don't blow off work to take long lunches."

"I'm not looking for a long lunch." He slid a little closer. "I'm here to coerce you into an afternoon of sweaty sex."

Her mouth went dry. She met his gaze—light brown eyes, dark on the outer ring, lighter in the middle, like liquid amber.

"There's a hotel just around the corner." He dropped his voice. "Room service from a four-star restaurant. An awesome view from the upper floors."

There it was again, that sexy vibration in his whisper. It worked on her like a tuning fork. Her body adjusted instantly to its rhythm. It had been two weeks since she'd bitten his hand to suppress her tendency to moan during sex. Two full weeks since he'd shoved one of her naked legs over his shoulder, grinding into her while she fisted the mattress.

And if she didn't break eye contact with him right now, she'd be hopping onto the cabinet, spreading her knees, and making an even bigger scene in front of all her curious and suddenly hungry coworkers. Besides, she knew him well enough to know that this spontaneous tryst was a distraction, in part. A ploy to get her to ignore all that other stuff that she could read in his eyes.

She slipped the vase in the sink and shoved the faucet on so that it would fill with water fast. "Bad day, huh?"

She noticed that, physically, he pulled back only a fraction—but mentally, she sensed that he reared back about two hundred miles. Oh, yeah. She hadn't forgotten how much he despised his desk job on Wall Street. She hadn't forgotten how he'd confessed his yearning to do something else—*anything* else. So she kept her gaze on him long after the water overflowed the vase.

"Two weeks, Kelly." Trey crossed his arms, blithely changing the subject. "When is this friend of yours going to leave your apartment?"

"I don't know." She hardly saw Cole these days. He stayed out late and slept even later, completely oblivious to the fact that he was a serious kink in her previously awesome sex life. "It's complicated." And it was time to change the subject so Trey wouldn't figure out more than he needed to know. "It would help if we could go to your place now and again."

"It's Parker's place until September. And these days Parker's there all the time." Trey pushed away from the counter as she unwrapped the cellophane and pulled the rubber bands from the stems. "Wendy cut him off cold turkey."

Kelly tried to mute her surprise. Wendy hadn't said anything about that at the tapas place last week. In fact, Wendy had been unusually quiet.

"Yeah, some asinine idea about wanting to make the wedding night special. The guy is climbing the walls."

Kelly slipped the roses into the vase. She didn't like talking about Wendy to Trey. It felt like talking out of school, and the longer she kept this secret, the more it felt like a betrayal. Then Trey came up behind her and wrapped his arms around her waist, enfolding her in nearly six feet of warm, strong Wainwright, and she forgot about Wendy, about flowers, about breathing.

"They've got cable, pay-per-view." He spoke into her hair, carefully nudging the pencil shoved in it. "I'll even promise to sit through *Doctor Who.*" He tightened his grip. "Once we're done."

She had a voice of her own. Somewhere. "I've...I've got a weekly progress meeting at three."

"Reschedule."

"I'm one of the team. Presenting the new networking protocols."

"I love it when you talk like that."

He pulled at her sundress, making the hem climb up past her knee. Against her shoulder blade, she felt the throb of his runner's steady heartbeat. His lips closed over the tip of her ear.

"I can manage," she said, her muscles clenching, "maybe an hour."

Only then did he release her.

On unsteady feet, Kelly took the vase and tried not to stumble back down the maze. As she neared her cubicle, she spied Min Jee on her toes, deep in whispered conversation with Matt, a twenty-something with bleach-tipped hair who worked in the adjoining cubicle. Kelly rounded the partition and slipped the vase across her desk. Min Jee started, and Matt dropped out of view.

"I'm heading out for lunch." Kelly avoided Min Jee's eyes by searching for her cell phone amid the Post-it notes on her desk. "If Karen asks where I am, give my cell a buzz, would you?"

"Sure thing, girlfriend."

Out of the corner of her eye, Kelly caught Trey shaking his head at Min Jee, wordlessly gesturing that Min Jee shouldn't call at all. Kelly straightened in mild annoyance, ready to bust up the conspiracy when she caught sight of the second shocker of the day.

It happened in ultraslow motion. Cole rounded the corner of the far cubicle, his head bobbing. His lanky silhouette loped up the narrow aisle as he searched the nameplates. She saw him lift his curly head. She saw him catch sight of her. His expression bloomed into an open, friendly smile.

And all her systems froze.

She struggled to reboot, her mind working as sluggishly as a dinosaur-grade operating system on a grandfather-generation Pentium processor, trying to pick out the last time Cole and Trey were in the same room together, wondering if they'd even recognize each other, wondering if there were any possible way to change the trajectory of these imminently colliding particles to avoid the inevitable nuclear explosion.

"Hey, Kelly." Cole approached, his freshly shaven face unusually bright. "I was in the neighborhood so I thought I'd stop by."

Trey pushed away from where he leaned against the partition, his focus shifting with curiosity.

"Hey," she stuttered, searching frantically for something to say. "Hey. I . . . um . . . that was nice."

Cole gave a quick chin nod to Trey and Min Jee before turning his attention back to her. "Listen, I just landed a client. A nice fat one. Let's celebrate. I'll take you out for lunch."

Min Jee's mouth dropped open. Kelly caught the glimmer of light winking on Min Jee's tongue stud.

"Sorry, buddy, but she's got plans." Trey thrust out his hand, a good bit of solid shoulder following close behind. "Trey Wainwright here. And you are...?"

Cole instinctively moved to shake his hand, but at the sound of Trey's name, he stiffened like the Tin Man.

Kelly wished she could just curl into a tight little ball and not imagine the stuttering flow of Cole's thoughts as Trey's name rang in his head, as Cole searched Trey's face and no doubt recognized the strong resemblance to Wendy. Kelly rifled through her lackadaisically Catholic childhood in search of prayers that would prevent Cole from remembering the whole ugly affair, but all she could come up with were fishermen's prayers, and not all of them were saintly. Besides, there was no way in hell Cole had forgotten what had happened that terrible weekend. Cole had threatened to make a road trip to Princeton just to pummel the guy—the very man standing before him—for Trey's intimate and public bragging about his redheaded conquest.

Then her body moved on its own. She stepped between them, placed a hand on Cole's chest, and tried to catch his attention. "Cole, I know this is a shock to you, but let's talk about this later."

He took two stumbling steps backward.

"We'll have lunch tomorrow, okay?" She silently pleaded for calm, for understanding. "We'll talk then."

Weaving, Cole spread his feet a little father apart. His gaze shifted to where Trey was standing behind her and then focused with a piercing intensity back on her face. "What the fuck, Kelly?"

Oh, God.

"All those phone calls." Cole scraped his fingers through his crisply curling hair, his mind working through the past two weeks. "Now I get it. You closing your door, locking yourself in your bedroom, whispering secrets. Those calls were from *him*, weren't they? You've been *seeing* him."

"Whoa. *Whoa.*" All six foot something of Trey loomed beside her. "What's this about your bedroom? Who the hell is this?"

"Cole is my friend," Kelly said, turning slightly toward Trey, speaking slowly, as if to calm a child. "He's the one I told you about. The one staying at my apartment."

"You told me you had a girlfriend staying at your apartment."

"No, no I did *not*." She met Trey's wary gaze. "I told you I had a *friend* staying—I never said it was a guy, because I knew you'd act like *this*." She took a deep breath, struggling for calm. "Trey, this is Cole." She held out her palm. "He's Dhara's ex-boyfriend."

"Oh my God, Kelly." Min Jee slapped a hand over her face. "You're living with your best friend's ex?"

"No. No!" Kelly glared at her office mate as heads popped up all across the room, like prairie dogs from burrows. "Cole is my *friend*," she explained. "He's staying on my *couch*."

"This is wrong. So very wrong." Cole backed away, his palms up. "I am totally out of here."

"Damn right," Trey said. "You walk your ass right out of here."

Cole paused, his gaze a challenge. Kelly swung out an arm to hold Trey back.

"Stop it, both of you. Don't go all Neanderthal on me."

Kelly heard someone muttering for security just as Cole made a surly half salute and turned on his heel.

"Don't leave, Cole. Wait!"

But Cole loped with impossibly long strides down the aisle. She panicked. She couldn't let him leave. He'd go looking for information, and the first person he'd call would be Wendy.

"You," she said, swiveling on Trey, "you don't leave. This is *not* what you think."

"Right."

"He could ruin everything. Don't you get it?" Her jaw was tight with frustration. "He will tell your sister."

Trey looked at her out of hooded eyes, a look that made her blood run cold, because although they were still the same whiskey colored eyes that had gazed upon her with passion only minutes earlier, now they gleamed, impenetrable.

"Whatever. Do what you gotta do." He swaggered into her cubicle and sprawled on her chair. "I'll just make friends with Min Jee here."

"Honey," Min Jee said, "it's me who's going to ask the questions. I had no idea Kelly had so much going on."

Kelly turned away, ignoring them both. Trey was angry, but he hadn't stormed away, so he must believe her at some level. She would deal with him later. On swift feet, she headed toward the elevator banks, avoiding both Lee's curious look and the avid stares of the guys working on the routers, who were likely to dislocate a vertebra if they strained any harder to see what was going on. She met Cole at the elevator bank, where he pressed the button with increasing annoyance.

"Didn't realize I was putting such a cramp in your style, Kelly. I'll be out of your apartment tonight."

"You don't have to do that."

"Nothing has changed, has it?" He glared at the lights above the elevator door, rising too slowly for his taste. "You can write code that'll make this company millions of dollars, but you wouldn't know an asshole if he came with a blinking label."

"Promise me you won't say anything."

"Right. I get it. Nobody knows. I know Wendy doesn't." He took one turn, and then, as Min Jee would say, he was right up in her grille. "Because if Wendy knew, she'd get the girls together and chap your ass for falling for her asshole brother again."

Kelly tried very hard to suppress the fury that rose up within her. "You," she said softly, "don't know anything about it."

"I know that guy fucked you before. And it was your first time. And then he wrote all about it, in lurid, full-color detail."

Yes, folks, the rug matches the curtains.

She flinched. "That was fifteen years ago."

"People don't change. He's going to hurt you again. It's just a matter of time."

The elevator rang, and the doors slid open. Cole made a move to step in, but paused as two burly men in blue swaggered out, one talking into a mouthpiece on his collar.

With a chilling sangfroid she didn't even know she possessed, Kelly's arm shot up. "Over there. Two guys. Human resources."

The men nodded and strolled off. Cole slipped into the empty elevator.

"Wait." She slapped her hand on the frame to stop it from closing and then wedged her foot against the slider. "I made you a promise, Cole. I haven't said a word to the girls about you—your job, your apartment, anything. Now you have to make a promise to me."

"I'm not making you any promises."

"Wendy deserves to hear this from *me*."

He shot a glance at her. A strange, bruised, disbelieving glance that cut her to the bone. "For Wendy's sake, I'll hold. But I'm not going to hide this from everyone forever."

Kelly stepped back and the elevator slid shut. She watched the numbers drop while she wondered how she'd gotten herself into this situation. How she'd gotten herself tangled up in so many lies.

She had to get out of this office. She swiveled to return to her cubicle only to be greeted by the sight of a dozen heads shooting down, like some geek Whac-A-Mole game.

And this time when she advanced down the aisle, it was a long, hard walk of shame, and she made a point of keeping her chin high but her gaze averted. She arrived at her own desk to find Trey in full flirt mode, deep in conversation with a giggling Min Jee.

She must have looked utterly wrecked because the cocky smile he'd turned to her froze and then faded. He shifted his weight so he wasn't leaning so close to her office mate.

"We need to get out of here," she said, "before the security brutes figure out it's me causing all the trouble."

"Let's go."

He stood up, sidled by her, and headed down the aisle. She caught his hand and tugged him to a stop. Her throat felt like sandpaper, and her head was beginning to throb. She wove her fingers with his and stepped very close.

She spoke quietly to the knot of his tie. "Are you still interested in lunch?"

He made her wait through long, agonizing moments.

"Cover for her, Min Jee. She's going to be very late."

⌒⌒

Kelly leaned back in the upholstered chair, naked under the terrycloth robe emblazoned with the logo of the hotel. She stared out the window, watching the line of yellow cabs zoom down the canyon of lower Broadway. She still felt languorous from a vigorous bout of sex with Trey, who was at the door to the hotel room right now signing for room service.

All in all, she thought, her heart pinching, a fancy hotel suite in a snobby Manhattan hotel wasn't a bad setting for the end of a relationship.

A tall glass of ice tea appeared before her. She followed bare arm to bare chest, to Trey's grinning face.

"I figured you'd be thirsty."

She took the glass and forced a smile. The sheets of the bed behind him were a knotted tangle, the pillows askew, and the comforter in a heap on the floor. Jealousy, she'd discovered, was a lusty bedfellow. For though she'd explained all the way to the hotel the somewhat edited reason for Cole's presence in her apartment—and Trey with feigned casualness had conceded he believed her—he'd nonetheless jerked her into his arms the moment the door to the hotel room closed behind them.

It was a reflex, she told herself. A very primitive need on his part to stake his claim. To think of his lovemaking in any other way was just to make a romantic muddle of it, and the last thing she needed right now was a false sense of hope. She would keep her feet flat on the floor—brace them, like she did on the trawler in a rough sea—and not let her wavering emotions unsteady her from what she knew was best.

Trey slipped two silver-domed plates on the table, along with linen napkins, silver utensils, and tiny crystal salt and pepper shakers. Before he sat down, he took away the silver domes. On the china plate before her, fragrant and warm, lay a crusty panini sandwich. Apparently, arugula was a kind of lettuce.

She savored two bites before she set the sandwich back on her plate and watched him tuck into a steak.

"I am sorry." She twirled the glass of ice tea in its puddle of condensation. "About the whole thing with Cole."

He shrugged and waved his knife, cutting off the whole discussion.

"It is going to cause some complications," she added.

His chewing slowed. "You said he was leaving your apartment."

"Oh, he is." She traced her plate's rippled gold edging. "The guy can't bear to look in my face anymore. In any case, that's not the kind of complication I'm talking about."

His shrug was a flex of the shoulders, and his attention stayed on his food. "You think he's going to tell my sister."

"I *know* he's going to tell your sister." She curled her freckled legs up on the cushioned chair. "Maybe not today, maybe not tomorrow. He hasn't spoken to her in a while. But eventually, he will."

"So let him."

"Just like that?" Over the past months, she had prided herself on learning to understand every flicker of Trey's facial muscles. She'd made a study of it, forcing herself to develop that particular skill with this particular man. But she couldn't read anything in his expression now, as he sat with his head down, his shock of hair just showing the first signs of thinning. "Trey, we've been lying to her for over three months."

"Technically, I haven't. She never asks who I'm seeing. She's got her hands full with this wedding."

"That's an excuse." Kelly knew Trey didn't want any friction with his sister. He'd once confessed that Wendy was the only person in his family who'd even had an inkling of compassion for him since he'd been forced out of his position in that London bank. "You didn't want to deal with the shit storm, either."

"If she had asked me, I'd have told her flat out." The knife flashed in her direction. "It's *you* who wanted to keep this on the down low."

Trey continued to cut his steak into bite-size pieces. It was certainly true that she'd suggested they keep the relationship a secret. If the girls knew, they would have called an intervention, and she wouldn't have been able to explain to them why she'd forgiven Trey.

Because what he'd confessed to her at Wendy's engagement party in January—blessedly alone in the light-bedecked winter pavilion—was a glimpse into the boy Trey once was, and an insight into the man he'd become.

"Kelly, here's the thing a lot of women don't know. To a young guy, a pretty girl is like a lioness in lipstick. If he approaches her right, she might give him a chance to get to know her. If he fumbles, or stutters, or says something asinine, she'll cut him cold. Those pickup guys gave me confidence. I didn't realize, until long after, that they asked way too much in return."

Now she watched him eating across the table, while her gaze lingered on the red highlights gleaming in his hair. That night, his confession had seemed so heartfelt, his expression so vulnerable, and it had taken a great force of will to calmly reassure him that all was forgiven, and then, even more calmly, to walk away from him. Only when he pursued her six weeks later did she loosen her grip on her libido, and then her heart.

Now she had to prepare to leave him again, with as much dignity as a fisherman's daughter could muster.

"Do you remember that brunch we shared a few months

ago," she murmured, running her fingers through her tumbled hair, "that dim sum place near my apartment?"

It was one of her favorite local finds—a tiny storefront Cantonese restaurant that served massive amounts of steamed dumplings and rice noodle rolls, along with bottomless pots of fragrant jasmine tea.

"I remember you originally offered me a breakfast of powdered milk, store-brand instant coffee, and frozen cans of orange juice."

She flushed, remembering the look of horror as he perused the contents of her kitchen that first rainy March morning before suggesting in his most polite way that they go out for brunch.

"I'd have eaten anything after that." Trey pointed a piece of steak at her. "And I believe I did—chicken feet, right?"

"They called them phoenix talons," she confessed. "That waiter spoke English, you know. He just wanted to see the look on your face. He did that to me, too, the first time I showed up."

"Yeah, I figured there was a reason every Chinaman in the room was grinning."

"It wasn't all bad."

"Oh, no. Those buns with the bean paste—"

"Three orders, I remember."

"Yeah, they were something."

"And do you remember when we went bowling?"

Trey laughed into his napkin. "I think that was the first time I understood what it was like to be a minority."

The two of them had been the palest people at the lanes

off Times Square, a lively bowling alley that—despite all the new neon lighting, fancy fruit drinks, and shiny polished lanes—still exuded the smell of stale tobacco and cheap spilled beer, a particular blend that she always associated with the ten-pin bowling alleys of her youth.

She remembered teasing him about his reluctance to wear rented shoes. "If I remember correctly, I whooped your ass."

"Oh yeah, I sucked. The rum shooters didn't help."

"You know," she said, picking up her sandwich, "that might have been my favorite date of all."

She bit into her panini, not really tasting it, sensing as she did his sudden stillness. His fork and knife clinked as he laid them on the plate, and she felt a little tremor inside her. It was going to take more strength than she thought to make sure this lovely affair ended with as much dignity as possible.

"What's going on in that techie head of yours, Kelly Palazzo of the Gloucester Palazzos?"

"Come on, Trey." She felt a swelling pressure in her throat. "We had a really good run of it, didn't we?"

He looked at her as if she'd just sprouted wings. "Whoa. Whoa."

"I don't want to ruin all this." She gestured to the hotel room with its down comforter and flat-screen TV and impossibly big bed, meaning so much more than the place. "I mean, it's really been great, Trey. It's been exciting and incredibly romantic, and you've just been . . . well, you've been wonderful. But I know you didn't get into this expecting forever."

"Hold on—wait a minute."

"I understand you better than you know." Her breath caught in her throat; it hitched against her will. "I know, from Wendy, that you rarely stay with a woman more than a few months—"

"Hey—"

"—and I don't want to make things difficult. I told myself, way back in March, that if things got complicated—messy— well, I promised that we would just skip that part and go right to the end."

His face mottled. "You're breaking up with me."

"I'm Kelly Palazzo." She held up her hands, palms out. "I'm a working-class girl from the wrong part of Gloucester. The only reason I got into Vassar is because I hooked the admissions officer with the sob story in my essay—you know, about how my father's living depended on the seasonal runs of whiting and how I nearly broke my mother's budget insisting on bags of lemons so I could scrub the smell of fish off my skin every night."

She could tell, by the way his eyes widened, that she was going too deep—into waters he'd never be able to fathom.

"Do you have any idea what it means, for a girl like me, to attract a guy like you? It's fairy godmother stuff, Trey. I'm a freakin' geek. After our little scene in the office today, my social cred went up, like, a trillion gigabytes. But midnight is coming, and the ball is over." She leaned across the table and covered his hand with hers. "Let's cut bait now, before everything gets complicated. That way, we'll both leave with good memories."

His thumb came up from under her hand to stroke her

fingers. He fiddled with them while a line deepened between his brows. The sound of cab horns and squealing tires drifted up from the street.

"You're always taking me by surprise, Kell."

She shivered a bit at the sound of the nickname.

"I mean, if I didn't know you better, I'd think you'd practiced all of that." Hurt brown eyes, wide and wounded. "That you were playing me, somehow."

"Trey, I wouldn't know how to 'play' anyone."

"You're making it too easy." He shifted his weight against the chair. "I mean, one word, and I'm cut loose entirely."

"No anger, no hurt feelings." Damn her eyes, prickling already. "And absolutely no regrets."

How long could she do this? She focused on the wink of a gold fleck in his left eye, becoming more blurry as tears gathered. Then, to hide the tears, she dropped her gaze to the naked V of his chest, growing more and more blotchy under the influence of some internal struggle.

The silence stretched. Her heart swelled, choking her. She tried, very hard, to smile.

Trey tightened his grip on her hand and fixed her gaze across the silver, china, and linens. His face looked strange. There was no laughter in his brown eyes, no devil-may-care Wainwright looking for a quick and easy joke to slip them both out of the moment.

"You're not like anyone else I've ever dated." A muscle moved in his cheek. "The girls I've known have certain... expectations. You don't. You take me as I am. It's weird. And it's really good."

And for a moment, she felt like a very tiny, charged particle in a very quantum world—a world where you can know where you are or how fast you're going—but never both at the same time.

"Kell," he said. "I am not letting you go."

chapter eight

Wendy leaned back against the stern pulpit of Parker's forty-foot sailboat, shading her eyes against the sun winking between the jib and the mainsail. "Hey, Parker, the telltales on the jib are fluttering. You want me to trim it?"

"I got it."

"I'm right here," she said, picking up the handle by her feet. "I can crank the winch—"

"That's my job." Parker came out of the forward cabin clutching a glass of cranberry ice tea in one hand and a frosty microbrewery beer in the other. "We made a deal. Your only purpose today is to soak up some sun and give me an eyeful of that fine, blue bikini."

Wendy took the drink out of his hand, hoping Parker didn't notice the strain it took to make her smile reach her eyes. She handed him the handle for the winch and then slid down the pulpit to settle on the port bench.

She let her gaze linger on her fiancé. The sun blazed on his hair, bleaching more white streaks in the blond mop that flopped in barbershop perfection over his brow. That hank of hair had always begged for her fingers to run through it, even when he was a ten-year-old stealing her pencils at their private Montessori day school. Of course, he'd long grown out of the skinny brat phase, maturing into the athletic young man whose diffident, let's-not-take-this-too-seriously attitude had gradually coaxed her out of the brooding celibacy of her post-Soho days. For a girl so battered by stormy seas, Parker's arms had proven to be a peaceful harbor.

Yet now the sight of him, lean and sunburned, only pinched her heart. For though she'd carefully avoided the subject as Parker tacked out deeper into Long Island Sound, eventually, Wendy knew she'd have to bring up Birdie again.

"Now that's what I want to see."

Parker squinted in her direction, grinning as he pulled off the handle of the winch. She blindly patted her shoulder, wondering if a bathing suit strap had slipped off, but she was wearing a bandeau and everything was in place.

"You sitting there," he said, "with your long legs stretched out, making me look like the luckiest man in the world."

She made a soft hitching sound. She planted her tea in the cup holder, then rose to her feet. She wrapped her fingers around the rail ropes that curved around the stern, gripping them so hard that sharp bits of fiberglass dug into her palm. "Hey, Park, how about we go out a little farther today? Maybe into deeper water? We haven't done that in a while."

"Who are you," he laughed, as he tucked the handle back where it belonged, "and what did you do with my fiancée?"

"I'm just in the mood for adventure."

Deeper water meant gusty wind, bigger swells, and a straining lean to the boat. Deeper water meant she'd have to concentrate on helping Parker sail in order to battle the currents around the tip of the island. Deeper water meant she had more time to avoid the inevitable.

"Well you know, I'm always jonesing for speed." He gave her an odd look as he made his way back to the wheel. "But I thought you'd want to relax today. You know, just take it easy."

Yes, she knew she should be enjoying the swift, clean cut of the *Livibell* through the rippling water, the feel of the sea breeze in her hair, the unscheduled, unstructured afternoon free of fittings and floral appointments, rather than battling a fierce longing for an unfiltered cigarette. "Maybe I just want to fight the boat a little."

Or just win a fight for a change.

She winced. Part of her itched for the battle. Part of her was royally pissed that Parker didn't want Birdie at the wedding. But she was determined to be mature about this. She understood the need for diplomacy. She'd been struggling to identify with Parker's point of view while cultivating an argument strong enough to change his mind.

"Well, it's true I haven't had this girl of mine out of the marina for days now." He eyed the sudden fluttering of the mainsail as he palmed the wheel a bit. His ears seemed perked to notice the changing pitch of the wind through the ropes. "You think she feels a little neglected?"

Wendy thought not. Some of the guys at the club loved

horses—bought them, stabled them, raced them, and talked endlessly about them. Other guys loved yachts—the bigger, the more customized, the better. Parker's passion was more visceral. He liked the way the water felt rushing past the fiberglass hull; he liked the rasp of the ropes in his hand; he liked the way the bulging sails harnessed the power of the wind. She'd often figured that he'd marry this boat, if it were an option.

But stating the truth wouldn't further her goal. "I think," Wendy said, "that it's always dangerous to take a girl for granted."

"Maybe she's just jealous that I spent last week at another regatta, feeling up another boat's rudder."

"You cheating bastard, you."

"She has to know," he said, sidling her a glance, "that for all the time I spend away, she's my one and only girl."

Wendy met his dark blue eyes with a prickle of guilt. She knew Parker was true-blue loyal. With the boat and the regattas, there was no room in his life for another lover. Yet into her mind, unwittingly, slipped the image of a sexy Brazilian electrician, an artist with an unforgettable face.

"No, we stay in the sound today," he said firmly. "I promised I'd give you a relaxing day, and that's what you're getting." His gaze drifted from the sleek upsweep of her hair all the way down to the pale pink polish on her toes. "Gotta keep to the plan."

"What plan?"

"Lunch."

Then she looked ahead to where he was directing the

boat. She saw a familiar shallow-draft curl in the shoreline. She glanced at him sharply, but he kept his profile toward her. They'd been to this cove often enough that she knew why he'd chosen it. The knowledge brought a wave of irritation.

"Hey, Parker," she said, struggling to tame her tongue, "just remember you're cut off."

His lip did a little pull. "Yeah, I remember."

"I warned you a long time ago. Three months before the wedding, no more horizontal rumba."

"I completely respect your opinion."

"It's the only way to make the wedding night special."

"I know you've got my best interests at heart."

"Then why are we heading to the old parking spot?"

"Just lunch. Lobster salad from Brennan's. Fresh rolls. A bottle of Dom. Strawberries dipped in dark chocolate."

She knew, in his own guy way, this was Parker's method of apologizing. He'd brought along her favorite food from a roadside seafood deli at a marina twelve miles up the road. *And* he'd made the trip to the farmers' market downtown for the dipped strawberries. But it annoyed her that he would fall back on food and sex while a quarrel still lingered between them.

"Hey, hey." Parker laid his hand on her arm, sensing, perhaps, that he'd gone too far. "Listen, it's just lunch."

"Right."

"Not that I'll say no to any dessert you offer."

"Parker."

"I'm only human, Wendy. And that bikini is killing me."

"I shouldn't have come out today."

"Yes, you should have. You need to relax. You're not yourself. It's like when I'm with you, you're not even *here*."

She imagined, fleetingly, a pair of tilted brown eyes, wistful with regret.

"Cove first," he added, "and rough water later, if that's what you really want. Today, I'll grant you any wish."

"Then let me have Birdie at our wedding."

The words cut through the screeching of the gulls and the flapping of the mainsail. They fell into a strange pool of silence, and hung there.

And Wendy remembered a moment at last year's annual charity gala, as Wendy watched her mother talk with a generous donor about some new acquisition for the museum. Mid-sentence, the donor made some rude joke about the ethnicity of one of the museum's employees. Her mother stiffened, frozen for a moment of uncomfortable silence, then discreetly changed the subject.

By the sight of Parker's suddenly blank face, there was no way to discreetly ignore what Wendy had just blurted aloud. She didn't want to ignore it. She was tired of pretending that the issue hadn't been churning in her stomach ever since their truncated discussion at the country club.

Parker gripped the wheel against a windy gust shooting around the headland of the cove. "So that's what this is about."

"You know it is."

"We resolved that issue at the club."

"We didn't resolve the issue." She remembered the looks

they'd received as they'd discussed the issue in low tones outside the yellow parlor. "We just stopped talking about it."

"Your own mother doesn't want Birdie at the wedding."

"God forbid there's any unpleasantness."

"She's not wrong." Parker reached for his beer, took a good long swallow, and then squinted out at the curving coastline. "You told me the seating arrangements have been finalized."

"There's nothing so written in stone that it can't be adjusted for one or two more guests."

"So you expect me to just forget the dinner we had with Birdie last year."

Wendy suppressed a wince. It had been the first time the three of them had gone out in public. Birdie had misbehaved. She'd made a terrible scene in the restaurant. Birdie hadn't meant to...she was just overexcited, uncomfortable, and unsure of Parker.

"Birdie," Wendy said with conviction, "will behave at our wedding."

The breeze tossed Parker's hair wildly. "Wendy, for God's sake, you know you can't guarantee that."

No, she couldn't. Birdie was chaos, Birdie was blessedly unpredictable. Wendy remembered a day in her teens when she and Birdie ran out to the little shed where a towering drift of snow from a storm nearly met the roof. Wendy had called her friends—Miss Porter's girls—to join her in sledding, but they had refused. They were too old for that, they said, as they headed out to Vermont for the weekend. But Birdie wasn't too old for sledding. They'd pulled out their toboggans, climbed the roof, and sailed off it down the long, sloping hill to the frozen pond.

Birdie was never too old for fun.

"Does it really matter if she behaves badly?" She thought of Dhara's engagement party, where one of the uncles had tried to break-dance to Usher. "Aren't weddings supposed to be filled with family drama? Birdie is our own homegrown family drama. Why leave her out?"

"Because people will stare."

"We've invited lots of ignorant guests to our wedding."

"People will walk wide circles to avoid her."

"Birdie doesn't care about that."

"Why would you do this to her?"

"Really, Parker? You're asking me why I'd invite my only sister to our wedding?"

"You'll embarrass her in front of everyone we know. Do you think James won't make mocking imitations—"

"Parker. She'll laugh along with him. She won't care." Wendy fixed him with her gaze. "Or is it *you* who will be embarrassed, to have at our wedding an adult with Down syndrome?"

The eyes he turned on her were harsh. Wendy felt an urge for a cigarette—as bitingly keen as when she'd first quit, years and years ago. Her accusation wasn't completely fair, and she knew it. Parker had dutifully trudged up to Birdie's assisted living facility with Wendy many a long Sunday. It wasn't completely his fault that Birdie didn't warm to him. Wendy shared a special relationship with her sister, cultivated in the bubble of their childhood, insular and fierce.

Parker, awkward in Birdie's presence, couldn't help but be viewed as an intruder.

That stung nonetheless. Birdie didn't act that way around anyone else. Dhara had met Birdie when Wendy wanted a second opinion on the situation with Birdie's heart defect, and the two of them had gotten along fine. Kelly had spent a Thanksgiving with the Wainwrights during one college year, when Birdie still came home for the holiday and Trey was abroad, and Birdie still asked after her. It was actually through the eyes of her college friends that Wendy came to understand how disruptive Birdie's presence could be, how unusual were Birdie's unpredictable moods and awkward social inhibitions. Birdie lived at the physically and mentally more challenging end of the spectrum. Birdie simply wasn't the TV-ready version of Down syndrome.

But Wendy had grown up with her. The rollicking chaos of Birdie was what she adored the most.

"She's my sister," Wendy said, mustering up all the well-practiced arguments. "She's my *only* sister, Parker. The girl I shared my childhood with, the woman who is among my best of friends—"

"Then have her at the wedding." Parker put his shoulders into steering the boat around the headland winds, his muscles straining against the salt-and-wind-faded Princeton crew team tank. "Okay? Just arrange for her to be there, Wendy, if that's what you really want."

Wendy wove a little, unbalanced by Parker's sudden capitulation. She felt like she'd just swung a fist through thin air.

She said, "You'll support me when I tell my mother."

"Yes."

"Even though she'll fight this."

"Yes."

"But you think it's a terrible idea."

"Yes."

Wendy grasped the stern ropes. She thought of all the compromises she'd made for Parker's sake. She'd allowed their honeymoon to coincide with a Greek regatta, where Parker would be spending a full day sailing around the isles without her. She'd agreed when he'd asked her to cross two names off the guest list, artists from her Soho days. (*For God's sake, Wendy, you think that crazy Ukrainian is going to remove his ball gag? And what if your Lebanese friend decides to make naked performance art out of the Viennese Waltz?*) She'd compromised with him, in a hundred little ways, thinking that was how happy marriages were made.

"I'll agree to have Birdie there," Parker said, as he let the jib go slack and he steered the boat to a good mooring, "because you want it so badly. Isn't that why you've been pulling away from me these past weeks?"

Wendy felt the ghostly shadow of a paint-flecked hand against her palm. She saw, in her mind's eye, a shock of crisp, dark hair. And around her, the salt-sea breeze smelled oddly of turpentine.

"Yes." She spoke quickly, roughly. "Yes."

"Then by all means, bring Birdie to our wedding."

She slid down onto the port bench as Parker set the wheel and abandoned the back deck to work on the sails. She took a shaky sip of her ice tea as Parker climbed over the deck, set out the anchor, and tied ropes with the quick hands of a man who raced boats regularly.

She'd won the skirmish.

The victory shouldn't feel so hollow.

Moments later, a shadow fell across her face. Wendy looked up to find Parker leaning over her.

"Listen," he said, his voice conciliatory. "I don't want to make a big deal of this. In three months, this wedding will be over. Your mother's meddling, this whole thing with Birdie, it'll all be in the past."

She dropped her gaze to the sailor's knot necklace she'd given him for their fifth anniversary, swaying from his neck.

"And you and I," he continued, "we'll be drifting on a yacht in the Aegean Sea. We'll be sipping ouzo and basking in the Mediterranean sun. We'll be island-hopping, eating moussaka, and growing fat on baklava."

He cupped her face in his hands, drawing her gaze back. She searched his dear, dark blue eyes for some sense of understanding. She was torn between the urge to push him away and an equally insistent urge to pull him closer. These past years, he'd been the partner in a tux dutifully beside her at every club function, smiling as she nattered on about art. He'd been the sweet lover accommodating her silence about her Soho past. He'd been the solid man at her side, snickering at her snarky jokes. She was glad he'd compromised about Birdie, but she wanted more.

She wanted him to love Birdie too.

"And then," he continued, "when our honeymoon is over,

we'll be back here. We'll be playing tennis at the club, knocking that damn arrogant new couple off the leader board. And, eventually, we'll look for a little house up in Armonk, or Larchmont, or wherever you want to live—"

"As long," she interrupted in a whisper, "as it's close to the marina."

"Yes." He smiled, slowly shifting onto his knees, clearly pleased that she'd picked up the familiar narrative. "Yes. A five-bedroom, close to the marina. And before you know it, you and I, we'll be settled in that fine house, starting a fine family."

A ripple of emotion trembled through her, an emotion she was too frightened to name. She didn't need to hear Parker spell out her future. She saw it clearly. It was a life as unruffled as the surface of an upstate lake. It was a life bathed in shades of golden afternoons.

"We'll vacation in Vail with Audrey and James," he continued. "We'll spend weeks in Newport for the regatta—"

"Stop talking, Parker."

"—and everything will be just as we dreamed, Wendy. Just as we always wanted."

She dug her fingers into his forearms. She stopped him the only way she could—with a kiss, a hard kiss, a kiss on his cold, salty lips that gave him no more reason to speak.

~~ chapter nine

W ill you please stop complaining, Mother?" Marta slung her tote over her shoulder and leaned toward the curb, searching far down the street for the red awning of the café. "We're only a few blocks away from the street fair."

"*Loco,* Marta. This is just crazy." Her mother's gently padded thighs labored as she tried to keep up. "I mean, look at you, with those ridiculous sunglasses, dragging me down the back streets of Brooklyn on some scheme. I thought my daughter was a lawyer. Yet here you are, acting like some sneaky actress in a Colombian telenovela."

"I'll have you know these are designer shades," Marta said, lifting her sunglasses high enough to give her mother an arch look. "And I am *not* being sneaky. You and I are just making a little detour from the Bedford Street fair because I suddenly remembered a great bakery nearby. A little Italian café that I happen to know because of Tito."

"One that Tito still goes to," her mother retorted, "every Saturday morning at ten o'clock."

"Information that you yourself dragged out of Uncle Pedro." Marta slipped into Manhattan walking speed. "Come on, Mom, didn't you think I was eventually going to act on it?"

"Marta, *mi hija,* my darling little girl, just think for a moment." With short-nailed hands that could deftly fold the banana leaf of a *pastele,* her mother gestured to the expanse of the quiet side street. "Do you really think Tito is going to believe that you—a big-shot junior partner—just happened to be wandering around this neighborhood at nine thirty in the morning?"

"The biggest fair in Williamsburg is six blocks from here. Lots of people are here. How is this weird?"

"For starters, you haven't taken a Saturday off in seven years."

She flinched. "*He* doesn't know that."

"And why would he think that you've changed from when he last knew you?"

"Because now that I'm a junior partner, I can take a day off now and again. And so, we just happened to be so close to this café, and I remember it had killer cappuccinos, and there we go—a perfectly viable excuse—"

"For hunting down an old boyfriend."

Marta tried very hard not to sigh. She wasn't really *hunting.* She was just engineering a casual meeting. Gauging the situation. Seeing if there might still be a spark with the man she now knew she should never have let go. She would have much preferred to have Wendy or Dhara or Kelly along on this adventure, but that was a no-go. If they even *suspected* she was contacting Tito, they'd plant her butt on the hot seat of an intervention. And with reason. She was clearly breaking at least two major rules: initiating a relationship before six months had passed and committing the same romantic mistake twice.

So here she was, stuck with her mother, who had been utterly giddy when she'd first mentioned wanting to see Tito again. In fact, her mother had risen up from the kitchen table where she'd been drinking her third cup of coffee and started pacing, checking her calendar for upcoming family events, verbally listing who she could pump for information, and when and where she would see them. But when Marta had given her the details of today's plans, her mother had turned completely sour.

"There," Marta said, fixing on the sight of an awning halfway down the block. "There it is."

She had begun to worry that the café might have closed as they passed kosher butchers, tiny bodegas, and check-cashing storefronts. The little café appeared to be the only reminder that this part of Brooklyn was once predominantly Italian-American. She'd never seen it in the light of day. Back when she and Tito were an item, he used to bring her here after a night of salsa dancing at a nearby Bushwick club. Even at two in the morning, the place would be full of revelers, shouting and laughing over tiny, hot, bitter cups of espresso—or cappuccinos, dusted with nutmeg.

Ducking her head, she headed toward the café, rewording again and again what she intended to say the first time she laid eyes on Tito. After her experience with Carlos, she was just beginning to realize how little she had appreciated her old boyfriend. Oh, she'd always appreciated his generosity, for law school had left her no cash for going out. She'd appreciated his patience too, for he'd sensed her reluctance, at first, to become involved with a man ten years older than herself—especially one from the old neighborhood who had been all but hand-picked by their respective *abuelas*.

But she'd never truly appreciated how he made her laugh so easily with old family stories, how he relaxed her by teaching her to dance, how he charmed her into putting the books away for a few hours and taught her to just have *fun*.

What a husband he would have been.

"This is it?" Her mother paused as they neared the café with its rickety chairs and tables and a ripped and faded awning. "Really?"

"Yup. Best coffee in Brooklyn."

Her mother wrinkled her nose as she squinted into the dim interior, the only light a little TV mounted in the corner set on some foreign sports channel. "You know that Tito's *abuela* is having an eighty-seventh birthday party in two weeks, right?"

"Three times you've told me that, Mom. Since this morning."

"Your own grandmother is throwing it. She'd love to see you. Everyone would. You've been a no-show at every family event since your cousin Rico's wedding. And I know—for sure—that Tito will be there."

"Great. That'll give Uncle Pedro an opportunity to waggle those caterpillar eyebrows of his, and Aunt Fidelia to make remarks about who'll be the next bride." Her heart gave a little skitter. "And my nieces, they'll have an opportunity to dance around singing 'Tito and Marta sitting in a tree...'"

"So instead," her mother said, gesturing to the deserted neighborhood, "we sneak out here and pounce on him?"

"Mom, I'm not doing any pouncing." Marta took her mother's arm and pulled her under the awning. She chose a table strategically situated by the window, but in the shadows, so that anyone looking in from the bright June morning would not easily see her. "We'll have a coffee. Tito will come by. We'll all have a nice polite conversation...and then we'll see."

We'll see, indeed. Marta felt vaguely nauseous as she hooked her tote over the spindle of her chair. Tito would have every right to ignore her today. No ugly arguments or unforgettable words had heralded their breakup. It had been a quiet thing. Just thinking about it buried Marta in confusion and shame.

It had been a typical law-associate day. She'd been sprawled at her desk in the middle of her cubicle, piles of papers everywhere, her mind buried in a huge deal. She'd heard her name, and she looked up to see Tito standing in the doorway, sporting a new suit.

She'd completely forgotten that they'd made a lunch date.

"Oh, Tito." She glanced at the papers strewn around her. *"I just...I just can't."*

"You have to eat, Marta."

She'd stared at him in panic, willing him to understand. The papers had to be filed the next day. She'd had six boxes of documents yet to review, and two partners whose approval hinged on the quality of her work. Past Tito's shoulder she'd glimpsed one of those partners come into view, buttoning his suit jacket on the way to the elevator. He'd looked curiously at Tito. Marta had practically heard his thoughts as he stitched together the relationship. She re-

membered that a flush had risen up her cheeks, a warmth
full of mortification for Tito and his ill-fitting suit and his
scuffed shoes better fit for dancing.

But that wasn't why she'd hesitated. She'd hesitated because the weekend before Tito had talked in a soft voice
about dreams, and hopes, and how beautiful her babies
would be.

She'd felt herself tremble uncontrollably.

Babies changed everything.

"I'm sorry, Tito." Her voice caught. *"I can't have lunch with
you today."*

Tito had looked at her for a long moment. He'd turned
slightly, caught sight of the partner's curious gaze, and then
brought his attention back to her. He didn't speak for what
felt like hours.

"Ah, mi bonita, *you'll never marry a man like me."*

Now Marta looked blindly out the window of the little
Brooklyn café, wondering why she hadn't chased him down
the hall all those years ago. Why she'd just sat frozen at her
desk, listening to his footsteps as he walked out of her life.

"Buon giorno, signora, signorina. Caffè?"

She started. She glanced up at the café owner, a grizzled
ape of a man wearing an apron. She blinked, not believing
her eyes. This was the same man who used to wait on her
and Tito, right down to the rusty streaks on his apron. The
last time she'd seen him he'd been ranting at the TV with
a crowd of customers, while everyone watched Italy play
Brazil in soccer.

Some things never change. Maybe Tito hadn't changed.
Maybe she could start up the old relationship. She was ready

this time, ready for love, marriage, ready for babies. Then she could put Carlos behind her—every bad relationship behind her—and finally be happy.

"*Cappuccino, et una sfogliatella, per favore,*" she said, pulling off her sunglasses as she remembered two things in rapid progression. This curmudgeon of a man loved when a customer tried to speak Italian, and he loved pretty girls. "*Per la mia mamma, anche.*"

That might have been a pleased light in his eyes, as he dipped his head and turned back to the counter, or it might be suppressed amusement. She spoke only restaurant Italian, and badly, so it was possible that she'd just ordered two cappuccinos and a chimpanzee. She hoped it was the former, for depending on how things went, she might be lingering here for a good, long morning.

Her mother shifted her weight on the chair, slipping her purse onto her lap after considering all other possibilities. Marta released a slow sigh. Her mother was acting like someone had dared to take out a food processor to make the *masa* for the *pasteles,* instead of grating it by hand.

"Mom," she said gently, reaching across the table to tug her sleeve. "You like Tito, yes?"

"*Si,* of course. I love Tito. I *adore* Tito. You know I do."

"Then, please, just go with this. You should be happy that I'm making an effort to bump into him."

"I'm glad. I *am* glad, *mi hija.*" She slapped the table. "Especially after that disaster with Carlos."

Marta flinched.

"It's just that I hate to see you in this situation. It makes me crazy." Her mother leaned forward and gave Marta the laser-direct, urban-hospital-working-nurse look that dragged intimate secrets out of the most desperate people. "It's like you're little and shopping for boots again."

Marta closed her eyes. "Please, Mom. Not the boots story."

"It's the same behavior, I'm telling you. You're desperate for these boots, and we're out shopping. On a Wednesday night."

"The only time," Marta reminded her, "that you were available. You worked weekend shifts too, remember?"

"I worked weekends so I could afford to buy you and your sisters what you needed, no matter how crazy it was. And you, you needed these boots. We see them at Macy's. The perfect pair—the *perfect* pair. *Dios mío,* even the price is right, with my discounts. But no, Marta, you're not satisfied—"

"Are you really going to do this whole thing?"

"You said the buckle wasn't quite right. Two buckles, you wanted, and a different shade of leather."

Marta set her teeth on edge. Her mother would tell the whole story, from beginning to end, no matter how hard she tried to cut it off.

"So off we go. JCPenney. Payless. Half the nameless shoe stores in that big mall in New Jersey. Three nights, we're off looking for the perfect boots, dragging your sisters along. And then you decide—you know what? The boots at Macy's were the best—"

"—so we head back," Marta finished, "and the boots are gone."

"Gone!" Her mother threw up her hands like she was

tossing confetti. "Absolutely gone. So what does picky Marta Arroyo Sanchez end up with? *No boots at all.*"

Better no boots at all, she remembered, than knockoffs or something too funky or not the right color. Too many days she had shown up at the new school at Riverside with cheap jeans and ratty sneakers, long swinging hair with ribbons, a look that practically screamed *Hey! I just moved out of Washington Heights.* She learned fast that she could keep up academically with the girls in the classroom but her barrio sense of fashion marked her as a whole new category of oddball.

With her books and her basketball, her paper lists and her lanky legs, she was oddball enough.

"Okay, the boot story is done." Marta dragged her face out of her hands. "You want to bring up that thing about my *quinceañera* party or the time I ignored Uncle Pedro when he rumbled up to Sacred Heart in that juiced-up Buick? Or are we good for now?"

"The point," her mother said, scaling her Virgin Mary medallion back and forth on its long gold chain, "is that you're lucky Tito is still single."

"I get it; I get it."

"If you'd been asking about Tito last year, it would have been a different story. Last year, he brought two girlfriends home to meet his *abuela.*"

Marta stifled her unease. She knew a guy like Tito wouldn't be single forever. At every family event, he brought a pocketful of coconut bars and *dulces tipicos* and mango candies for the kids. He'd swing around the little ones and wrestle with the older boys. And when he finally emerged from the tumbled pile, he'd make teasing remarks about how good she'd look in a long white dress.

But eight years ago, she had still been in her twenties, and she'd had a darn good reason for pushing marriage and babies far, far down the Life Plan list.

"The Mexican-American girl from Arizona," her mother said, "I met her one Sunday in Washington Heights. A doll, she was, sweet as could be. But no, not good enough for Tito's *abuela*. She spoke trash Spanish, she says, and so Tito lets her go. But when Tito brought home that Russian girl from Brighton Beach—oh." Her mother stopped swinging her medallion long enough to bury it in her fist and raise it to the sky. "A thousand Hail Marys, at least, every single morning. The poor old woman wore out her knees."

Marta glanced longingly toward the counter where the owner was taking his time with the cappuccino. "Honestly, Mom, do you think his grandmother would love me so much if she didn't know that my family came from the same village in Vieques?"

"All I'm saying is that you should thank God he's still *single*. Aunt Azucena tells me there's been no one for months and months. And your Aunt Fidelia told me at Jojo's baptism that Tito didn't even bring a date to Eduarda's first communion last May."

Marta jerked up from the cradle of her hand. "Oh God, Mom, tell me you didn't say anything to Fidelia."

"I just asked about Tito," she said, avoiding Marta's eye, "I asked about a lot of people."

Fidelia was the biggest gossip in the family. Her mother may as well have posted it on the Facebook family page. "So now the whole Puerto Rican World Wide Web knows I'm sniffing around Tito again."

"Whose fault is that, when you're doing crazy things like this? You have a knack of making yourself a curiosity."

"Mom, any unmarried girl over the age of fifteen in our family is an object of curiosity. You think I haven't heard the rumors? If it weren't for Carlos these past years, Fidelia would be whispering that I'm a lesbian."

"Well, I'm hoping," her mother said softly, "that Tito is your last pair of boots."

Marta tried to field that verbal hit to the solar plexus. Nobody, nobody could find that spot quicker than her mother. Nobody, nobody could strike it with the same unerring force.

"*Attenzione! Caldo.*"

Marta jumped. The café owner slid two mugs of cappuccino across the table. The milky foam, swirled with caramel streaks, steamed visibly. Beside them he placed two curled claws of a flaky pastry, oozing fresh white cream that Marta estimated would be the equivalent of three hours on the treadmill.

"*Buon appetito.*"

Marta's churning stomach did an extra little flip for good measure. She watched her mother take a sip of the cappuccino and lick the foam off her top lip.

"Ay, Marta! You were right. Good coffee, very very good. But those..." She made a face at the pastries between them. "*Dios mío.* A full day's worth of calories and fat."

Marta nudged the plate closer. Her mother had a terrible sweet tooth. "We'll walk it off later at the street fair."

Her mother hesitated, eyeing the pastry. "Two miles, at least."

"That's a promise."

Then Marta raised the cappuccino to her lips only to set it right back down. In the building across the street, the door to the gym swung open.

Tito stood framed in that open door.

A tingling started in Marta's fingers and worked its way to her toes, then started its way back up all over again. She'd forgotten how fit he was. His chest under the gray T-shirt was a little more barrel-vaulted, his hair a little more salt than pepper, and his swagger as bold as always. There on the sidewalk stood the man she'd once loved, swinging a duffel bag in his hand.

"Ay, Marta," her mother murmured. "I last saw him across the pews at Santino's confirmation, oh, what, two years ago? He hasn't aged a day."

Marta felt a little light-headed. She clattered her cup into its saucer. She really needed to calm down, to act natural, to pretend this was just a casual encounter of two old lovers. Maybe two new lovers.

Her mother tapped the table to get her attention. "Come on, Marta. He'll be here in a minute. Fix your lipstick." Her mother's quick eyes took in Marta's crisp, white shirt and the few gold chains swinging around her neck. "That top button doesn't need to be done."

"Mom!"

"A little cleavage wouldn't hurt. What's the problem? Why must you always dress like you're going to work?"

Marta undid a button just as she noticed a taxi pulling

up in front of the gym. She stilled as Tito approached the taxi. Why would Tito be getting into a cab? It was Saturday morning, after all, and Tito always came to this café after the gym for coffee and a cigarette, before venturing to the bodega for the afternoon shift.

Her mind raced as Tito leaned down to the passenger-side window. About five years ago, Tito's father had retired to a beach condo just up the coast from West Palm Beach. Tito was now in charge of his father's whole empire, spread across all five boroughs, a chain of buoyant little neighborhood stores that stocked rows and rows of Goya canned goods, *sofrito* and plantains, and candles embossed with the image of the Virgin Mary next to lottery tickets and Chiclets and cigarettes. Perhaps the heavier duties he had now didn't allow him the same indulgences he'd enjoyed when he was just the carefree manager of one store.

Then suddenly, Tito straightened up, tossed the driver a bill, and pulled open the passenger-side door. A woman unfolded herself from the back of the taxi. A tall, slim African-American woman, wearing a full headscarf and a flowing dress.

"Mom?"

Tito took the woman's hands. The couple slid unerringly into a rumba. As if from a very long distance, Marta noted that they danced very well. The woman had a nice line to her back and professional grace.

"Mom?" she repeated, watching how the couple's feet moved as if they danced on a smooth parquet floor. "Have you heard...has Tito taken up dancing competition again?"

Her mother made a strange, choking sound.

Then Marta looked again and saw what her brain was denying. She saw how Tito's gaze lingered on the woman's face. She saw how his smile dimmed to something wistful, an expression that was terribly, terribly familiar.

"Come on, Marta." Her mother shot up and grabbed the cardigan off the back of her chair. "We need to leave. Through the back exit. Right now."

Marta stumbled to her feet, knocking the table slightly, sending a splatter of coffee over her untouched pastry. Her legs didn't seem to be responding to her urgency. She grasped the handle of her tote, jerked it toward her, rattling the chair.

This wasn't possible.

A Puerto Rican mother and her two hundred and seventy-two blood relatives couldn't be wrong.

But as Marta stumbled through the back room, tripping over boxes to the alley exit, Tito's loving laughter rang in her ears.

chapter ten

Look, here she is. Prettiest doctor in the whooooooole damn place."

Were it any other patient making comments on her looks, Dhara might have made a diplomatic but pointed remark before launching into a discussion of the patient's medical situation. But the man lying in the bed with a sweat-stained fedora on his belly was old Mr. Rivers. Those words, spoken in his whiskey-roughened voice, came across as echoes of a courtlier past.

"Glad to see you in good humor, Mr. Rivers." Dhara picked up the chart hooked at the end of the bed. "You're feeling better today?"

"Dewey, girl. Just call me Dewey. Everyone else does." He lifted the fedora off his stomach and gestured to the man seated at his bedside. "Ain't that right, Curtis?"

The grizzled saxophone player—a fixture in the room since Dewey had been brought here to recover from the week's multiple procedures—lifted his face from fiddling with his sax. "Dewey it is," he said, as he glanced at Dhara over his Coke-bottle glasses, "to everyone but them who owe him money."

Dewey laughed, a deep chuckle that weakened into a choking cough. "Now it's me who owes everyone else money and that won't work out so well for them, now will it, Dr. Pitalia?"

"There's still some juice in your motor." She scanned the chart for the latest EKG results, electrolyte levels, and vitals. "We'll just have to see. You may be up and playing the trumpet before you know it."

"Yup," he said, nodding against the pillow. "Surely I will, in a choir of angels."

Curtis waved a finger at him. "Maybe you should brush up on the fiddle, boy, just in case the devil's coming your way."

"Ain't no devil coming my way."

"Sure about that? I was with you in Juárez, you remember."

Dewey's face split in a grin, showing a full set of strong, tobacco-yellowed teeth, a grin that squeezed his eyes into merry crescents and made his chest bob with quiet laughter. Curtis laughed too, a deep-chested rumble. Dhara gazed at both of them with affection, the power of their friendship a palpable thing.

She laid the chart at the end of the bed and slipped the buds of her stethoscope in her ears. "Well, let's hear what's going on in there, shall we?"

"Oh," Dewey said, "here comes my favorite part of the whoooole day."

"You're a dog, Dewey."

"Mm-hmm, maybe I am, but you'd be thinking the same thing if you had this sweet-smelling child with the glossy, black hair leaning over you."

"Maybe I ought to have a heart attack myself then. You always did hog the stage."

Dhara listened more to their banter than she did to the murmuring rumble, whooshing hisses, and telltale pitches of Dewey's straining heart. This sort of examination wasn't really necessary—she already knew what was going on inside him from the sheaf of lab tests attached to his chart—but patients, especially the older ones, expected it. And there was no gauging the power of simple human touch.

Dewey had an old-tobacco scent, though he claimed he hadn't had a cigar in years. It was as if the lazy blue smoke of too many late-night jazz clubs had cured his skin. During the weeks he'd been in the hospital, she'd learned that he, Curtis, and a variety of other aging musicians now living in a brownstone on 136th Street had once played in all the best clubs in New York. Dewey liked to boast that he'd learned the trumpet at the knee of Satchmo, though Curtis called him on it, saying that seeing the great man play one night at the Apollo didn't count for nothing.

She took the opportunity while listening to his heart to compare what she'd read on the chart to what she heard—noting the gurgle of a chamber not completely emptying, the *shhhhh* of backflow from problems with a valve, the odd and slightly off-beat, scrambled electrical signals. His heart was managing all right, but mostly by improvisation.

Dhara straightened and pulled the stethoscope from her ears. "I'm going to scale back on your meds a bit, Dewey." She picked up the chart and clicked her pen. "I'll send the nurse in a little later."

"Fine, fine, Doctor." His attention had already drifted to the shining brass instrument in Curtis's hands. "Curtis, why don't you play the lady something bluesy? Something slow, something real Yardbird. That's ol' Charlie Parker, Dr. Pitalia."

Curtis swung his sax around and fixed his lips on the mouthpiece. The plaintive sound of a soulful riff filled the room. Dhara bowed her head to the chart, trying to find some hope in the numbers blurring before her. No matter how many times she scanned the test results, she could see only one conclusion. When a heart labored through so many hard playing, hard working years, the options for treatment become fewer and fewer.

Dhara hooked the chart at the end of the bed and lingered a moment, watching the two men. This kind of devotion was a lovely gift. She mostly saw it among elderly spouses— a husband joking about his attempts to cook for himself, or a wife teasing her ailing husband about how she was going to employ a brawny young man to change the lightbulbs once he was gone. All the while, thrumming beneath their banter, shimmered a gentle, loving vibration, the same sort of devotion she sensed in this very room.

It might be a few days, it might be a few weeks, but with Curtis playing the saxophone at his side, Dewey would probably have a gentle passing.

And for reasons she couldn't completely understand, the

thought of Desh drifted through her mind. She remembered the way he lobbed the ball to the end of the bocce court in one fluid, graceful motion. She thought of the way he offered his arm when she hopped about, trying to get gravel out of her sandal. She thought about when she looked up and found his deep, kind gaze resting upon her.

Her beeper went off, startling her. Curtis didn't flinch in his playing. Dhara glanced at the device hooked onto the pocket of her lab coat and saw that a patient in distress had come into the emergency room. With a nod to both men, she made a silent exit.

She took the elevator to the lower floor and walked briskly to the nurses' desk.

"Dhara!"

She turned to find a woman leaping out of a chair. The redhead, wearing pink fluffy slippers and an oversize Spock T-shirt, charged across the hall to meet her.

"Kelly." Dhara's mind shifted into emergency mode and sifted swiftly through the possibilities. "Is it Wendy—Marta?"

"No, no—"

"Someone you work with?"

Kelly seized Dhara's arms, her face stricken. "No, it's not any of them."

And Dhara stared into Kelly's wild blue eyes, watching her expression as Kelly's mouth opened and closed with indecision.

And in an instant of terror, Dhara knew.

Cole.

Dhara strode into the flurry of activity, slipping into professional mode to keep herself from trembling. Surrounded by nurses, residents, and the attending ER doctor, Cole lay on a hospital bed. His appearance was just as Kelly had described it—as gray as an old flounder gasping for air at the bottom of a boat.

Dhara let instinct guide her as she took her place among the staff swarming around his bed. She ran her fingers over his brow to get his attention—and tried not to think about how many times she'd done that before, in different circumstances, loving the way his hair resisted her efforts to straighten between her knuckles.

His panicked eyes rolled to her, and she imagined she saw recognition in the hazel depths.

The attending doctor presented her with rapid-fire particulars, dragging her attention away from his face. "Patient came in complaining of shortness of breath, palpitations, pains in his chest, in obvious distress. EKG presented with atrial arrhythmia and heart rate at 210 bpm. Administered Versed and cardioverted…"

She listened, her fingers still in his hair.

Our children will have your curls and my color—little urchins with curly black hair.

"…blood gas level, complete blood panel, chest X-ray being developed right now. We'll be taking him to ICU to wait for the tests."

Dhara glanced back at Cole. His eyes were still fluttering.

He'd just woken up from the Versed, confused at the activity. She considered what she knew. Considered whether it was within ethical bounds to use her personal knowledge of the patient to order a few tests beyond the ordinary. And then, with one eye on the jagged pattern of his EKG, she beckoned to the nurse gripping a chart and a fistful of blood vials destined for the lab.

Dhara wrote an order for one more test.

Cole rested peacefully in the ICU. Dhara had taken the opportunity to return to the waiting room to reassure Kelly that he'd come through the crisis. She'd promised to tell her more when the test results came in. Now Dhara slipped her way back quietly, needing a moment now that the crisis had passed, to look at him not as a doctor but as a woman.

The first moment she'd ever laid eyes upon Cole Jackson it was fall of her junior year, and the enormous sycamore in front of the library had just begun to drop its yellow leaves. She'd been distracted by a physics problem, mulling it over as she kicked her way home. She probably would have walked right by the students playing Frisbee had a Frisbee not careened its way across the grass and scraped to a stop at her feet.

She'd looked up to see Cole loping toward her, wearing a pair of jeans that sagged on his hips and sporting a faded T-shirt from some Portland bluegrass festival. The breeze had smelled like apple cider as it caught under his hair. Only then could she see him clearly—a lean face, a wispy beard darkening the line of his jaw. His smile had widened as he bent over and retrieved the Frisbee. Then he'd straightened, revealing a pair of laughing hazel eyes.

Now he lay gray against the pillow, his hair flattened with sweat, looking older than his thirty-seven years. He was still hooked up to an IV and an EKG, and the machine whirred quietly beside him. As she'd focused on working on his body today, one part of her mind had noted the familiar landmarks—the tight constellation of freckles on his chest, the little mole that marked him just to the northwest of his navel—but they'd paled in comparison to how he'd changed. It had been nearly a year and a half since they'd broken up, and Cole was a man profoundly altered.

He shifted his head on the pillow. His lids fluttered open, and he fixed his eyes on her. Though woozy from the sedative, Cole started, and something bright passed through his eyes—something hopeful and exuberant.

He said, "Can't resist me, can you?"

She pushed away from the door frame and wandered deeper into the room, drawn by his raspy voice. "I thought I'd see how you're feeling."

"Oh, you can't hide behind your medical degree. I know you too well." His shoulders tensed as he tried to push himself higher in the bed. "I know exactly why you're here."

"I'm here," she said, crossing the space that separated them to place a gentle hand on his shoulder, "to make sure you don't overexert yourself."

"It's my classic good looks." Lines from the oxygen mask still lingered around his mouth. "My raw, animal magnetism. Admit it, I'm irresistible."

She noted that sweat glistened on his skin and smeared remnants of gel remained on his chest where they'd cardioverted his heart back into rhythm. She looked into his bloodshot eyes, rimmed with purple shadows, and felt a rush of admiration. It was just like Cole—even in a situation such as this—to act devil-may-care. She could tell that it took all of his energy to maintain the teasing expression on his face.

She reached behind him to adjust his pillow. "You're right, of course," she said, playing along. "I'd best alert the nursing staff to be on guard."

"Oh, yeah. I've heard about those naughty nurses."

"Might not be necessary." She pressed the lever to elevate the top part of the bed. "Your magnetism may be confined solely to cardiologists."

"How's that?"

"Well, there's nothing sexier to a cardiologist, you know, than seeing a patient stumble in clutching his chest."

He made a little grimace as he clutched the bed rails to shift upright. "I suppose there are better ways to get a woman's attention."

"You think?"

"Like throwing a Frisbee at her feet."

She turned her attention blindly to the lever, trying not to be distracted by the memory of an apple-cider wind.

"Or," he added, "tugging on that glorious hair of yours."

She stilled. She met his assessing eyes. Among the beeping of the monitor and the whirr of the machinery, the memory shimmered in the small space that separated them.

The memory of when he'd wrapped her long braid about his forearm as they made love.

His shoulder flexed as if he were about to reach up and touch her, but Dhara reacted instinctively, and she shuffled back a fraction. Embarrassed by the reflex, she toggled the lever a little more, and then, satisfied with the height, took a full step away from the bed.

Cole dropped his hand back to the covers, and his smile turned wistful. "I have a confession."

She shoved her hands into the pockets of her lab coat, bracing herself for what he might say.

"On that table, in the ER," he said, "I thought that you were an angel."

"Oh." She could hear the relief in her own voice and then tried to gloss over it with a shrug. "Funny, I get that all the time."

"But then you ripped those electrodes off me."

Below the low edge of his hospital gown, a few welts glowed an angry red. "Sorry. We move fast in the ER."

"It got me worried that I might be going to a different place. Someplace where there are no angels."

"Don't." Dhara paused to gather her scattered wits. She really had to be more professional in front of her patient, even if the patient used to be her lover. "You're going to be fine, Cole." Even speaking the words, she knew they might be lies, for a quick glance at his EKG showed that all was not yet in perfect order. "You're in good hands in this hospital. The best of hands."

"Clearly."

"It's very important," she added, "that you get some rest. Your heart has been under a terrible strain."

"I love when you go all doctor on me."

"Please don't do this. This wasn't your finest moment."

"Can't knock it. It did get me here, with you standing beside me. While I lie in bed practically naked."

A slow, creeping heat rose up her throat. He shouldn't do this. He shouldn't remind her of the many times she'd crawled naked into bed beside him after a long weary shift, brushed full-length against his hard body, and gave herself up to him. It wasn't fair to remind her of the good times they'd had and then blithely ignore all the bad stuff that had pulled them apart. The bad stuff that had landed him in her ER.

"Here's the real question, Cole." She drew in a shaky breath. "This drama certainly got my attention. Did it finally get yours?"

And there it was, the eight-hundred-pound beast in the room, the roaring monster that had destroyed their relationship. She saw the struggle in the spastic twitch at the corner of his eye, in the swift dimming of his self-deprecating amusement, in the way he suddenly took excessive interest in the fraying hem of the hospital linens. She saw it, too, in the unhealthy tone of his skin, and the fragility of him—in part because of her own failure to stop this from happening.

And then that monster, in all its thrashing, flicked its sharp tail back at her, lashing her with the usual hefty dose of guilt. Maybe she should have stuck around longer. Maybe she gave up on him too soon. Maybe she took the easy way out, shucking him and his boatload of issues behind.

She remembered it hadn't seemed easy at the time.

"You know," he said, his voice gravelly and rough. "I didn't plan this."

"I know." She resisted the urge to fix the covers sliding down his chest. "Nobody gives himself such a serious arrhythmia on purpose."

"I mean, of all the hospital emergency rooms in all the towns in all the world, I didn't mean to walk into yours."

"Yeah, well." Her voice was doing a strange, breathy thing, as she remembered when they'd watched *Casablanca* one late night when the heat had gone off in her building, burrowed on the couch under a mountain of blankets. "I guess you didn't have much choice."

"Hey, our little redheaded friend can bark orders like a general when she wants to. Very colorfully. She wasn't going to bring me anywhere but here."

A stray thought wandered through her mind, of why he was with Kelly, and why Kelly hadn't mentioned that she'd still been in touch with Cole. Especially in light of all that was going on with Dhara's marriage.

"Can't say I'm not glad," he added. "Glad that you were on call. Glad to see you again." His chest rose as he took a deep breath. "Damn, Dhara. It's always like this with you. I don't see you for a while, and then I do . . . and I'm dreaming of angels."

She looked away to the scuffmarks on the tips of her sensible shoes, while the heat that warmed her cheeks now burned all the way to her brow. Thank God her skin didn't betray her, as Kelly's or Wendy's might. Surely Cole couldn't see how his words were affecting her, digging up a whole heap of emotions she'd tried to bury.

"I was starting to wonder," he said softly, "if I'd ever get the chance to see you again."

"Of course, you would have. College reunions. Wendy's wedding. We have too many mutual friends. Too much history. We'd cross paths eventually."

She'd been bracing herself for that. The awkwardness of the inevitable first postbreakup encounter. What was she going to say? What was she going to do? How was she going to introduce him to Desh? How was she going to handle it, blithely, calmly, and with sincere hope that he'd found someone else, someone better for him, someone with more patience, more backbone, someone not so woven in to a wild tapestry of a family?

She hadn't planned on seeing him struggling for breath on a hospital gurney.

"Yeah, well, after this tumble into the light, there may be no more college reunions or weddings for me—"

"There you go again, Mr. Theater Minor."

"Hey, it's true. Which is why I can't think of a better time than now to say I'm sorry."

Sorry.

The word reverberated. She had fifteen years of knowledge of this man and all his laughing ways. She'd spent the last year of their relationship slowly coming to understand his terrible secrets and all his skillful deceits. But now, from the sheets of this hospital bed, he was looking straight at her—no wavering gaze, no scoffing, no verbal overinsistence. He was still woozy from the effects of the sedative, which made it all the more sincere.

What she saw was real regret. Open acknowledgment. Acceptance.

She reached for his hand. "I'm so sorry too."

Sorry that she'd dragged Cole from family gathering to family gathering, overwhelming him with relatives, thinking that by spending as much time as possible amid the close network of the Pitalia clan, he himself would somehow feel more comfortable among them. She was sorry that Cole had a feckless mother and a bastard of an absent father. Sorry that he couldn't confess to her the real demons that haunted his days.

His fingers slipped around hers in a sensation so familiar it was as if the years together had dug grooves in their skin. "You were right all along. I just...fought it. I was an asshole."

Not always, she remembered. There was a time when everything had seemed to be going swimmingly. Her mother was thrilled that Dhara had finally brought a man home to meet them. The parties began, every weekend, and she'd watched with amusement as the news spread through the family, and everyone vied to be the first to have them over.

But then a letter from Memphis had flummoxed him. It had come from his father. The father he'd met only one terrible, terrible time.

She glanced down at their entwined fingers and thought:

I shouldn't be doing this. I am getting married in less than three months.

I'm just comforting him, she told herself.

Long before she and Cole had become lovers, they had always been the best of friends.

⌒⌒

Dhara found Kelly in the corner of the waiting room, a tattered copy of *Popular Mechanics* by her side. Kelly twisted a thin plait in her hair, watching an episode of *SpongeBob SquarePants* on the teeny ceiling TV.

"Hey, Kelly."

Kelly leaped up. "Any news?"

"He's stable and resting." Dhara had prepared her little speech. "We're going to need to do some tests over the next few days. I have to call his mother, she's next of kin."

"Don't bother," she said, stretching her arms over her head to pull the kinks out of her back. "I put myself down as his sister."

Dhara gave her an arch look. "I'll pretend I didn't hear that."

"What do you think his mother is going to do," Kelly said, "when you tell her Cole is in the ICU?"

"Absolutely nothing."

Dhara had met Cole's mother once, on a quick trip she and Cole had made out to Portland just when things were getting serious between them. His mother had welcomed her by offering weed she'd cured in her own barn. Dhara found herself working in the kitchen with Cole's mother's bushy-browed, pot-bellied, ex-logger boyfriend, while Cole fixed fences, weeded the field, hung a door that had been rusted out, and put new screens in the bedroom windows. All while his mother lolled in the kitchen like a hippie ex-debutante. When Dhara finally left, she confessed to Cole that she hadn't realized until then how thoroughly he'd raised himself.

"I have to call her anyway. It's the rule." Dhara suddenly realized what she hadn't fully registered when she'd first seen Kelly in the waiting room. Kelly was wearing a pair of baggy sweats, an oversize T-shirt, and pink fluffy slippers. "Kelly, why are you in your pajamas?"

"I put these on as soon as I got home from work. Cole was there, and he had made some dinner and said he wasn't feeling well, but I thought it was just some virus going around."

Dhara blinked at her, trying to process, waiting for Kelly to explain why Cole was at her apartment after work on a Tuesday when he wasn't feeling well, while Kelly was comfortable enough to be in pajamas. Dhara's mind was unwilling to make the logical leap to what absolutely *could not be*. Because Kelly, of all her friends, had been the most insistent that Dhara belonged with Cole.

"No, no, no!" Kelly shook her head, suddenly understanding the implication. "It's not what you think."

"You're not sleeping with my ex-boyfriend?"

"Of course not! That's the second time this week I've been accused of that."

"Excuse me?"

"He is—was—just living with me."

Dhara dropped into a waiting room chair, too gob-smacked to think.

"No, no, not like that!" Kelly swiveled on a heel, pacing in a small circle. "You must know what I mean. He was just staying with me. As a *friend*."

"As a friend."

"Yes! I mean, it's not like I have a *love life* or anything, or that I'd be able to keep a secret that big from you or Marta or Wendy. Geez."

Dhara sat stunned and relieved, but wary too, because this didn't make sense. "Maybe you can tell me why he's staying at your apartment when he has a place four times the size on Maiden Lane?"

"I can." Kelly bounced to the edge of the seat, her hands working in her lap. "But it would mean I'd have to break a promise to him."

Dhara gave her a look that she hoped spoke volumes, because right now all kinds of weird thoughts were flying through her head.

Kelly shifted her weight, apparently uncertain. "Would it help his health, if I told you the truth?"

Ethics were a bitch. "No," Dhara admitted. "I have a pretty good idea what's happening with him."

Kelly sucked in a swift breath. "Is it serious?"

"It could be." Dhara rolled her shoulders, only now realizing how drained she was from all the drama. "I'm not even sure I'm right. I just think... Call it instinct."

Kelly's face spasmed, tight with uncertainty. Dhara

watched her, knowing that Kelly would spill soon enough if she just waited her out in expectant silence.

Kelly closed her eyes and sank back into the chair. "All right, then. He's going to kill me. Mostly because you're not going to like hearing this." She sighed. "About three weeks ago, Cole was evicted from his apartment."

Dhara started.

"He couldn't make the payments because he'd been fired from his job, just a few months after you two broke up."

Dhara absorbed the information with a sick feeling growing in her stomach and a terrible rush of lightheadedness. Shifting her weight on the seat, she planted her elbows on her knees and sank her face into her hands, forcing herself to breathe steadily, breathe steadily...

Evicted. Unemployed. She scraped her fingers against her scalp. She thought she'd been doing the right thing. She thought she'd been removing one of the pressures that threatened to tip him over the edge. She thought that after she'd left him he would pull back, maybe realize how he was ruining his life, maybe ask for help to get better. And now she sat in a hospital waiting room, realizing that her decision to leave Cole may have been the very thing that sent him reeling.

"Dhara?" Kelly slid a hand on her shoulder. "Are you all right?"

No. She felt as if she were going to be sick all over this hideous, battered blue carpet. What kind of doctor was she—what kind of *woman* was she—to leave him?

"How long," Dhara said, forcing herself upright in the

hopes of calming her stomach, "has he been staying with you?"

"About three weeks, except he was away last weekend, and then he came to get his stuff today because he's moving out."

"Have you noticed anything unusual?"

"Like what?"

"Anything. Eating habits, sleeping habits. Has he been sick?"

"Yeah, come to think of it, he'd been sick a couple of times." Kelly wrinkled her nose. "He didn't always tell me though. I could tell by the smelly towels."

"Vomiting?"

"Yeah. He didn't seem interested in food, though he'd eat it if I put it in front of him. I didn't have much opportunity though. He kept weird hours."

"How weird?"

"He wouldn't come home until after two or three in the morning almost every night, and so he'd be asleep when I left. If he weren't filling my whole living room with his stuff, I would have hardly known he was there. Are you looking for symptoms or something?"

"Sort of." Dhara rubbed her face and sighed. The time for keeping secrets was long over. "There is something I haven't told you, Kelly. I haven't told any of the girls. It's about me, and Cole, and his situation."

"Let me guess. The reason you two didn't marry is because Cole can't handle your family."

"Partly."

"Raised by that mother?" Kelly said. "Screwed up by

that father? It's a wonder Cole can manage a relationship at all."

"Listen, like you, I'm breaking a promise by telling you this."

"For goodness sake, Dhara, what are you talking about?"

Dhara took a deep breath, then took Kelly's hand and spoke the words she never wanted to speak aloud. The truth she hadn't been absolutely sure of, until today.

"Cole is an alcoholic."

chapter eleven

Walking cross-town was not the quickest route between Kelly's apartment in Hell's Kitchen and the hospital on East Sixty-eighth Street. But Kelly knew the subway would be a crush because of the Yankees–Red Sox game and the Gay Pride parade, so she opted to hoof it. Three blocks later she realized she'd forgotten about the street fair on Ninth as well as the swelling influx of Saturday visitors. Her trek across Manhattan became an obstacle course of pretzel carts, crick-necked tourists, tin-drum bands, and half-naked men wearing strategically placed feathers.

Rushing the last block to the hospital, she glanced at her cell phone and groaned as she dropped it back into her messenger bag. She was a good half hour late to the first real intervention she and the girls had ever attempted.

Kelly hurried through the glass doors, signed in at the desk, and headed straight to the elevator bank. She fussed with the strap of her bag as worries pecked at her. She thought she knew Cole to the bone, but he had been living in her apartment for weeks and she'd never suspected any problem. Dhara had told her that he'd always been high functioning, hiding bottles in the laundry basket and filling his Starbucks thermos with anything but coffee. But as Kelly entered the elevator and stabbed the button for the Cardiac Step-Down floor, a cold drip of fear slipped down her spine. It was one thing to confront Marta about her men issues or Dhara over an arranged marriage. It was another thing to confront a man whose own father denied his paternity, handed him a wad of dirty twenties, and shoved the devastated eighteen-year-old onto the first bus out of Memphis.

Kelly prayed that Dhara remembered to have a professional present. If Cole lashed out...There'd be more than one intervention today.

Kelly located his room and found Cole propped upright in bed, the window shelf beside him laden with flower arrangements and balloons. He looked more like his old self than when she last saw him. Above the neckline of his hospital gown his chest was shiny with sweat.

"Sorry, I'm late." Kelly mustered a smile for Cole's sake as she shrugged off her messenger bag. She set it with a clunk by the wall. "Pedestrian traffic slowed me up."

"Hey, Kelly." Wendy stood by the bed pulling wax-wrapped sandwiches out of a brown paper bag, turning the sandwiches this way and that, as if to decipher the cryptic markings on the wrappings. "You didn't pick up your cell when I called for lunch orders so I just bought you an Italian hero with the dressing on the side. That okay?"

"Um...okay."

Kelly tried to catch Wendy's eye. They usually didn't eat during an intervention. Talking around a wad of salami wasn't conducive to telling a buddy that he was screwing up his life. But Wendy, tossing a sandwich to Marta, missed her silent query. So did Marta, who was swaying by Cole's bedside to some tinny music coming through the earbud of her iPod.

"I just adore Jamaican accents," Marta said. "They sound like tropical waves and kettledrums, and they make me think of hot nights and fruity drinks. What was that doctor's name? Dr. Aghanya? Damn, why are all the good doctors married?"

Kelly looked from Wendy to Marta and back again, unable to read the strange currents in the room. "Someone want to tell me what's going on?"

"As usual, *chica,* you're late to the party."

"Party."

"My going-away party." Cole laughed. The laugh hitched as if caught in his throat. "It's the driest damn party I've ever been to. Something I'd better get used to after today."

Kelly cocked her head, not understanding. She cast an appeal to her friends, but no one looked her way. Nobody was looking at anyone else, either, just going about his or her business. It was like one of those zombie apocalypse movies, the scene after the blast of a sound-dulling grenade, when everyone wandered in the wreckage and tried to act normal.

"If you'd been here twenty minutes ago, you would have caught the fireworks." Wendy tossed a wrapped sandwich to the far end of the bed. "Cole was a monster. He got so riled up he called me a jerk."

"I believe the word I used was *asshole.*"

Kelly, flummoxed, glanced at the institutional clock clicking above the door. "I'm only a half hour late."

"Like I couldn't figure out what you guys were cooking up." Cole cracked open the soda Wendy handed him, his smirk doing a fair job masking whatever other emotions battled beneath. "So I'm sitting here, waiting for my discharge papers, and suddenly Wendy shows up, and then Marta, and then Dhara comes in with this doctor with a clipboard, and I'm looking at the three Vassar girls and a Rastafarian standing at the end of my bed, and I think—oh *shit*."

"He collapsed," Marta said, patting Cole's arm, "like a hostile takeover whose funding cratered."

Cole made a scoffing noise. "Like I was going to say no to a month in an upstate rehab resort. It has a golf course. Three tennis courts. A French fucking chef. I'm likely to make more business contacts there than I've made in the last eight years on Wall Street."

Kelly shot a glance at Wendy, who'd taken a seat in one of the four chairs aligned around the bed, figuring the only one who could bankroll that kind of rehab facility was a Wainwright.

"You'll get to meet my uncle Tad," Wendy said, her voice falsely light. "He cheats in poker, and he's a lousy loser, but you laugh so much at his stories that you don't care."

"You can close your mouth, Kelly." Cole raised his soda in a self-mocking little toast. "Scrooge needed three ghosts to knock some sense into him; I only needed three Vassar girls."

Kelly felt like a newly landed fish still trying to swim.

She'd come here expecting to see the uglier side of Cole, the part of him that had driven Dhara away, caused him to lose his job, forget his bills, and be evicted from his apartment. The part he'd been so skillfully hiding, for more years than she cared to imagine.

Instead, as she tried to process this change, he abruptly straightened in the bed, by some illusion looking instantly broader, heavier, and more substantive. Dhara had just walked into the room. The air was full of funny little eddies, so strong that Wendy and Marta exchanged a glance, a glance that Kelly intercepted and understood.

"Dr. Aghanya is filling out some paperwork you'll need for rehab, Cole." Dhara focused her attention on the chart before her. "But even with that, I'm afraid I can't delay your discharge much longer."

Wendy put her sandwich on the paper in her lap. "Do we need to leave?"

"No, not yet. In about a half hour. I can stay for a little while, at least. Celebrate the moment."

Kelly witnessed Dhara glancing up at Cole slowly, as if her friend knew the act would be painful. Kelly noticed the wary softness in Dhara's eyes, the undeniable traces of old affection. She saw, too, how swiftly Dhara turned her attention away, asking Wendy which sandwich was hers, busying herself hanging the chart, sweeping up the sandwich, and retreating to one of the chairs.

Five days he'd been in this hospital. Today he'd agreed to rehab. Dhara was not yet married. For the two of them, Kelly felt a fluttering of hope.

"All right," Cole announced, trying to break the awkward little silence, "I have a confession."

"No need, darling." With one hand Marta made an exaggerated sign of the cross. "You're completely absolved."

"Yeah, well, you'll want to hear this. It's my dirty secret. I've always wanted to be a part of one of your interventions."

Marta made a little grunt of disbelief. "You probably thought they were girlie pajama parties."

"Hey, do I not, right now, have four good-looking women surrounding my bed?"

"Oh, you are so misguided." Marta pulled out her earbud. "Take it from me, Cole. Real interventions are no fun."

"I'm not complaining." Cole's gaze centered, once again, on Dhara, who found sudden interest in the contents of her pita pocket. "It's not so bad to be surrounded by people who really give a damn."

A chorus of *aw*'s rose up, and Wendy and Marta leaned over to fold Cole in a group hug. Kelly watched the swift catch-and-skitter of gazes between Cole and Dhara with keen interest, noticing how quickly Dhara bent her head over her sandwich to hide a soft smile.

Maybe happily ever after really did exist.

"About this girlie pajama party thing," Cole added as the girls settled back down, "just so you know, I'm always open for that too."

"Oh, honey," Marta said. "That's just asking for another heart attack."

"No, no, he didn't have a heart attack," Dhara said. "Arrhythmia, brought on by withdrawal, a lot less serious."

Marta shrugged off the explanation. "Just no more hospital visits, okay? These places give me the creeps. No offense, Dhara."

"None taken."

"All right," he said. "Next time I'll do something less dramatic. Like reveal some really big, ugly secret."

And Cole's gaze slid, pointedly, toward her. Kelly froze with the sandwich halfway to her mouth. She saw in Cole's eyes a friendly urging, a kind but firm insistence.

I made the leap, his look said. *Your turn.*

Goose bumps rose on her skin, and not because of the hospital air-conditioning. Kelly sensed the girls picking up the volumes of nonverbal communication now passing between her and Cole. She squeezed her sandwich. She wasn't ready for this. She and Trey had just taken one fragile step closer to a deeper communion. Their relationship was like the first soft coating on a new mollusk, needing time to grow solid and sure.

But battle-hardened Cole pinned her with his red-rimmed gaze, leaving her nowhere to look.

"Guys," Kelly heard herself say, "I have some news."

She set her sandwich down. On shaky legs, she hauled herself out of the chair. She looked at each of her friends, and before her throat could close up, she yanked the pin from the verbal grenade.

"For the past three months, I've been dating Trey Wainwright."

Kelly had been involved in enough of these interventions to know how swiftly the girls worked, but amid the shouts of denial and the fierceness of their fury, she marveled at how lightning-quick they rearranged the furniture. Soon it was she, Kelly Palazzo, sitting in a lonely little chair at the far end of the room with Wendy, Marta, and Dhara by the bed, and Cole in the middle, openly bemused to find himself on the other side of an intervention.

Wendy's skin had washed to parchment white. She leaned near the window with all the flowers and balloons, bracing herself on the windowsill while her elbows bent under her weight. Kelly couldn't quite tell if it was shock or distress, but Wendy seemed utterly incapable of speech.

Marta, taking her cue from her frozen friend, opened the argument. "*Chica,* what were you thinking, starting things up with Trey after all these years?"

"You know how strongly I fell for him."

"I know he broke your heart."

"No, that's not true. He didn't have a chance to." Kelly gripped the arms of the chair. This was going to be a long, hard afternoon. "You guys stepped in the middle too soon."

"He wrote about your hookup on a public forum!"

"He apologized."

"Because Wendy *made* him!"

Kelly dared a glance at Wendy, who still leaned precariously against the windowsill. "He stopped hanging out on that forum right after that," Kelly informed her, "and he dropped those guys cold."

She knew this to be true for she'd joined the forum with

a fake nickname and sought him out for months after. Blessedly, in vain.

"So hallelujah, he learned his lesson," Marta said. "That doesn't explain why you'd set yourself up for punishment again."

"I didn't set myself up for anything. Trey chased me."

"Oh, *Dios mío*." Marta crossed her arms. "Kelly, Kelly, that only makes it worse, don't you see?"

"How? How could the fact that he *sought me out* at Wendy's engagement party and *repeatedly apologized* possibly be a bad thing?"

"Because you're a challenge again. He's a player. He wanted to see if he could get you back, after all he'd done." Marta collapsed into the closest chair. "I just can't believe this. You're a freakin' genius, and you *know* what kind of man he is. No offense, Wendy."

Wendy waved off the words blindly.

"Here are the facts you guys don't know," Kelly said, counting them on her fingers. "Trey personally apologized to me at Wendy's party. I accepted his apology. Then I walked right out on him."

"Wait." Marta balked. "You walked out on him?"

"When I next saw him, it was months later. He was standing in the rain, hoping to catch me as I left work."

She remembered the day she'd stumbled out of her office into a gusty wind and a sudden March downpour. She'd stood in the shelter of the overhang, struggling with her umbrella, only to notice amid the dozens of people pouring out of her building the sudden movement of a man leaning against a signpost. The signpost said NO STANDING ANYTIME. And Trey stood there, his hands deep in his pockets, seemingly oblivious to the fat raindrops soaking the shoulders of his suit as he gave her a slow, hopeful smile.

It had felt like Christmas in March.

"Since then, Trey and I have spent a lot of time together. We've eaten out. We've gone bowling—"

"Bowling!" Marta canted forward. "Trey went *bowling*?"

"We've had long, long talks during some long, long mornings."

Wendy made a strangled little sound.

"This is so twisted." Marta dropped her elbows to her knees. "You know it too. Otherwise you would have told us months ago."

"This is why I didn't." Kelly gestured to the new configuration of chairs. "I knew I'd end up here. Having those rules banged over my head like they're as important as the ten freakin' commandments. Listening to you trying to talk me out of dating the most exciting man who has ever come into my life."

A spatter of raindrops against the window sounded loud in the sudden silence. Wendy had her face in her hands, and Marta was biting her lip, while Dhara pulled nervously on her earlobe. They looked like the three monkeys who see, speak, and hear no evil. Only Cole, on the bed among them, looked at her with a somewhat apologetic smile.

"Listen," Kelly said. "I know this is a shock to you all."

She knew they meant well. She knew they were trying to protect her now, just like before. She remembered shaking with emotion in the Terrace apartment that terrible weekend, with Wendy in her tennis whites speaking truths she didn't want to hear. Wendy was a voice of authority; Wendy, so blithely self-assured, who carried the same sort of effortless confidence as her brother, as if the world were paved solely for their footsteps. She remembered her heart aching, but feeling grateful that these three women cared so much to speak the truth.

But she really wasn't that young girl from Gloucester anymore. And love never followed rules.

"When you called me off Trey all those years ago, you were right. Trey was a jerk, and I was totally gutted. But I'd always wondered how it might have turned out, had the situation played out differently. Now I have a chance to find out."

"Trust me, *chica,* there are lessons you don't want to learn."

"And one of them is that this isn't a healthy relationship." Dhara ran a finger over her brow, as if following the line of a growing headache. "You two are so very different, Kelly. Be honest. Isn't this less about affection and more about awe?"

Kelly took sudden interest in the fabric pills on her thrift-store skirt. She remembered a few weekends she spent at Wendy's home during college. The housekeeper served tea in the parlor every afternoon at four p.m., whether anyone was home or not. There it would appear, on the server, a shining silver pot and all the accoutrements: little silver colanders to sieve out the loose leaves, plump porcelain creamers with real cream, bowls of cubed sugar topped with miniature tongs, and a gold-rimmed plate with slices of lemon cake, still warm from the oven.

It was an old family tradition.

"Sometimes," Kelly murmured, "I don't think you understand who you are, Wendy. You and Trey Livingston Wainwright."

Kelly looked down at her hands. She thought of a day she'd spent with her father by the Isles of Shoals, hauling up the first net with the sun just starting to peek over the horizon. She'd stood on the deck in rubber boots picking out the flounder from the hake and the pollock and tossing the dogfish over the edge back into the sea. Then, amid the squirming silvery pile she caught a glimpse of something orange. It was a lovely fish, the color of a tropical sunset, with two barbels jutting from under its mouth.

She called her father down from the wheelhouse and held it up for him. She could see from his expression that he'd never come upon a fish like this before. "An odd one," he'd said. "Blown up by the hurricane, I 'spect." He turned it gently in his callused hands. "What a strange, lost little beastie."

Like herself. Kelly Palazzo, the once-famous Gloucester baby. Adopted by a local fishing family after being abandoned on the firehouse steps.

Wendy shook herself out of her paralysis. She took a few stumbling steps to Kelly's side, as if her legs had fallen asleep and she was having trouble working them. She sank to her knees beside Kelly's chair. "Kelly, you've got it all backward. It's you who doesn't appreciate who *you* are."

Kelly shook her head in dismissal. They all knew her

story. But she was beginning to think when you actually *had* a family, it wasn't possible to understand how, all her life, this abandoned creature had felt very much like that odd fish pulled out of the sea.

"It's precisely *because* of your history that you have this amazing opportunity. You can be whomever you want. You can do whatever you want." Wendy slipped her hand over hers, squeezing until her knuckles went white. "No one has any preconceived notions of who you are, what you should do, or how you should behave."

"Yeah," Cole added. "And I'll just remind you that even a biological family can be full of shits."

She met Cole's gaze, his rueful smile, the silent acknowledgment of their similarities, and the gentle reminder to buck up, be strong, listen.

"This is family business," Wendy said, clearly unnerved at the turn in the conversation, "so I don't usually talk about it to anyone. But since you're so deeply involved, I no longer have a choice."

"Wendy, I understand him better than you think."

"He's had four jobs in eight years. Fired from each one. The last one he landed only because of my father's strong-armed influence. Did you know he has three DUIs, and that's why he was sent to London?"

"Yes, I know all that—"

"Did you know that once in London, he just bugged out of his job? Right after making a series of trades that lost the company *millions*." Wendy looked away, her face tight. "It was a legal mess. In slightly different circumstances, it might have been a criminal one. Fortunately, the Wainwrights can afford the wiliest British solicitors." Wendy ducked her head but not quick enough to hide her rising color. "My father finally tracked him down sailing in the Greek isles with a crowd of Eurotrash. He was sleek, tanned, and evidently unconcerned. Like a toddler who, wrapped up in a new toy, completely forgets the mess he'd left behind."

Kelly sat very still, remembering the afternoon he'd shown up at her office, blowing off work for the day. A worry needled her, something she hadn't wanted to examine too closely.

"Honestly," Wendy said, her voice a frustrated sigh, "back in college I think he got in with those sleazy pickup guys because they taught him how to be successful with girls. He'd wanted to be good at *something*."

"Wendy—"

"Let me finish." Wendy pressed against the arm of the chair. "I love my brother. I understand him better than anyone—both the good and the bad. Which is why I can tell you with full certainty that you're putting your heart in the hands of a man-child. He won't mean to, but Trey will break your heart."

"Oh, Wendy. I know he'll likely break my heart." She hugged her own arms. "I chose to get involved with him anyway."

Wendy rocked back on her heels. She cast an appeal toward Marta, Dhara, and Cole, but the three of them looked too shocked to respond.

"I'm playing a game of probabilities," Kelly explained.

"The way I see it, all the relationship possibilities for Trey and me—good, bad, or neutral—they're like a big probability distribution." She raised her hands as if to embrace an invisible beach ball. "A three-dimensional map, where an electron could be in an S-orbital at any given time."

Four pairs of eyes blinked at her.

"If you had an electron probability cloud," she said, "and you were to suddenly take a picture, you would catch one possible outcome. You'd probably find that electron somewhere in a doughnut shape around the nucleus—"

"Kelly, Kelly," Cole quipped, "do you really think about this kind of stuff?"

"—but amid that range of probabilities," she persevered, "there's always the one or two outliers. A few improbable results. The most probable result is that Trey and I won't make it, like you've been saying. He'll break my heart."

"Oh, *Dios*."

"But you see, there's that one, far-flung possibility." She drew in a hopeful breath. "One rare but not statistically impossible outcome. It *exists*. It could happen. Trey and I could someday, possibly, fall in love."

Wendy gripped her head in her hands. "Kelly, the world doesn't work like this."

"Yes. Yes, it does."

"Why? Why would you risk your happiness, your future, your heart, on some glimmering impossibility?"

"Oh, God, Wendy. I'd be the bigger fool if I didn't try."

~⌒~ that weekend

A ll these rules are useless," Wendy insisted. "There isn't a rule in the world that could have protected me from Josef."

Wendy plucked at a noodle with her chopsticks, feeling shaky and cold, even though she'd wrapped herself in a sweater. She'd spent the previous night in Josef's dorm room, their limbs spilling over the twin bed. She still had a crick in her neck from the discomfort. Between her legs throbbed residual warmth she was trying very hard to ignore.

"Talk about a predator," Kelly muttered. "Josef puts Trey to shame."

"I still can't believe it." Dhara slipped her bare feet onto the chair. "Six months you were with him, and we never had a clue. You know I always liked him."

"That's just the problem." Wendy tossed the chopsticks onto the paper plate. "He fooled us all."

Fooled her, most of all. First, through fascination: unlike any other guy she'd ever met, Josef was an actual artist, an older student from the Czech Republic who would disappear into the theater workshop to weld pieces of scrap iron into spindly, rough-edged sculptures of the human body. She'd come upon him there one day, his brawny arms gleaming as he wielded the blowtorch.

Then he'd fooled her through flirtation: with his sexy Eastern European accent, he'd asked her on real dates, to picnics by Sunset Lake, to plays on campus, flattering her by showing an interest in her life and her family. Now she flinched, thinking of all those long conversations about her father's business, about the Wainwright and Livingston line of ancestors and their blueblood bearings. At the time, she'd thought he was charmingly curious. At the time, she thought he was adorably empathic. Now she knew he'd been taking notes.

In the end, he'd fooled her through fucking. In his artist's hands, she was as malleable as clay. She'd still be writhing in his bed if she hadn't seen those files on his computer.

"I know exactly what went wrong." Marta strode out of the bathroom, her chin raised, as if daring them to ask her if she'd just peed on the stick. "You didn't trust your instincts."

Wendy looked up at her roommate. Marta talked of instincts as if Wendy had them, when her experience until now had consisted of the comfortable Parker Pryce-Westons of the world. Whatever protective instincts she had against Josef had long been abandoned. To every word of Czech whispered into her ear. To how she felt under the expert guidance of his hands. To his compelling foreignness.

"Three months ago, you broke up with him," Marta reminded her, flopping next to her on the couch. "You told me that something about him just wasn't right."

"I didn't know he was keeping files on every trust-fund girl on campus," Wendy argued. "I didn't know he was fucking his way to the richest and quickest route to a green card."

"You said he blew hot and cold. One day he was into you, the next moment he was irritated with you. You never knew where you stood."

"He's an artist." Wendy tugged at a loose piece of merino wool, rolling it between her fingers. "It comes with the package."

"*Chica,* you're thinking with your loins, not logic. And believe me, I know what I'm talking about."

She met Marta's eyes. A stranger would say they were wide and brown and steady—but Wendy saw right through to the terror flowing beneath. She took Marta's cold hand in hers.

"Here's another rule," Marta said, trying hard to hide the hitch in her voice. "Never go back to an old flame, Wendy. It's like making the same mistake twice."

Marta was right. Wendy should have followed her instincts months ago. She should have had the strength of her convictions. She should have shucked Josef like last year's haute couture.

But in her heart, she understood the deeper problem. She was fatally, helplessly drawn to the mysterious other. The rule-breaker. The exotic. The man with the courage to peel off his public face and display his true self to the world. The man driven not by money or ambition or commercial success, but by curious inner passions.

Artists were her weakness.

They would always break her heart.

chapter twelve

W endy had come to the inescapable conclusion that Kelly Palazzo was the bravest woman she knew.

Granted, it was a crazy sort of courage. Self-delusional and heedless, and bound straight for heartbreak. Wendy knew her brother better than anybody, and Kelly better than most, and the two of them together was such an explosive combination that in the twenty-four hours since Wendy had sat in that hospital room listening to Kelly confess, she still hadn't wrapped her mind around the news.

But Wendy knew this much was true: she herself was no Kelly Palazzo. Unlike Kelly, she'd given up her past. She'd tossed that studded leather choker in the trash. She'd settled herself in a fine, comfortable life, with a fine, comfortable man whose happiness lay in her hands.

So today, as she stood amid the maze of white tents that formed the display grounds of the Hudson Valley Art Fair, she thought of Kelly and tried to channel a measure of her courage. She would need it, to make this final good-bye.

"You like the painting."

Wendy started. His low voice came from just behind her,

like a warm breath against the nape of her neck. She wondered how long he'd been there. When she'd first arrived, the older woman in the next booth selling hand-painted pots had told her that the artist had slipped away for only a moment. Then Wendy had lost herself in the painting before her.

"I'm stunned, Gabriel." She mustered her professional voice, a nice solid wall between them. "I've been standing here trying to figure out how you captured the light so well."

"I washed the whole thing with a pigment I found in this art store in Rockport, Massachusetts," he said. "It has crushed seashells in it. Gives it a sheen."

He came to her side, blocking her from the frisky gusts of summer wind that billowed the sides of the tents and sent crumpled food wrappers skittering along the grass. He wore dark jeans and a black graphic T-shirt, but she couldn't see any more out of the corner of her eye, with the wind whipping her hair around her face.

She focused on the large canvas propped up on an easel before her, depicting a collection of ordinary glassware. Four glass vases clustered on a windowsill. One was small and sleek and crystal clear. Another was classically shaped but shockingly scarlet. Exotic curves marked the third, in emerald green. The last stood behind, tall and arrow-straight, an earthy shade of amber. It was a simple painting of bottles. But light poured in through the painted window and seeped through the various colors, setting each one aglow. The whole effect was one of glorious contrast, of beautiful fragility.

"This reminds me a little of Derondi Raffick," she murmured. She sensed the turn of his attention. "You wouldn't know him. I'm afraid he's struggling still. I met him when I worked in the city. His work was more abstract than this." She'd been unable to sell Derondi to anyone but herself. Her inability to close a sale was the fundamental fault that hastened the end of her art gallery career. "He used bold, tropical colors but he painted them with clarity and an edge, as if they were cut from stained glass. This painting reminds me of that."

It reminded her, too, of the first time she'd seen Derondi's work, dragged into the studio by the frighteningly skinny artist in paint-spattered jeans and a T-shirt so big that his shoulder jutted out of the stretched collar. She'd been struck by the contrast of the richness, clarity, and color of his work compared to the world-battered appearance of the man.

It was a truth that always unhinged her. Artists were fearless. They poured their whole selves on canvas.

"I'd like to know how he managed that. I use a thin oil. It can be tricky, temperamental." His voice dropped. "I'm glad you came."

The familiar frisson washed over her, that tingling intensity of awareness. At the museum these past weeks, this had been her sign to back away, to beg off because of work, to end their conversation—whether it be about art or work or his son—because their banter had unwittingly slipped beyond some dark line.

But now his job at the museum was finished. He was no longer her contractor, she his client. Here, under this open sky, they were together in some sort of fluid in-between zone, their connection uncertain and dangerous.

"I was curious to see what you would paint." She gestured to an image of candy-red geraniums straining toward an unseen sun, and then another, of a bowl of sea glass in a pool of summer light. "Your talent...it's astonishing."

"Those are strong words, coming from the assistant curator of a museum."

"A regretfully small, very conservative museum," she corrected, pulling her hair off her face again as the wind whipped it around. "A museum without a wing for contemporary art. The last time I suggested an exhibit of local artists in the foyer, the board balked."

"Let me guess. Jesus in urine?"

"Not quite that bad. Just nudes. Lots and lots of nudes."

"I imagine that wouldn't go over well with school groups."

"No, but I'm sure the seniors would have loved it." She avoided his eye a little longer by squinting more closely at the painting, seeing how the green bottle now looked motherly, the scarlet, like a young girl growing into womanhood. "This is like a puzzle to me. The longer I stand here, the more I see."

"Stop. You'll give me illusions of grandeur."

"I can't possibly be the first to say this to you."

"You're different, Wendy."

She stared more fixedly at the canvas, unnerved by the change in his voice.

"You and I have similar tastes," he explained. "Every day in the museum, you stop in front of that little painting by Jervis McEntee, the one where the light is on the mountain."

"I love that canvas. It's bright. Hopeful." She gestured at

his painting with her chin, trying to focus the conversation where it belonged. "Like this."

"If you're not careful, my head will swell, and I'll end up quitting my job, uprooting my son, and taking out a second mortgage."

There it was again, that teasing vibrato, the light tone of voice that he used whenever their conversations veered to intimate territory.

"Well," she said. "I wouldn't want you cutting off an ear or anything."

"Or losing myself in an absinthe binge in some Montmartre café."

"That does sound destructive."

Then, forgetting herself, she turned to face him, unprepared for the impact of those upturned eyes, the broad cheekbones, the flattened bridge of his nose, the exotic beauty of him bathed in the gauzy light of the overcast day. Thick fingers of wind tousled his hair.

Between them came a sudden stillness, a sharp contrast to the bustling activity around them—a young mother racing a stroller through the grass to make her child laugh, the whirling chaos of a vendor working his wares at a nearby wooden-toy booth, and the ringing of bells from handmade wind chimes being knocked about by the breeze.

With a slow, uneven breath, she absorbed a thought: A man shouldn't be allowed to look like this.

Then she dropped her gaze to the graphic on his T-shirt: a smaller version of the very painting she'd been admiring. She told herself that a sailor could stave off seasickness by keeping his eyes fixed on the horizon. And she could stop the seismic shaking of her world if she just fixed her sights on returning their relationship to professional parameters.

"I still have some contacts in the art world," she heard herself saying, in a little rushed voice. "It's been a while since I worked in the city, but I know at least one gallery owner who'd be interested in looking at this."

Something in his demeanor shifted. It was an imperceptible thing, like the slow ebbing of the wind. He squinted at the overcast sky, as if he were more concerned with the weather. "I can't ask you to do that, Wendy."

"I want to do it. My favorite thing to do, in my wild city days, was to find new talent."

She felt a sudden, piercing ache for those days. For the unpredictability and the first excited rush upon seeing something new, something exciting, something exotically different. Like this painting.

Like this man.

"I can't do gallery openings." He shoved his fists in his pockets and tilted back a bit on his heels. "Evenings are difficult."

Because of his son, she suspected. The one he spoke of with such affection, the one he left the museum early to pick up at school on Mondays, Wednesdays, and Fridays. The son whose mother was never mentioned, but also, apparently, never around.

"My friend Roger will love you even more if you act the recluse," she said. "It adds a little mystery."

Then he looked at her with the strangest expression. He looked as if he was about to speak but then his jaw went

tight. In the uncomfortable silence, she slowly began to realize that her offer of help must have sounded condescending.
That in her attempt to solidify the ground beneath her feet,
she'd shifted the conversation from a discussion between
equals to casting herself in the role of the rich patron—and
him as the poor struggling artist.

She was saved from her own awkward attempts at apology by a few splatters of rain. Gabriel opened his palm, saw
the moisture on his hand, and then squinted up at the sky.
A thrumming patter swept across the field of canvas booths,
the undeniable sound of a hard summer deluge.

"Oh, no," she murmured. "Can I help—"

Before she could finish her sentence, the skies opened.
He moved into action. He seized the big easel, painting
and all, and hefted it around the wrapping table to stand it
against the pole on the far corner of the booth. Panicked,
she glanced at all the propped paintings and seized a smaller
one, folded the easel flat, and followed his lead. He plunged
back out, pulled in two more while she slipped out of the
protection of the booth to seize another one as rain pum-
meled her shoulders. She bumped into Gabriel as he passed
with two more crushed in his arms.

All around them, vendors pulled in their wares or drew in
the jangling canvas flaps where they'd hung racks of beaded
jewelry, children squealed while racing out of the maze,
and couples jogged past, hunkered under twisted umbrellas,
their feet sending up sprays of mud.

"Here, put those back there," Gabe said, slapping two
more paintings on the table before she could grab another.
"I'm pulling the flaps."

While Wendy braced the bigger easels and paintings as securely as she could against the far back of the booth, Gabe unhooked the booth's canvas flaps—heavy with paintings—and folded them in, knocking the fringe flap over the grommets to protect the paintings from rain. He gathered the last of the smaller easels and leaned them against the table before cutting in to where she stood, in the small space between the back booth wall and the bristling forest of easels.

Trapped in the little canvas tent, she asked, "Are they okay?" She finger-combed her hair off her face. "Is there anything I can do?"

"If we wipe them, they should be fine." He grabbed two clean rags from a box under the table and tossed one blindly toward her. "Especially around the edges."

Wendy set to the work, clicking the frames against one another as she swiped the beaded water away while the rain pounded a fierce rhythm on the roof. A rumble of thunder rolled in the distance. They both looked up, as if they could see through the roof to the sky. And then, after a brief snagged glance, Wendy returned her attention to wiping a frame.

She thought, with a tremor, *We may be here for a while.*

And she became keenly aware of the close confines of the space, humid with the pounding rain and cluttered with table, easels, paintings, boxes . . . and a tall, looming, strangely quiet Gabriel.

She shook out the rag violently, searching for a dry corner, reminding herself she was a Wainwright, socially finished at Miss Porter's School for Girls, and surely she could make polite conversation with Gabriel for just a little while longer, until the rain ebbed and she could, with grace, say a last good-bye to him, his art, and his exotically beautiful, unforgettable face.

"It'll pass," he said, as if he could read her thoughts. "I saw it on the Weather Channel this morning."

"Occupational hazard, I suppose." Another rumble of thunder rolled above them. "How much do you trust your weatherman?"

"I trust my senses more. I can smell it." He collapsed one of the smaller easels, making a careful pile on one side of the table. "This is like an *abroholos*. A summer squall. Strong, soaking, but quick."

"I guess we'll just have to see."

"You should stay for a while." His voice was tight, as he continued to methodically wipe the frames. "Then you can leave without getting soaked."

She hazarded a glance toward him. His back was toward her. The bent nape of his neck was beaded with moisture, and the rain had darkened his shoulders and back with an elongated *V*. And suddenly she found herself resisting the impulse to move across the space that separated them. She found herself battling an urge to wrap her arms around him and place her forehead on his shoulder blade.

Then she squeezed her eyes shut and did that dangerous thing: She dared to envision Gabriel in Parker's place, sitting on the floral couches of the club parlor and eating lemon cake with her family. It was a reverie she found herself drifting into in the wee hours of the night, when sleep loosened her grip on her good sense. Inevitably, the whole scene morphed into some twisted Tim Burton version of *Alice in*

Wonderland, where Gabriel swelled too big for the room and the teacup shattered in his hand.

"I hope this rain doesn't mess up your schedule too much," she said, wincing as if she'd been pelted by shards of china. "You wouldn't have happened to have brought a book or something?"

He shook his head.

"Not even *The Sound and the Fury*?"

He paused, a rag hovering just above the glass.

"It was in your tool box," she explained. "I couldn't help noticing you were reading it. It's one of my favorite books."

"My sister gave it to me. She said it would help me better understand my son."

Wendy tried to puzzle that out. *The Sound and the Fury* was a difficult book. She couldn't quite make the connection between it and a young boy. She stood in confused silence, acutely aware that he was continuing to fold and unfold the rag.

"My son," he said softly, "is autistic."

She paused in her wiping. She turned toward him. Not once in the last month had he said anything about his son having any sort of disability. She thought about all the comments he'd made and suddenly remembered the special school his son attended on the weekends, and his comments about how difficult his son could be to handle, about how grateful he was that his mother-in-law lived nearby.

"And not mildly autistic," he continued into the silence. "Not even close. He's not an easy boy to understand, in any way."

Wendy remembered that the main character in *The Sound*

and the Fury, Benjy, was mentally disabled, and that whole first difficult stream-of-consciousness, time-warped section was written in his distorted point of view.

"I guess," she said, thoughtfully, "that the character of Benjy could be considered autistic."

"Hell if I know." Gabriel tossed the rag on a pile of paintings and leaned a hip against the table. "As a baby, he spent most nights screaming. We thought he had food allergies. But later, there were other signs. Miguel can spend hours spinning the wheel of a toy truck. It took a while to have him diagnosed. My sister thought the book would help me understand how his mind works."

"Oh, God, Gabriel. This must be impossibly hard, for both you and his mother."

"For me, yes. For my *ex*-wife, not so much."

Ex-wife.

"She couldn't handle Miguel." He crossed his arms and eyed the roof of the tent, now bowing under the weight of moisture. "The first time she found him banging his head repeatedly against the bars of the crib, she bought a one-way ticket back to Brazil."

Her knees went a little weak, thinking about how his young son handled the loss of a parent. "You're doing this alone?"

"My mother-in-law lives here. She takes her daughter's place in my son's life. And I've got him in a school—a very good school. They say there's a window for autism, a period of time when you can pull him through." He shrugged, a great roll of movement, as if he were forcefully shouldering off a thirty-pound pack. "My wife and I, we were just kids. Neither one of us knew what we were getting into. And Miguel would be a challenge for anyone."

"You must have the patience of a saint."

"No." He made a humorless, strangled laugh. "That's just the problem. With me as his father, poor Miguel is doomed."

"I don't believe that. You're doing an incredible thing, raising him alone at home. There's no teacher, no doctor, no therapist, better than family." She turned back to the easels, wiping blindly, as he tilted his head in growing curiosity. "I mean, being alone must make every little decision so hard. Whether to take him out to a park, face the curious looks of strangers—"

"I gave up caring about that a long time ago."

"And the routines." She twisted the rag, letting the water drip onto the ground. "I know how important they are to kids who struggle to figure out the world. You must feel like you're walking on a high wire trying to keep that in balance. I can't imagine."

"Sounds to me like you can."

She'd said too much. She was dangerously close to bringing up Birdie, and all the turbulent emotions that went along with her. Then, just as suddenly, she didn't give a damn.

"I have a sister. Her real name is Sarah Catherine Livingston Wainwright. But when I was six, I called her Birdie, for the way she flapped her arms when she got excited."

Birdie loved to swim, she loved to fold paper, she loved to paint with her fingers. Wendy's job, for most of her youth, was to get Birdie ready for bed. She'd done it every evening until she went off to boarding school.

Gabriel shifted his weight against the table. Quietly, as if afraid to upset the paintings or stop her from speaking.

"She has Down syndrome, and not the kind you see on daytime TV. She also has what's called an endocardial cushion defect in her heart. She has trouble with her kidneys and hearing problems. She's mostly deliriously happy, but sometimes she becomes frustrated with her limitations and expresses this in ways that most of the world would not consider socially acceptable."

Wendy stopped, the lump in her throat interfering with her ability to speak, remembering how she'd bounded into Birdie's room after her first break from boarding school, bringing her back a stuffed bear wearing the pink-and-gray school colors, only to find the room empty.

"By the time I was fourteen, my mother chose to send Birdie away to an institution in upstate New York. She was, my mother insisted, at a better place. It is a nice place, at least it seems to be. All I knew was that she wasn't home anymore, to bring to my house what it lacked the most. Noise. Laughter. Chaos. It feels good to have someone knock over a teapot once in a while."

She wiped and wiped and wiped, but for some reason, the frames weren't getting drier. She wiped and wiped, wishing she hadn't said anything at all. Knowing that Birdie's situation was far better than Gabriel's son's situation must be, as Gabriel struggled to afford a very special school, as he juggled the very difficult and disparate responsibilities of work and being a single father.

She heard him move. She squeezed her eyes shut, for he was moving closer and she didn't think she could bear him to be so close right now.

"It usually takes," he said, glancing at his watch, "about

three minutes after I make that announcement about my son for a woman to find an excuse to say good-bye."

She glanced past him, toward the folded flaps. "It's pouring out. Maybe I don't want to ruin these shoes."

"Helen Vivian Livingston Wainwright might give a damn about the shoes," he said softly. "But I know Wendy doesn't."

Wendy ducked her head. She'd once read a tell-all article about a washed-up reality star who admitted that she hid her old identity from anybody she met, having learned, during her long decline, that admitting to her erstwhile celebrity always triggered the same set of awkward personal questions and then changed the relationship in some irrevocable way. But with Gabriel, her money, her standing, her name, didn't seem to mean anything.

"You are a puzzle to me, Wendy."

She lifted her eyes only enough to see his sneakers, spattered with mud, and above them, his long, long legs.

"Just when I think I've got you figured out, you tell me something like that, and I've got to rewrite the whole book on Wendy."

It was too much to have all six foot something of him standing next to her, stealing all the oxygen. She was wedged in this corner, barred by the waving canvas sides and the leaning pile of easels and frames. She lifted her gaze a little higher and saw his strong arms and the dusting of dark hair upon them. Saw, when she dared, the clean cut of his jaw. She smelled the sugar in the coffee he must have drunk not too long ago, and even noticed a single crystal in the corner of his mouth.

Her heart pounded. She should get a hold of herself, tell

him she needed to leave, find an excuse strong enough to send her out into the rain. His breathing was too loud in the small space. She should just push past him, push him away. She was engaged to Parker, rock-steady, oh-so-familiar Parker. Parker was a good man. Parker deserved loyalty. And she shouldn't make the same mistake with Gabriel as she'd made with so many free-spirited artists who only played at love.

But even as that thought passed through her mind, her heart whispered, *Gabriel is not like the others.*

His voice, a soft rumble. "I didn't think you'd come here today."

"I lied to my mother." Her voice sounded strangled. "I was supposed to choose the wine. A Sancerre and two pinot noirs, maybe a California sauvignon blanc. I told her I had a summer cold."

"You said good-bye to me at the museum."

"I did. I thought I did."

"I can't get you out of my mind, Wendy."

"Gabriel." Her heart tripped. "Don't."

"I've been trying to. God knows I've been trying. But since the day I first laid eyes upon you, I've wanted to ask you to a picnic in the park, just so I can see the way sunlight plays on your hair."

She made a sound, a strangled sound—part gasp, part denial; she no longer knew.

"Here's the problem," he said. "You've got that promise on your finger. And I can't rip it off you."

Beyond the cocoon of their tent, lightning flashed, and as it faded, a blue evanescence lined his face. His hand engulfed her jaw. His palm rasped against her skin. He tilted her face up, forcing her to look him directly in the eye.

"I know you're taken," he said, his voice fathoms deep. "I know I should leave you alone."

"No, no, it's me who should go."

"I've got nothing to offer you. I'm a single father with an autistic son, working two jobs. My life is chaos."

"Gabriel—"

"You're too good for me."

"I'm *not* good. I'm a liar and a che—"

"No."

"—and I'm not myself," she stuttered. "I haven't been myself in years."

She felt something then, rising up from some deep place inside her, primitive and undeniable, summoned by Gabriel from a place where the *real* Wendy existed—not the one urged since youth to fall into line with the expectations of the world—but the wilder one who yearned for unattainable things: the chaotic jubilation of Dhara's gregarious family; a small measure of Marta's earthy lustiness and single-minded ambition; Kelly's fearless determination to put her heart in immediate and terrible danger.

And now, most especially, this honorable, hard-working, beautiful man.

"Tell me good-bye." He shifted his body to weave a thigh between hers. "I'll let you go. You can go back to your world. I'll miss the hell out of you in mine."

Those eyes. Full of unreadable currents. She felt the long painful turning of her heart, three uneven beats, tripping over one another. The heat of his gaze warmed her lower lip, and her mouth swelled with the sensation. The blood moved beneath her skin, tingling.

He made a low, rumbling moan. His lips swooped down. She closed her eyes at the heat and moisture and hungry pressure. His hands trembled in her hair. In a blur of feeling, she lost all sense of the world and succumbed to the slippery, tumbling sensation of her own heart opening wide.

Then he pulled away, breathing hard. He scraped a hand down her side. He splayed his fingers over her hip and tugged her against him. He waited, his face fierce, in his eyes an unspoken question.

She opened her mouth but words caught. She was breathing as if she'd run three miles.

I can't.

She surged up on her toes.

I can't say good-bye.

chapter thirteen

In times like these, Marta had to remind herself of how she felt when she tried out for the basketball team at Sacred Heart, the Catholic high school her parents had enrolled her in after moving out of Washington Heights.

Sacred Heart was nothing like her old middle school, a cozy nest of two hundred neighborhood kids, where the volunteer lunch moms served rice and beans and the whole place sang with Spanish. No, it had taken her about five minutes of walking through her new high school's scentless halls, plastered with the school's shamrock emblem, to realize that the Fighting Irish basketball team was the center of social life—and the clearest, quickest way for this oddball to fit in.

She'd played basketball before, but these Maeves and Mollys were fearless and quick. Marta was thrown out in the first cut for being repeatedly knocked to the gritty gym floor. She practiced all summer and then tried out again her sophomore year only to be hip-checked out of the lineup by yet another competitor.

So she nursed her bruises, pondered her weaknesses, and

then practiced with her male cousins in the driveway of their Riverdale house. By then, she'd found her social circle with a group of brainy friends—but making the basketball team wasn't about social status anymore.

When she entered the gym her junior year, even the coach rolled his eyes, which only stiffened her resolve. This time, when Marta got the ball and saw one of those sturdy blondes coming right at her, she turned her flank. The two collided. Marta absorbed the hit and budged—but didn't tumble. She hooked that basket with nothing but net.

Bruised, out of breath, and still standing at the end of try-outs, she faced the coach with her hands on her new secret weapon—her swiftly ripening, center-of-gravity-changing, and very fine hips.

The coach, with a little nod, allowed her on the team.

Now as Marta climbed out of the taxi in front of the Three Dancers bar in Soho, she silently bid a *hasta la vista* to lying Carlos and *adios* to darling Tito, forever gone from her life. She'd wasted too much time hiding in her apartment, dodging concerned phone calls from her friends as she nursed her wounded ego, a pomegranate Cosmopolitan, and the remote control. Having pondered her weaknesses, she'd finally come up with a perfect strategy. She'd signed herself up for a speed-dating event.

Marta swung into the hipster bar, adjusting the weight of her Italian leather briefcase and checking her cell phone for the time. She'd come directly from work, where she was elbow-deep preparing papers for the SEC concerning a complicated corporate merger, but she'd managed to pull herself out of the boundless depths of document review to arrive with five minutes to spare.

About ten women clustered on one end of the long bar. The sight gave her pause. The image of their cocktail dresses multiplied in the mirrored walls like the colorful splatters of a Jackson Pollock painting. Marta slowed her pace and tugged on the jacket of her brown suit, conscious of the hemline just skimming the top of her knee. She felt like a plain sparrow about to swoop into a flock of cockatiels.

A perky brunette stepped into view.

"Welcome to Big Apple Speed Dating! You must be Marta Sanchez. You're the last to arrive. So glad you could make it!" The brunette put a check on her clipboard and then, with a bend of her knees and a sweep of her hand, gestured toward the bar in a way that would do a Texas cheerleader proud. "Go ahead and get yourself a drink. I'll be talking to everyone in a few minutes, telling you all how it works and laying the ground rules. After that, we'll let the guys in."

Fixing her gaze on a top-shelf bottle of liquor, Marta braced herself for the long walk across no-man's land. She'd been told that this speed-dating event was for thirty-five- to forty-five-year-old single, professional men and assumed they'd be looking for single, professional women. Perhaps she'd miscalculated, for she passed at least one hair poof, two unnatural blondes, and three boob jobs—and felt herself sharply assessed and coming up thoroughly *boss*. She barely acknowledged the cute bartender before ordering a glass of the Glenmorangie single malt, neat.

While he poured the drink, she stared into the mirror behind the bar, trying to pick out her own reflection—brown hair, brown eyes, dark clothes—against the bar's dim background. She reminded herself that her well-laid plans had never failed her. She reminded herself that this was just a first stride in the process. If she just followed the road one step at a time—like she always did—it would eventually lead to a white picket fence.

Yeah, but next time I'm wearing a red dress and Christian Louboutins.

See? She had learned something already.

"New to this, aren't you?"

The gravelly voice emerged from the dim end of the bar. A woman, toying with the olive in her martini, leaned forward into a pool of yellow light. Her streaked hair was swept up and agreeably tousled. The stranger assessed Marta with eyes that crinkled at the corners and then gave her a rueful little smile.

"Yes, it's my first time," Marta conceded. "I didn't realize it showed."

"The clothes." She gestured to Marta's suit with the pick from the olive. "And the briefcase. Very nice, by the way. Louis Vuitton?"

"Prada."

"Ah." The woman reached under the bar and briefly hefted a slim tooled black leather job. "Tumi."

Marta gave it an admiring nod and then, raising her scotch in a toast, she took a healthy sip. From what she could see in the dim light, the woman was slim and well tended in the way of executives who diligently spent lunch hours working out at the gym. The black suit was conservative, but a bit of red lingerie peeked just at the V of the jacket. Unlike the chicks clucking on the far side of the bar, this woman was more of what Marta had expected for an event billed for high-wage-earning professionals.

The woman spoke again in that whiskey-tainted, cigarette-smoker's voice. "Don't worry too much about them, hon."

"I'm sorry?"

"The competition." She gestured to the gaggle with her chin. "The guys that'll go for that type, well, they're not the kind you're looking for, believe me." The woman leaned over to offer her hand. "I'm Sophia, by the way. Sophia Martin."

"Marta Sanchez." Marta gripped her hand then slipped onto a barstool close enough to talk. "It's a pleasure to meet a coconspirator."

"You a lawyer?"

Marta raised her brows. "Oh, you're good."

"Lucky guess. Where do you work?"

"I'm a partner," she replied, lingering on the word with delight, "at Sachs, Offsyn & Reed."

"Ah, yes—Sacks of Sin and Greed. I know that firm well." Sophia pulled a card out of an outside pocket of her briefcase and slipped it across the granite surface. "VP of Operations, Hodges Pharmaceuticals. We had a fire in a plant ten years ago. The lawsuit is still going on. One of your colleagues—"

"Bill Offsyn, yes." Marta handed over one of her own

business cards. "I'm in corporate—not litigation—but I'm familiar with the case."

"I'll try not to hold it against you."

Sophia laughed, and Marta noticed the playful grooves around her mouth. They made Sophia look mischievous and a lot of fun, but also gave away the fact that her age was on the far end of the range. Marta thought it was a good thing for both of them that the event planners had chosen to keep the lights flatteringly dim.

"So," Marta asked, lifting her glass, "you've done this before?"

"Fifteen notches on my Manolo stiletto, hon."

Marta nearly choked on her scotch.

"Hey, the first five hardly counted. There's a skill to this, you know." Sophia glanced at Marta's briefcase. "You've got your list in there?"

"List?"

Sophia raised one very cleanly waxed eyebrow. "Your list of Vitally Important Questions."

Marta felt her cheeks go warm. Of course, she had a list. She'd spent many a stolen hour this past week sitting cross-legged at her kitchen table with a mud mask drying on her face, trying to compose the perfect queries to tease out—in five minutes or less—everything she needed to know about a potential husband.

"Oh, hon," Sophia said kindly. "Please tell me it's less than five pages."

Marta clanked the drink back on the bar. "Six and a half, actually."

"Greenhorn."

"You wouldn't say that if you knew my checkered past."

"Hon, I'll meet your checkered past and raise you two divorces."

"Oh, my. Does your list fit in that briefcase?"

"It fits in here." Sophia tapped her temple. "After all the hard time I've served, I've boiled it down to three basic questions: Does he have kids? Does he have an apartment? And does he have a job?" She mused a moment as she swirled her quickly disappearing martini. "Though I must say, the presence of kids is becoming less of an issue."

Surely she was joking. Not about the kids, but certainly about the job and the apartment. Marta watched Sophia's amused expression, trying to tease out whether Sophia was amused at her own joke, or just amused at Marta. The incredibly animated woman on the phone had assured Marta that she was going to meet a bunch of *professional* men. That meant a job. That meant an apartment.

A sudden raucous clanging made Marta all but leap out of her shoes. She swung around on her barstool to see the perky brunette shaking a huge brass bell like the one Sister Magdalene used to shock students into silence.

"Ladies, ladies, thanks for coming to our speed dating event tonight! For those of you who've never done this, here's how it works." The perky brunette gestured to a line of numbered tables like a game show host gesturing to a new washer-dryer. "You'll all be sitting here at individual tables, and then we'll invite in the men. They'll sit down, one at each table, and you've got five minutes to chat. Five minutes, ladies! Make them count! When the time's up, I'll ring this bell, and the men will shift to the right. It's that simple. At the end, you fill out the form sitting on each table to pick out the guys you'd like to see again. If he's asked for you too, then that's a match! We'll give you each other's email addresses, and you guys can take it from there. Got it?"

The cockatiels raised their drinks and made excited chirping sounds. Marta took a good, long slug of her scotch and then gestured to the bartender for another.

"All right!" The cheerleader pumped her fist. "You all seem like you're in a good mood. Don't forget to tip the bartender, ladies, Sam deserves it! You'll have a chance, halfway through the evening, to take an eight-minute break and order another drink. Remember, there's a two-for-one special tonight." The cheerleader glanced down at her clipboard. "Okay, I'm happy to tell you that you'll be meeting fifteen men tonight. Fifteen thirty-five- to forty-five-year-old single, professional men, ladies. Are you ready? Take your seats, get comfortable—I'll get the guys."

Santa Maria. Marta mentally made the sign of the cross. Sophia, with a gravelly little laugh, slipped off her barstool, hauled up her briefcase, and then took Marta firmly by the arm.

"Poor lost lamb." Sophia led her toward the closest tables. "The first time is always the worst."

Marta sank into a chair behind table number 15. "You were joking about the job and the apartment?"

"Such a little virgin." Sophia tossed her briefcase on the floor. "Listen, Marta—it is Marta, yes?—part of my job in management is to make quick but accurate judgments about people, and I've got a good vibe from you. So here's what I'll do. I'll cut through the crap for you, all right? When these guys file in, I'll point out the ringers and dingers, you got it?"

"Sophia, I'd appreciate that," Marta said. "But how do you know—"

"Shh. Here they come."

The men poured in, drinks in hand, from an adjacent room. Marta scanned them quickly and, considering the conversation with Sophia, with more than a little dread. She perked up as she saw some promising prospects. One was an older man with a bit of silver in his hair, a well-preserved guy with a nice square-jawed face. Another candidate was dressed in a very expensively tailored suit and looked dashingly European. A third swaggered in sporting a fitted T-shirt. He was clearly an athlete of some type, with a quick half smile.

"Okay, here's the deal." Sophia leaned in her direction, keeping her voice low. "The guy in the Italian suit? With the swept-back hair? He's the ringer."

"What's a ringer?"

"The bait, hon. He's dashing, he's romantic. Every girl in the place is getting damp panties looking at him." Sophia hissed her breath through her teeth. "This one is particularly hot. I swear, they salt the crowd with at least one guy like this every time. The sight of him keeps us all coming back. But he won't make any matches to anybody, you'll see. Well, maybe to the blonde with the big boobs."

Marta felt a twinge of disappointment. He was clearly

the best-looking guy in the group. As he sat down at the first table, he made a very Gallic shrug, and she heard what sounded like a French accent. Already, she was imagining a transcontinental relationship and sex on an airplane.

"Okay, hon, see the one with the silver hair? The nice-looking guy with the firm jaw? He's recently divorced."

"Sophia, come on."

"Look, his suit fits loosely around the middle, like he's not being home-fed anymore."

"Maybe he's just working out or losing weight."

"He's wearing wrinkled pants, like he left them in the dryer. And his tie isn't quite right. All a man like that is looking for is some easy tail."

Marta leaned back, disbelieving.

"Trust me on that one. Okay, the one with the good build?" Sophia chin-nodded to the athlete, just taking a seat at the fourth table. "He's a total dinger. Twenty bucks says he doesn't have a job and he's living with his mother."

"Sophia, you can't—"

"The jeans. They're ironed."

Marta noticed, with sudden alarm, that there was most definitely a crease in the denim.

"And that young one," Sophia added, "with the off-the-rack suit?"

The man Sophia referred to had a bright face, cleanly shaven, and Marta thought he looked cute, if a little puppy-ish for her taste. "No, no, you can't possibly knock him. It'd be like stepping on a kitten."

"Hon, the first thing he'll do is ask if you've accepted Jesus as your personal savior." Sophia fixed her with a direct, open look. "I'm not pulling your leg. I've met this guy before."

A strange, squeaking sound came out of Marta's throat. She glanced longingly toward the exit, imagining herself rising from this chair and fleeing the bar. Her boss, Nathan, was still at the office, running his fingers through what was left of his hair. The table in the conference room groaned under piles of papers in which were hidden the vital elements she would need to posit the argument that the SEC had no reason to step in and prevent the merger of these two rare-earth mining companies. How much nicer it would be to spend the evening ferreting out those precious little nuggets of lawyerly dysprosium, cerium, and yttrium—and lose herself in a world she understood.

"Oh, hon, I'm going at it too hard, I see that. But it's not all bad, believe me. Look, here's my best piece of advice." Sophia leaned even closer, for the guys were nearing their tables. "Go for the husky one."

Marta blinked. Sophia was nodding to a short guy whose thinning hair formed a Caesar-ring around his head.

"He has no confidence, none at all." Sophia's voice dropped to a hush. "Look at the way his gaze is darting around. He's taken stock of his competition, and he knows he hasn't got a chance with those party girls. A guy like that, Marta, he'll *worship* you. And I'm calling dibs."

Marta felt the muscles in her neck tightening. "Sophia, is this what you usually do at these events?"

"Honey, my goal is success." Sophia tugged on the hem of her suit jacket to show a little more red lace lingerie. "My goal is to find a marriageable man. My secondary goal is to avoid having my ego crushed by discovering on Monday morning that because I went for the obvious ringers and dingers, I don't have a single match."

Marta felt as if a one-hundred-and-forty-pound point guard had just slammed her off the court. Her ears rang. She couldn't breathe. She told herself she was not like Sophia. She told herself that it was date-weary cynicism she was hearing. She told herself that she shouldn't let Sophia's whiskey-voiced advice destroy her well-laid plans before she'd even started.

"Why?" Marta clutched her chest as the question wheezed out of her. "Sophia, why do you keep doing this?"

"Because I've got big plans, hon." Sophia plastered on a wide smile as a guy approached her table. "And I want my white picket fence."

chapter fourteen

C ole, I'm not sure we should be doing this."

Dhara settled at the desk in her apartment, pulling a robe across the tank top she'd worn to bed. Cole's pale face loomed on her computer monitor. A glance at the digital clock showed that it was eleven at night. She hadn't heard a word from him since they'd separated the afternoon he'd been discharged from the hospital. He'd been drifting in and out of her thoughts, a dark cloud of worry. Tonight, she'd taken his phone call with bated breath. She thought it might be something serious, something medical.

It wasn't. He sounded lonely.

He sounded like he needed a friend.

"You're my doctor, Dhara. Nobody will question it. I just told them I wanted to consult with you."

"About online poker?" In another computer window, she busily logged onto the Web site. "I don't think this falls within the normal bounds of a doctor-patient relationship."

"I didn't give them specifics. For all these guys know, I could be asking you about heart palpitations or unspecified pain."

"You're not fooling anyone. They're experts at addict behavior."

"True. But they've been giving me a free pass these last couple of days, while they taper me off the meds."

"How's that going?"

"Fine."

"Because sometimes when—"

"It's fine, Dr. Pitalia. No problems at all." He ran a hand through his hair, making it stick up wildly. "Are you logged on yet? I don't see your username on the list."

She let the subject drop. There were medical folks at the rehab facility monitoring his progress. If there were a real physical problem, he would have consulted them first. She knew he didn't want to discuss his situation with her. Especially not now, in the gloom of their respective bedrooms, as they connected to an online poker chat room where, in the tentative early days of their relationship, they'd spent many an idle hour.

"The real problem," he said, "is that tomorrow is my first group session. This conversation of ours is the last sane contact I'll have with you and the rest of the whole wide world. Tomorrow, I'm isolated with the other loons."

She flinched at the description. "Cole, you understand there are reasons for those rules?"

"Oh, I understand. Tomorrow we go digging into my psyche. You know that isn't going to be pretty. Don't want to let those dragons out into the world. Got to keep them caged."

"So you can slay them, Cole. So you can slay them."

"That's really why I called you tonight. I need one last

night of normal living before they excavate my brain. I wouldn't want to spend it with anyone but Dhara Pitalia."

She dropped her gaze, concentrating on the five cards being digitally dealt to her on a background of green baize. She never knew how to react when he said things like that. His words triggered warm feelings, but also confusion and guilt.

"You know," she said, slipping a loose tress behind one ear, "we're probably being monitored."

"By who? Krishna? Ganesh?"

"No, no. The rehab people."

"No way. Cut me three cards."

"They probably watch all your communications with the outside world." She gave him three cards and cut herself two. "They're trying to separate you from bad influences."

"You're my doctor, not a bad influence."

"Unfortunately, there are some unscrupulous doctors who might supply prescription drugs, and so your counselors would be remiss if they didn't monitor even these conversations."

"Well, they won't monitor this. We have doctor-patient privilege."

"You signed away all that when you entered the facility."

"Fuck, really?"

"They are doctors, too, you know. We're all trying to help."

"Well, I said 'cut me three cards,'" he said, tilting his head back in his bare-walled room, as if shouting to some hidden microphone. "That's absolutely not code to send me three bottles of Jack. We're just playing an honest game of online poker here."

"Cole!" Dhara laughed. "There might be people sleeping."

"Are you kidding? This place is full of vampires. We sleep all day, and we're up all night. I've got a full house, by the way." He leaned into the monitor with a smirk. "You know, being here is a lot like being at your mother's house trying to figure out a way to sneak around the relatives for a moment alone with you."

Her breath hitched. She remembered one particular night Cole had spent at her family's home. When he got up in the middle of the night, he bumped into her father in the hallway. She felt a shower of fresh shame. "Cole, you insisted that you were just going to the bathroom."

"Oh, no. I lied. I was totally looking for you."

"Cole!"

"I'd have started peeking in bedroom doors if your father in his underwear hadn't glared at me like he was about to shoot me with Brahma's arrow."

Once again, she turned her attention to her cards, stumbling for a response. She saw them—a face card, two clubs, a blur of red diamonds—but couldn't seem to make any sense of the hand. She didn't know whether to laugh at his audacity or chide him for being disrespectful.

"Sorry, Dhara." He cleared his throat. "I shouldn't have brought that up. I know you don't like to talk about the past."

"No, no. It's okay." She shoved the curl behind her ear again, though it was already snug. "You won, by the way. All I have is a pair of threes."

"It's just that we have such a history, you and me." Cole pressed the icon to deal a new hand. "And old habits are hard to break."

"Well, that's why you're at rehab, right?" she said brightly, hoping to veer away from the intimate. "You're there to break some bad habits."

"Yes, but not all of them. There are some habits I'm very fond of, Dhara. Some habits I'm hoping for a chance to start up again."

Dhara fixed her gaze on her keyboard. She stared at the letters of the middle row, faded to flecks of white. She felt a knot develop between her eyebrows as she remembered that tomorrow she'd be traveling to New Jersey with her mother, to peruse henna designs at a small shop in Edison.

Oh, Krishna, what was she doing? She was engaged to another man. A woman engaged to one man didn't idly chat online with a former lover. Even if that former lover was still an old friend.

"Cole," she murmured, "why don't we just stick to five-card stud, okay?"

⌒⌒

Dhara saw Desh long before she reached the bocce courts in John Walker Park. He was standing with two older men watching a third lobbing a red ball. As the ball landed, Desh laughed with a quick flash of teeth.

Her heart did a little lurch. She tugged nervously on her *dupatta*, the long blue scarf that matched the tunic and loose pants of her *shalwar kameez*. Her thoughts clattered like so many bocce balls. Maybe it had been a mistake to wear the traditional Indian garb today. Maybe she should have transferred the ailing jazz musician to hospice by now. Maybe this rain was going to destroy her hopes for a distracting game. Maybe there was no gentle way to break a good man's heart.

Desh caught sight of her. He raised his hand to indicate he'd be there momentarily. She hoped her smile didn't look shaky and feeble. *Oh, Krishna.* Marta said guilt was a Catholic thing, fed to youngsters along with the host and the blessed blood, stoked into flames in the confessional box. Several of her colleagues insisted it was a Jewish thing, passed on through the long-suffering maternal line. Dhara thought the Hindu trumped them all: bad behavior meant bad karma and came with the threat of being reincarnated as something slithery.

And if she didn't let go of her *dupatta* soon, no hot iron would ever be able to smooth the folds.

"Sorry for the wait," he said, jogging toward her. "We were on the last round. We were up twenty bucks, and Paolo would have killed me if I forfeited."

He took in the sight of her *shalwar kameez* with what looked like honest pleasure. Shirt clung from the spattering rain, translucent over the swell of his shoulders. He was blinking rapidly. He'd worn his contact lenses today—no doubt, for her.

"I didn't mind the wait." She held the palm of her hand toward the sky. "Think we can get in a game before this gets too bad?"

"No chance. The skies are about to open. Have dinner with me instead."

She hesitated. Dinner meant sitting across a rickety table with nothing to distract them from the topic at hand.

"Just something quick," he said. "Someplace where we can order at the counter."

"Sure." Her heart hovered somewhere in the vicinity of her larynx. "I suppose I could eat."

"Italian or Chinese?"

"Whichever is closest."

He set out at a jog, crossing the park toward the storefronts on the facing street. She followed in his wake. A rumble of thunder startled her. He took her arm, guiding her as they stepped off the sidewalk, watching carefully for oncoming traffic before pulling her across the street. They made it to the other side just as the heavens opened.

Desh drew her deep into the restaurant as other customers tumbled in behind them. The place was bright with fluorescent light, scattered with a half dozen battered tables, and smelled of frying meat and steam.

"I know it doesn't look like much," he said, as he led her to a two-person table in the corner. "But this place has the best Kung Pao Tofu outside of Chinatown."

"Sounds good. That's what I'll have."

She sat down and fussed with her wet hair, watching him as he ordered at the counter. The back of his jeans were dusty, as if he'd crouched at the end of the bocce court. She noticed a fold in his shirt, cutting clean across from his left shoulder blade to his right hip. His hair was trimmed sharply at his nape.

Strange, the details you notice when you're about to say good-bye.

He returned with two Styrofoam cups and handed one to her as he sat down. "It's not the best tea, but you look like you could use something hot."

She cupped it in her hands. "Thank you."

"How is your friend doing?"

She startled, meeting his gaze.

"The one," he added, "who came into the emergency room a couple of weeks ago."

Dhara tried not to choke on her tea. His gaze was steady, nonjudgmental but full of unspoken questions. He kept his silence with a half smile while she tried to figure out how he could possibly know.

"My mother," she blurted, nearly spilling the tea over her hand as she clattered the cup back on the table. "She must have said something to my aunt Nisha. Nisha's husband is a good friend of one of your cousins."

"Haresh." He nodded. "I saw him last Sunday at my aunt Deepti's house. I was playing carrom with my uncle Raj when Haresh wandered by and asked me how you were holding up. I thought it was an odd thing to ask, until he told me a good friend of yours had shown up at the emergency room and given you quite a scare."

A friend. She hadn't told her family that the friend was Cole, although Aunt Nisha had a sixth sense about these things. Dhara wouldn't put it past her female relatives to make very specific inquiries.

"It's a strange coincidence." He swirled the tea in his cup.

"Him showing up, after all this time, in the middle of marriage arrangements."

Dhara paused, wondering how much she should say. Cole certainly hadn't planned to come gasping into her emergency room. That had been Kelly's idea. In any case, Cole's situation had been building up for so long that it was only a matter of time before he'd show up somewhere in an ambulance. She considered whether it would be an acceptable breach of medical ethics to divulge to Desh the details of Cole's situation, but then she dismissed the idea. Cole deserved his privacy, and Desh deserved not to be burdened.

"I am sorry you had to find out this way, Desh."

"The last time we met," he said, gazing out the window toward the bocce courts, "you made a point of telling me how important he once was to you. It could not have been easy to see him on a stretcher."

Two images came to her mind: Cole, gray and waxen, gasping for breath, lying on the emergency room bed; and Cole leaping up against a blue sky, all long muscle and sinew, stretching to catch a Frisbee on the lawn outside the library.

"It wasn't easy." She dug her fingers into the Styrofoam. "I don't think it will ever be easy."

She'd done nothing else these past two weeks but try to work through the foggy maze of her feelings, trying very hard not to let Cole's medical issues muddle the clarity of her thoughts, or Cole's lingering, hopeful glances during their poker session turn her mind away from the path she'd chosen.

Desh's voice came, flat and emotionless. "Is this going to change our plans?"

Dhara stared into her tea, seeing not the muddy liquid but Cole in the gloom of a Poughkeepsie winter, his cheeks angry pink, his grip on her hand softened by her mittens as he raced to Sunset Hill to go traying. She saw Cole, years later, at the Cape May B and B where they'd finally consummated their relationship. She still remembered the smell of the September sea blowing the window curtains. She remembered the crisp give of his hair under her palm.

"Yes. This is going to change things." Her throat tightened, making her voice a husky whisper. "I think, Desh, that under the circumstances . . . it's best to reconsider our arrangement."

Desh held her gaze for a painfully long time. Then he made a long, sighing sound like the deflating of a balloon. His head dropped so she could see the spot on the top of his head, that little pinpoint origin from which his dark hair whorled.

His chair creaked as he sank back. "I was afraid something like this might happen."

"Be angry with me, Desh."

"I can't be angry at you. I can see your pain."

"You're supposed to make a scene." The Styrofoam cup warped into an oval within the pressure of her hands. "You're supposed to call me terrible names, blame me for the embarrassment."

"I won't do that, Dhara."

"You're supposed to ask me to reconsider."

"I see your mind is made up. Schrödinger's cat can't really be alive and dead at the same time."

She blinked at him, not understanding.

"Schrödinger's cat," he repeated wearily, scraping his fingers through his wet hair. "It's a quantum mechanics thing. And a philosophical one too."

"One year of physics," she reminded him, "and one lost semester in philosophy."

He shrugged as if it didn't matter. "It's basically a cat in a sealed box. It's either alive or dead, depending on the state of some subatomic particle. You don't really know whether it's alive or dead until you look at it," he said, "thus sealing its fate."

Her heart turned over with sorrow at lost possibilities. "I really would have liked to introduce you to Kelly."

"The point is, you either feel one way or another," he said. "You only *think* you have two equal possibilities."

Oh, but she did. Between Cole, recuperating in an upstate rehab facility. And Desh, this quiet rock of a man, a cipher still, but one who understood her Indian side, the man who was taking the news of their breakup with stoic and philosophical sanguinity. Dhara wished she could reach across the table and finger away the line deepening on his brow.

"You'll waver between those two possibilities endlessly," he continued, "until the very moment you decide to take a good, long look at the situation. At that moment, the truth becomes unequivocal."

Unequivocal.

It didn't feel that way, this splitting of her heart.

"Marriage is a big step." Desh seemed to find great interest in the pattern of hairline cracks in the Formica table. "It should never be made lightly. I've come to know you well enough to understand you've thought hard about this. Apparently, that cat of ours is dead."

"Desh—"

He held up his palm. "Don't worry about my family. I'll smooth things over with the Boharas."

"Blame it all on me." She let go of the cup long enough to rub her temples with her fingers. "It *is* my fault."

"No fault. I'll let everyone know it's mutual. Amicable. For the best." He shifted his weight again, the rickety chair tapping the floor beneath him. "For what it's worth, I've spent the last month or so feeling like the luckiest man in the world. I hope that this man knows what a gift he has in your affections."

His words sank deep, pinching where she felt the sorest.

Just then, one of the restaurant workers showed up in a food-streaked apron and silently shoved two plastic plates in front of them. He pulled chopsticks out of his apron pocket and then ducked back behind the counter without even a *thank you very much.* Desh pulled the chopsticks out of the sleeve and separated them with a little crack.

She fiddled blindly with her own chopsticks. She'd just remembered that it was Monday, her Shiva fast. She wasn't supposed to eat before sunset. Then again, she may as well break her Shiva fast, because the point of a Shiva fast was to find her a nice boy to marry.

In his capricious generosity, Shiva had found her two.

Then Dhara was saved by her cell phone. "It's the hospital," she said, recognizing the distinctive ring tone. "I have to take this."

Desh nodded, his attention on his food. Dhara turned a shoulder for privacy's sake and took the call. She spoke to the floor resident, knowing what the news would be. She'd expected it to happen sometime during the evening and certainly long before morning. Dewey had been slipping away, his breath slowing in his sleep like the unwinding of an old clock. She'd been putting off sending him to a nursing home, knowing that would separate him from his buddy, who wouldn't be able to manage the train and two buses it would take to visit. As the night-shift resident relayed the details, Dhara heard in the background the mournful keen of a saxophone.

When she hung up the phone, Desh glanced up from his food. "Trouble?"

"One of my patients just died."

"I'm so sorry." He turned toward the counter to catch the attention of the man at the register. "I'll get a bag so you can take your food with you."

She didn't really have to go. In her profession, death happened all the time. The doctor on the floor would take good care of Dewey now. She could stop by the hospital after she ate, to pay her respects, and to listen to Curtis playing the saxophone by his bedside.

But Dhara made no objection as the worker took her food away. She'd told Desh what she'd come to say. It was probably best if she just slipped out of this restaurant before the sound of Curtis's mournful saxophone merged in her mind with the terrible realization that she was saying good-bye forever to a relationship that could have been very good.

While she waited for her food to be packed, she glanced away from Desh only to find herself contemplating his blurred reflection in the window. He was staring at his food. His thick black hair shone from the lights. She had the odd sensation that she was watching the two of them from a great distance. They looked just like any Indian-American couple sharing a meal. Like married folk, making plans. Talking of weekend duties, work troubles, children. They looked good together. They looked like they *belonged* together.

She once felt that way about Cole too. By reflex she summoned the old memories—Frisbee, traying, picnics in the park—and instead, with a strange stutter of her heart, she noticed that the images were fixed, like old photographs marked ochre from Scotch-tape stains. She probed deeper, seeking to turn the many pages of their shared history. On cue, fresh images came to mind.

These memories were not kind.

She squeezed her eyes shut, trying to block them out. The truth was, she had *always* worried about her relationship with Cole. In college, she'd worried that Cole wouldn't fit in with her voluble family. After she'd introduced him to her parents, and her mother and father had accepted him, she'd struggled with unease. As she'd discovered bottles of vodka in the garbage and the smell of vomit on his work clothes, her worry had vaulted into new territory. The more she thought about Cole, the more the reel of the good memories flickered and stuttered, like a Havan candle lit to disperse the evil spirits, sputtering out, drowning in its own liquid wax.

Desh's warm hand was suddenly on her arm.

"Hey, your food is ready." He tilted his head at the bag knotted on the table. "Do you want me to hail you a cab?"

She searched Desh's face. She let her gaze linger upon his high cheekbones, then the fathomless depths of his eyes. Then she looked lower, to the sweep of his throat, the hollow at its base, and the stretch of hard chest revealed by the two buttons undone on his shirt. She had just told this man she wasn't going to marry him. Yet warmth and concern radiated from him, all for her sake alone.

She couldn't speak. She knew, instinctively, that Desh would always be like this. He would face difficult decisions with equanimity. There would never be angry words, terrible fights, or blind uncomprehending resistance. Desh would approach the inevitable troubles of marriage and family with a simple philosophy and boundless kindness. There would never be discomfort. There would never be lies.

And Dhara felt the rush of the future like the pounding rain outside, fogging the glass so she could no longer see their reflection. Now she could see only Desh—flesh and blood. In that face, she saw her own children: a solemn-eyed boy with a calm, thinking manner, and a wild-haired girl with impish eyes and swift feet, racing away in the wake of laughter.

Desh squeezed her fingers. "Don't cry, Dhara."

It was so simple, really. So very, very simple, once she took a good, hard look at the truth.

"Remember, I can't hug you in public," he whispered, laughing. "A thousand generations of relatives are watching."

"Let them watch."

She leaned across the table. She pressed her lips against his mouth.

He jolted. She tasted soy sauce and strong tea. She felt the heat of his sudden breath. He reacted, rising from his seat and tilting his head for a better fit. He scraped his hand through her wet hair.

Long after they separated, they stayed like that, half-standing, staring into each other's eyes.

~⌒~ chapter fifteen

Kelly Palazzo sat in the deck chair and stretched her painted toes into the July sun. Behind her oversize sunglasses, she drank in the view of Long Island Sound, retreating from the back of a fifty-foot Navigator Pilothouse yacht. Trey leaned against the deck rail just beside her, his ankles crossed, casual in his battered boat shoes, plaid bathing shorts, and sun-bleached polo shirt, the sun striking auburn lights in his dark hair.

So very, very handsome. And all mine.

Her heart gave a stuttering flutter. She didn't know it was possible to be deliriously happy and nervously anxious, all at the same time. She was so thrilled to be with Trey in public with his friends. Yet she was so *nervous* to be out with Trey in public with his friends.

"I'm very impressed, Kelly." Audrey Eckensburg, the hostess and wife of Trey's good friend James, arrived with a bottle of sunscreen and sprawled on the deck chair beside her, all long, golden legs. "I just spoke to James about you. Wendy told him you practically grew up on the sea, but I had no idea how much you knew about boats."

She felt her skin warm. As soon as they'd navigated out of the marina, James had given her the grand tour of the yacht. When they got to the wheelhouse, Kelly couldn't help but gape at the panel of computerized instrumentation with its Captain Kirk swivel chair. She'd been full of questions, mentally comparing this wheelhouse to the one on her father's boat, with its scratched Plexiglas, worn knobs, and duck-taped seat.

"I suppose James isn't used to people asking him about the lifting capacity of the davit." Trey gave her a little wink as he gripped a long-necked bottle of cold beer. "Or being told he could haul up a hell of a lot of flounder, if the boat was set up to drag."

"Flounder? Oh, dear." Audrey laughed, showing off a pearly array of perfectly aligned teeth. "Such a lowly fish would never grace these decks. Nothing but marlin and the like."

Kelly gave a little shrug. It was inevitable that the truth of her upbringing would come up. So inevitable that she'd determined she wouldn't second-guess every question she was asked or worry too much that if she opened her mouth she'd say something spectacularly gauche. If she did, she'd spend the whole trip in a state of terrified muteness instead of trying to enjoy the moment.

"In Gloucester," Kelly said, "we didn't do a lot of marlin fishing. If we caught one, we'd probably be pissed because something that big would rip the netting."

"Gloucester. Ah, yes, Trey said you were from there." Audrey lifted a wrist laden with chunky bracelets, shaking them down her arm. "I think the Marshals have a sailboat moored there."

"My father had a fishing trawler, thirty feet long," she said, figuring the Marshals had one of the fancy sailboats in the new marina. "I used to work the decks with him during the summers."

"What Kelly is saying," Trey explained with a wry little smile, "is that her father was in commodities."

"Until the runs dropped off," Kelly added, "and we had to work within quotas, which killed our daily take."

"I see." Audrey lifted one perfectly winged, lovely brow. "So, in basic investor-speak, the bottom fell out of the fish stock?"

Trey and Audrey laughed. Kelly looked at both of them and joined in a few seconds late. She was just beginning to understand that these little jokes were a strange form of social lubricant, smoothing out the rough edges of conversation. Rough edges caused, without doubt, by her own social ignorance. There always would be gaffes, she suspected, since she and Trey were moving this relationship into the wide open, and, well, Kelly Palazzo was Kelly Palazzo.

Hey, she was the girlfriend of Trey Livingston Wainwright. That should be good enough.

Audrey's two children, Chad and Emily, tumbled out of the galley to hook their feet on the stern railings, watching the ocean churned up by the three-hundred-and-seventy-horsepower Volvo engine as they wove their way toward the open waters of the sound. The purr of the repressed power was so markedly different from the sound of boat engines

Kelly had heard all during her youth, a labored whine that sputtered and coughed as her father propelled his little boat into the bay.

"Emily—Emily—don't stand up on that railing," Audrey said, tugging on the edges of the girl's terrycloth cover-up. "Now, Trey, tell me the truth. I thought I heard Parker this morning telling you both that he was going to hold his bachelor party on his sailboat."

Trey glanced up toward the wheelhouse and shook his head in amused disbelief. "Yeah, that's what he said. James and I are going to try to talk him out of that. I reminded him it sleeps only four, and it's too much work."

"I've always admired Wendy's fortitude." Audrey lifted her glasses to give Kelly a significant look, kindly keeping her in the conversation. "Wendy doesn't seem to mind that Parker has another lover."

Trey leaned back over the edge of the gunwale to look ahead to where the yacht was heading. "I think that's why they get along so well. Parker would always choose the boat over the woman, and Wendy doesn't seem to mind."

"I mean, really, James loves this boat." Audrey gestured to the whole of it with her bracelets clattering. "But the minute I become a yacht widow, I'm calling for marriage counseling." Audrey straightened up suddenly. "Chad, really, must you keep kicking the boards like that?"

"Mommy," Chad asked, "what are they catching?"

"Fish, darling." Audrey arched her neck a bit to see past the rail. "Like the fish you had for dinner last night."

"Actually, it's a lobster boat." Even from her seat, Kelly

could see the mound of piled traps. "He's probably checking his traps and laying new ones in the water. See those buoys? They have distinctive markings, according to who the trap belongs to."

"Ah," Audrey said, "we have an expert on board. You're in for it now, Kelly."

"What about that boat," Emily asked, "the one over there?"

Kelly put down her drink and stood up in the hot sun. Holding her wide-brimmed hat against the wind, she glanced at the wooden boat hugging the shore. "That's an oyster boat. They're pulling a net full of them right now. That's what that big, round gray thing is." She scanned the little boat, acutely aware of Trey beside her. Acutely aware of his eyes on her figure as she stretched to see the boat better.

She knew she looked good. Marta had made her try on every string bikini they could find during a trip to a Jersey mall. Marta had literally dragged Kelly away from the conservative one-pieces she'd gravitated to, to protect her already freckled skin from overexposure.

Honey, that's what sunscreen is for. You're not on the rocky beaches of New England. You're going cruising on a yacht. You've got to look the part.

She did. She saw it reflected in Trey's half-lidded eyes, saw it in the way his gaze lingered on the gold clasps at her hips, the battered bronze cuff on her wrist, and the sheer cover-up that hid absolutely nothing. She'd spent more than two weeks in grocery money for this one tiny scrap of bathing suit, and judging by the way Trey's gaze lingered, it was worth every penny.

Suddenly, Trey's hand lay on her waist. His fingers were chilled from holding the beer, and their touch sent little goose bumps running all over her skin.

"Hey," Trey said, "I see the last buoy coming up." He walked around her, letting his fingers graze her side, her belly, all out of Audrey's view. "James is sure to punch it as soon as we get into open water. If you two don't mind, I'd like to take the kids up to the pilothouse."

As the kids squealed and skittered down from the railing, Trey addressed his question to both her and Audrey, yet his gaze behind his sunglasses rested solely on her. She sensed his eagerness to be off. She thought *she'd* be the only one walking on eggshells today, but somehow, Trey's quiet unease was strangely endearing. And as much as her stomach clenched at the thought of trying to make small talk with Audrey—a sweet but impossibly well-tended, stay-at-home mother—she knew Trey wanted to be in the wheelhouse with Parker and James.

Kelly wished Wendy had come. She could have used her guidance today.

"Please, go on up and take the kids," Audrey said, waving Trey away. "Until you're gone, Kelly and I won't have a chance to gossip about you."

His laugh was short and strangled. He paused for a moment, as if he were contemplating the wisdom of dropping a kiss on the top of her head. She willed him to do so. She gifted him an inviting smile. But he just lifted the beer in salute, then made a little backward shuffle before striding away.

"All right, Kelly." Audrey patted the seat of Kelly's deck chair as an invitation to sit. "The little boys are all gone now. You and I have to talk."

Kelly froze. She wondered how much Audrey knew about her and Trey's earlier connection. Kelly doubted Wendy would have told her that story, but Audrey could have heard it from James, who might know it from their Princeton days. Gawd, Kelly thought, sinking into the deck chair. She had spent half the night visiting Web sites about quick and easy guides to small talk, but she hadn't spent a single minute thinking about how she could describe the weird narrative of her and Trey's relationship.

"Now, you must tell me," Audrey said, settling her deck chair a foot closer to hers. "What in God's name is going on with Wendy?"

The question pulled her up short. Audrey removed her sunglasses to reveal a pair of concerned blue eyes.

"I don't believe for a minute that Wendy is dealing with a case of food poisoning," Audrey confessed. "That girl has a stomach of steel. We have a little tradition at Miss Porter's concerning raw oysters and senior year. I won't bore you with the gory details, only to say that Wendy set the house record."

Kelly paused, contemplating. Wendy had shown up at the marina this morning wrapped in a long-sleeved sweater and an ankle-length skirt, looking ashen and twitchy, like she could really use one of the emergency cigarettes she always carried in her purse. The original plan was to have three couples for their day-jaunt on the yacht. Wendy had arrived last, but as Parker hopped off the yacht to greet her, she clutched her midriff and looked as if she were going to be sick right off the edge of the dock.

"I don't know, Audrey. She looked pretty shaky to me."

"For weeks, she's been a wreck." Audrey settled back on the dock chair, tapping the arm of her sunglasses against her lower lip. "It's spreading beyond just my notice too. Her mother has been talking about her on the golf course. Our mothers," Audrey explained, "are part of a regular Thursday foursome. Wendy's own mother has been complaining that Wendy has been completely unreliable. And frankly, sometimes, Wendy doesn't answer my calls for days."

Kelly frowned. She'd been so anxious about the trip on the yacht that she hadn't given much thought to Wendy's decision to beg out. Wendy was sick; Kelly took that fact at face value. But now, with Audrey so suspicious, Kelly began to wonder. Maybe Wendy had bowed out of this trip because of her and Trey.

No.

Kelly's reaction was instinctive. This morning, Wendy had greeted her with a tight hug and then sent a casual wave toward Trey on the boat deck. Wendy had seemed distracted, twitchy, but not because of them. Something else was bothering her.

"The wedding." Kelly riffled through Wendy's difficulties with her mother, with seating plans, with the planner, with Birdie. "Wendy says it has been difficult."

"All weddings are difficult." Audrey waved the thought away. "Listen, I understand wedding stress. My wedding took place at the yacht club with three hundred and seventy-two guests, and I had to contend not only with my mother, but also with my stepmother-in-law, who we call the Botox Queen. The woman insisted on wearing a *tiara*."

"If this were poker," Kelly said, "Wendy would see your Botox Queen and raise you a Manhattan Wedding Planner."

"And I'd win that hand, no question—and Wendy would agree. No, it's not just the wedding. Wendy would say that's a rich-girl problem. Wendy would shuck that off. It's something more."

A teenage boy, sporting a white polo shirt emblazoned with the yacht club logo, suddenly approached from the gloom of the bar galley. He offered them both sweating drinks upon a silver tray. Kelly took a sip of the Sea Breeze, thinking it a far cry from her father's twice-burned coffee.

"She's been playing tennis like a fiend," Audrey continued, setting the glass down on the teak table between them. "She shattered Mrs. Mountebank last week in singles. Now Wendy's in contention for the championship. It's . . . so not Wendy. I had hoped," she said, "that she'd come on this trip with us. That I could pin her down, try to get to the bottom of it." Two lines of concern appeared between Audrey's brows. "Frankly, Kelly, I was hoping you could shed some light."

"Me?"

Audrey twirled a lock of hair around her finger, while staring at her bracelet with great attention. "Wendy's very loyal, you know. She really makes an effort to see me, even

though I've got a husband and a family now. It was kind
of her to choose me as her matron of honor, and I can't
tell you how excited I am about the bachelorette party at
the Wainwright cabin next weekend. I'm so glad Wendy offered it as an option—so much better than holding it in
some sleazy Hamptons club." She dropped her ponytail and
lifted her drink, bracing it on her clearly Pilates-toned belly.
"But though we both agreed on that...I know that Wendy
and I aren't nearly as close now as we used to be at Miss
Porter's. She spends most of her time with you guys—you,
and Dhara, and Martha."

"Marta."

"Yes. Marta." Audrey gave her a wistful little smile. "You
three, you're really her best friends. *You're* the people she
talks about. So I'd hoped you had some inkling about what
is going on with her, and maybe you could clue me in."

Kelly looked toward the swiftly shrinking shoreline, both
flattered at Audrey's observation and chagrinned at it, because beyond the stress of the coming wedding, Kelly didn't
really have a clue what was bothering Wendy. It was true
that there had been a lot going on among their little group
these past six weeks. Dhara announcing her arranged marriage had been a shock, as had Marta's breakup with Carlos.
Cole's hospital visit and rehab stint had been another surprise, as was her own outing of this relationship with Trey.

In any case, that was all family business, in a manner of
speaking. Kelly wasn't sure she could share any of this with
Audrey. Then she looked past Audrey's designer glasses,
plumping lip gloss, and perfectly lined eyes to the very se-

rious woman, clearly deeply concerned about their mutual friend.

"Frankly, Audrey, it feels weird talking about Wendy to you."

"I know what you mean." Audrey's nose crinkled mischievously. "Talking about her makes you feel vaguely guilty, like she could arrive any moment, and we'd be caught."

"Why do you think it's like that?"

"Because Wendy is the most private person I know. Generous to a fault. Always there when I need her. But sometimes, I think Wendy's afraid to really open herself up to anyone."

A good half hour later, Audrey apologized as the children tumbled down from the wheelhouse and dragged their mother out of the sun for a long-promised game of Chinese checkers. Kelly had already regaled Audrey with one particular night she, Wendy, Dhara, and Marta had shared senior year in Aruba, and Audrey had started in on a story about Wendy when she was captain of the field hockey team. As Audrey's children dragged her by the hand into the galley, Audrey, with a roll of her eyes, promised to give further details once little ears weren't around.

Kelly took the opportunity to strike out for the head, thinking that if Trey's other friends were half as sweet as Audrey, then the unveiling of her and Trey's relationship wouldn't be half as traumatic as she'd feared.

She slipped into the main area of the boat, gliding past

the galley where the young helper was laying out tiny sand-wiches and trays of summer salad. She sidled into the bath-room, expecting a confined space, only to find a granite-topped vanity, a huge mirror, and a glass-enclosed shower big enough to include a seat. It was bigger than the bath-room in her apartment.

And had about the same amount of privacy, she thought, as she did her business amid the sound of Trey's laugh and then the clipped vowels of Parker's familiar voice. Some quirk of architecture made their voices echo from the wheel-house to this room.

As she washed her hands, she paused, catching the sound of her name.

"Oh, Kelly's cute, Trey, no doubt about it," James said. "Especially for that type."

"You mean redheads?" That was Parker's voice, and it was accompanied by a hissing noise, as if he were drawing air through his teeth. "That's a new one for you, Trey. I always thought Kelly was hot. My compliments."

Kelly smiled a little, drying her hands on a plush towel, warming to Parker.

"Yeah, nice curves," James added, "but you better watch yourself, bro."

She stilled.

"Watch myself?" Trey said. "Watch myself how?"

"I'm just saying. You have to be careful. With a girl like that. Brought up like that."

Trey made a dismissive noise. "You're just pissed she knew what a davit was."

"Did you see her face when she looked at these controls? She lit up. The girl has never seen such a boat, and she grew up on the water. Total working-class, that Kelly of yours."

Damn right. Kelly didn't think she liked James all that much. He'd rubbed her the wrong way, showing irritation when he couldn't tell her the fuel capacity of the boat, brushing off her other questions with a roll of his eyes.

"I'm just saying," James continued, "that you have to think about this. She's not like that girl you dated last year—what was her name?"

"Muffy Stonebridge," Parker said, his voice full of wonder. "Ferocious butt, hair down to her knees."

The warmth she felt for Parker cooled a bit.

"Well, Muffy's family's got money in minerals," James said. "She's not looking for more. But this girl of yours? She's looking at you and all she's seeing is dollar signs, bro."

"No, no, you've got her all wrong."

"Listen," James persisted, "I know you like variety. I still remember that Lebanese girl you bagged at that bar in the Hamptons last summer."

Oh, Kelly *really* didn't like James. She wondered what the good-hearted Audrey saw in him, and what could possibly have brought them together.

"Oh God, yes," Parker exclaimed. "You get all the luck."

"Yeah," James added, "Trey likes to slum. He likes 'em dirty."

Anger, like a shower of sparks, prickled down upon her.

"Hey, easy, James," Parker warned. "Remember, Kelly is Wendy's friend. One of her bridesmaids."

"What? Jesus, Trey, you've got to be kidding me." James's chair squealed as it swiveled. "Never fuck one of your sister's friends."

Trey's protest—*Shut up, James*—sounded strangely muffled.

"What the hell are you thinking?" James continued. "There's nothing wrong with banging a redhead. But why are you bringing that kind of girl *here*?"

Then Kelly pressed against the granite countertop, waiting for Trey's response in the silence, and in that silence, she imagined him pushing out of his seat in the wheelhouse, his hands tightening into fists, debating whether it was bad form to punch the host. She waited, not expecting Trey to give a long speech on how much fun they had together, or how he felt like himself when he was around her, or how he stole time, even from work, to be in her company. She waited for Trey to give James a good knock in the teeth for being such an *asshole*.

She waited, her knuckles going white on the countertop.

She waited, her heart pounding in her ears.

She waited.

"Fuck, guys," Trey muttered. "Just show me how much power this boat has, okay?"

ᴖᴖ

Kelly stood alone at the bow as the wind whipped her hair off her face. The yacht raced across the sound, shattering a path through the wakes of lesser boats. She gripped the railing, her knees loose to ride the gentle heave and ho. She welcomed the occasional spray, a physical manifestation of a cold slap of reality.

Trey was still in the wheelhouse above her. She knew he could see her through the Plexiglas. That's why she'd planted herself here. Eventually, she reasoned, he would slither away from his so-called friends and join her.

"Hey." He arrived later than she expected, slipping one hand along the railing. "Aren't you cold out here?"

"No. I like the speed." She fixed her gaze on the far horizon rather than the sight of his polo shirt battered against his six-pack. "It makes me think of time travel."

Trey's laugh hitched in surprise.

"It's conceivable, you know." She tugged a strand of hair off her face. "Based on velocity, if you look at time dilation in special relativity a one-way trip to the future is possible."

He leaned a hip against the rail in an effort to catch her gaze. "Someday, I hope I actually understand you, Kell."

"The real problem is traveling to the past. Theoretically possible, but there are all kinds of tricky paradoxes."

"Bummer."

"And that's what I'd really want to do—return to the past." She gripped the rail as the boat took a sudden dip. "To one particular day in college when I was sitting by myself on a pub stool, waiting for my friends."

She saw the smile lines at the edges of his eyes deepen as he remembered. Then those wrinkles smoothed, as he grew uncertain of her mood.

"You know what I'd tell that girl, Trey? I'd tell her to keep waiting for her friends." She began to tremble, and not from the cold. "I'd tell that girl that the hot guy approaching her from across the room was a weak-assed, sniveling, grade-A fuckup."

She seized the fluttering ends of her gossamer cover-up and yanked them across her body. Fury made her shake. Fury that she hadn't ended this relationship the way she'd intended to—sweetly, softly, at the hotel when the moment was ripe. Fury at what a fool she'd been in the first place, for not listening to her friends. And most of all, fury at him, for his failure, over fifteen years, to grow a spine.

He froze, blanching to the color of his polo shirt. His gaze skittered to the wheelhouse.

"Yeah, this is me talking, Trey. Working-class Kelly Palazzo, the gold digger who's banging you for your money."

He shifted his weight and turned his attention to a small puddle of seawater beading on the deck. "You were in the head."

"The acoustics are damn good. Your friend James is a real charmer."

"I'm sorry you overheard him."

"I'm not. I'm glad I heard *all* of it. If I hadn't, I would never have believed that you'd let a friend cut off your balls like that."

"Hey, hey—"

"What? Did you forget I'm a fisherman's daughter?" She jerked her chin in the direction of the wheelhouse. "Go back to James. He'll remind you."

A muscle jumped in his cheek. He folded his arms. His

throat worked as if he were swallowing his own temper. "I know he's an asshole. But he was looking out for me."

"You're freakin' kidding me."

"You don't think that doesn't happen?" He leaned in to her. "You think there haven't been situations where I'm ass-over-tit for some girl who's thinking of nothing but my money?"

Kelly remembered Wendy and Josef in college. In her head, she acknowledged that the situation could cut both ways. It didn't make her heart feel any better. "So when James called you out on those other relationships, did you argue with him?"

"Of course I did."

"Then clearly you're not ass-over-tit for me. You didn't say a *word* in my defense."

"Fuck, I did!"

"I heard everything—"

"James is a bulldog." He cast an angry glare toward the wheelhouse. "He's a damn brick wall. He'll argue a point un-til he's three blood-pressure points from blowing an artery. Even if he's wrong—*especially* if he's wrong."

"Oh, so he's wrong?"

"Of *course* he's wrong." He jabbed a finger in his chest. "I know that. *You* know that—"

"How the hell am I supposed to know that? You just let your best friend piss all over me."

"You're blowing this all out of proportion."

"Like *hell* I am." In the wheelhouse, Kelly noticed three curious faces pressed close to the window, one of them Audrey, covering her mouth with her hand. Their voices were carrying, and Kelly worried, fleetingly, about the kids, so she lowered her voice a notch. "Do you have any idea what kind of shit storm I battled when I told my friends the news about us? Do you have any idea how hard it was to defend myself? Do you know how much I defended you?"

"That's different—"

"It's the same. Freakin'. Thing."

"You don't have a clue what it's like—"

"I understand that you're ashamed of me."

"Fuck, Kelly—"

"I understand more than that too." Her heart pounded in her ears. "I understand that despite all my hopes, you are the same heartless screwup that you were in college. Except this time you're stuck under a different alpha male's hairy thumb."

His pupils contracted to pinpricks. The yacht had slowed from its headlong race but it still bobbed in the wake of other boats. She braced her legs, riding the rock, while he came right up to her, close enough so she could smell the sunscreen she'd slathered on his skin that morning.

He spoke straight into her face. "You want the truth, Kelly?"

"That would be refreshing."

"I don't give a damn what James thinks. I don't give a damn what James says. We're here together. You and me. That means something. I don't know what else you want from me."

She searched his eyes. She waited for something more.

She waited for the phrase she'd yearned to hear since the very first night they shared together, the declaration she'd gambled her heart, her hopes, and her future to win. She needed to hear that truth now. Spoken loud and clear on the bow of a boat on the open water, a phrase that the wind would wrap tight around her heart and then carry in glorious victory all the way to the wheelhouse.

She waited, her heart pounding.

She waited.

And then she waited no more.

"I'm done with you, Trey Wainwright." She turned on one heel. "I'm done with you for good."

chapter sixteen

Her cell phone rang again.

Wendy perched in the corner of the couch, her toes digging into the leather. The blinds of her condo were shuttered. Thin stripes of daylight stretched across the floor. Hugging a pillow, she stared at the phone rattling on the coffee table.

Then it stopped ringing.

She tugged at the tassels of the pillow and felt her heart pounding against the fabric. She knew it was Gabriel calling again. She'd seen his name on the screen. She knew it was Gabriel calling, because he'd called once already.

Her phone beeped, and the voice mail icon appeared. With clumsy hands she reached for the phone and dialed, working through the menu to retrieve the message. In the crackling silence after the beep, she recognized the rhythm of his breathing. She heard him sigh into the receiver. She closed her eyes and tried not to remember how it felt when he stretched her out on that table in the tent, his mouth hot against her throat.

Gabriel's voice, soft in her ear.

"Listen," he said. "I know this is complicated, Wendy. But we can't leave things like this."

She began to rock, pressing her mouth against the pillow, squeezing the phone against her ear. She never should have gone to the art fair. She should have known she wouldn't be able to resist him.

"Just meet me somewhere. Anywhere. Times Square. Grand Central Terminal. I need to see you, *querida.*"

She buried her face in the pillow. She wanted to see him too. She wanted to move into his house and take care of his little Miguel and watch Gabriel paint marvelous paintings. She wanted to surrender herself to him as if she were a free woman, without guilt or hesitation.

A strip of light gleamed across her hand, sparkling the topaz of Parker's ring.

"Please, Wendy. Don't give up on us."

~⌒~

It was a gorgeous wedding dress. Made of thick ivory silk with a hand-beaded overskirt that glimmered under the lights of the chandelier. Wendy stared at her reflection in the five-paneled mirror, marveling at the workmanship. She imagined pairing the dress with black stiletto boots and a spiked collar.

Wendy's mother perched on a leather sofa coddling a cup of tea. "Oh, Stella, dear, you've outdone yourself. She's an absolute *vision.*"

"Simple and graceful." The designer glanced up at Wendy

from her knees, where she was carefully tugging the hem. "These silver Louboutins work perfectly. Just as you ordered."

"What do you think, Wendy?"

Wendy hardly recognized her own reflection. It was a wonder she hadn't noticed this during all the other fittings. This was a dazzling wedding dress, a thing of great beauty— it was just better suited for some other lucky girl.

"I will say this," Wendy said, plucking at the bodice's careful folds. "The dress came out exactly as planned."

That was the scary part. She'd labored over the design with her mother and Stella more than six months ago, coming in every six weeks to check on the progress. The dress had not changed. *She* had. All because on Saturday afternoon, Gabriel had made love to her under a tent in the rain.

"Really, Wendy, you have nothing else to say?" Her mother swirled the cup. "After all the trouble Stella went through hand-beading those Swarovski crystals on the overskirt?"

"Stella," Wendy said, as if prompted for her line. "The overskirt really is spectacular. My sister, Birdie, will adore it."

That was not what she intended to say. That was the least of what she needed to say. Birdie had been, until this moment, the very farthest thing from her mind. But since Gabriel's last phone call, she'd been like a sleepwalker, dreaming through the haze of her life, going through the motions while watching it as if from a very great distance...and yet seeing it with stunning clarity. The words had leaped to her lips of their own accord. This newborn creature living in her skin felt absolutely no urge to take them back.

"So this is why you've been silent as the grave all morning," her mother said. "I see you've made up your mind to bring Birdie to the wedding."

Wendy had made up her mind on many things. Lots of plans had to change. Despite the fact that there were three hundred and twenty-five wedding invitations in the mail. Despite the fact that there were potted, not-yet-bloomed specialty orchids on a steamer, navigating from Rio de Janeiro. Despite the fact that there were three designer bridesmaid's dresses and one matron-of-honor dress, cut, sewn, and awaiting Marta, Dhara, Kelly, and Audrey for the last fitting.

For in less than two months, there would be no sixteen-piece orchestra at her cocktail party playing the Meditation from *Thais* while her guests nibbled on salmon mousse on wafers. In less than two months, she would not be married to a wonderful man she'd known since second grade, a good man who deserved a better wife, a loving wife, a *faithful* wife.

Her heart squeezed.

"Oh, for goodness sake," her mother exclaimed. "I'll tell the wedding planner to arrange for two more seats."

Her mother brought the cup to her mouth and put her lips upon the rim, going through the pantomime of sipping. Very deliberately, she replaced the cup in the saucer without a clink. And Wendy glanced at her mother's reflection in the mirror, noting the sudden capitulation with a raised brow that she'd once pierced, and now was seriously considering piercing again.

In the stretching silence, the designer must have sensed the tension, for she mumbled something about fetching seamstress's chalk. She rose to her feet, padded across the floor, and then closed the door behind her.

"Don't look so surprised, my dear." Her mother pulled a mirror from her purse to check her lipstick. "I suspected you were going to bring this up, sooner or later."

It was a strange irony that the issue would come up when it didn't matter anymore. "I know you never wanted Birdie at the wedding."

"I love your sister, Wendy. I also know that you won't be doing Birdie any favors by insisting she attend."

"It wouldn't be a true family celebration without her."

"Oh, you'll have plenty of her. She will cling to you through the entire reception. She adores you above all others."

"Yes."

"And when you must make the rounds of the tables, she will become petulant. She will complain. And she will have a tantrum. Then she will have to be dragged to some distant room where the minder will spend the next hour and a half trying to calm her down."

Wendy closed her eyes and willed patience. She would not say the terrible things that leaped to mind. How her mother had sent Birdie away, when the family had the money to take care of her at home. How much more that act needled her, now that she knew someone like Gabriel.

She was not going to fight with her mother, at least not to-day. That fight would come later. She needed to marshal every ounce of her energy for the more difficult confrontation coming this afternoon.

She reached blindly for the row of pearl buttons up the middle of her back. "Help me get out of this dress, would you?"

"Wait for Stella. She has a few adjustments to make." Her mother crumpled her smooth brow. "And don't change the subject. I know you think Birdie has improved these past years, but that's because you see her only in a place where she is comfortable, where she feels safe, where there is a pre-dictable routine—"

"Please, stop."

"Yes, I see it's no use discussing this." Her mother spread her hands across her knees. "When you've got that look on your face, I should know better."

Wendy glanced back at the woman in the mirror, seeing only the flush of her cheeks, the strange brightness of her own eyes, the face of a woman who'd fallen hard for a Brazil-ian artist when she should have been planning a wedding to a wonderful man.

"You were like this before you insisted on taking the job at the art gallery in that terrible part of the city. I couldn't sleep, thinking you'd call me from your cell phone, bleeding in some alley—"

"Now you're just being dramatic."

"And that vulgar piercing in your ear, and those widow's weeds you used to wear. No, no," her mother said, raising the flat of her hand. "You'll have Birdie at your wedding. I'll try very hard not to say I told you so when she's screaming in Trip's office at the club."

Wendy let the remark pass. It didn't matter anymore. Birdie wouldn't be screaming in Trip's office at the club. Someday, Birdie would dance at Wendy's wedding.

Just not at this wedding.

Parker's sailboat lay low in the water, its gunwale only a foot or so above the pier. As she approached, she saw him bent over something. His plaid shorts came to just above the knees, his calf muscles firm and contoured. His blond hair was dark with moisture, as if he'd recently showered.

"Hey," he said, catching sight of her. "There you are."

Yes, here she was, cheating fiancée. He cast a warm smile upon her and she felt that smile like a shadow across her heart.

"Love the hair," he said. "You do that for me?"

She lifted her fingers to her hair, still pinned up from the trip to the salon that morning. She tried to run her fingers through it, but they snagged in the pins. "It's bad luck if you see it."

"Hey, not a word from me. Help me load, will you?" He gestured to a pile of gear on the dock. "Hand me some of that stuff so we can get on the water."

She slipped her purse off her shoulder and let it topple to the boards. She picked up the first bag, crinkling the paper. She smelled fresh grapes and caught sight of a bottle of wine. Then, tilting the bag, she saw the familiar logo of their favorite deli.

"I did some shopping," he said, reaching over to take it out of her hands. "Knew you wouldn't be happy with a ham sandwich and some beer."

Something inside her tightened. She reached for the next bag to hide her face. This was the man who suffered family Thanksgivings with her, clutching her hand under the mahogany table as the dysfunction flew. This was the man who'd raised the yachting cup toward her, blowing her a kiss after he'd won the club regatta last summer. This was the man she'd said yes to when he fell to one knee on this dock—in this very spot—offering her his great-grandmother's ring along with his bright shiny future.

"Another bad morning, huh?" He put the last bag in the boat and then held out his hand. "C'mon. A few hours on the open water will clear your mind."

Wendy looked at his hand. It was a strong hand, callused at the palms and fingers, the kind of hand that spent a lot of time pulling hemp ropes and cranking winches. An honest hand, an honest man. She had no memory of sinking down and folding her legs, but suddenly, there she was, sitting on the dock in a pool of cotton skirt with the sun-scorched boards burning against the backs of her thighs.

"Hey." He clutched the gunwale, ready to leap over onto the dock. "Are you all right?"

"Yes," she murmured, waving him back. "Yes, I'm fine. I just…need a minute."

She fumbled in her purse, searching among the chaos for

the familiar little pack, the emergency cigarettes she kept with her though she'd given up the habit years and years ago.

"Hey, Wendy...Are you sick?"

At heart, yes. "No, I'm not sick, just light headed."

"You should stop dieting. You look great."

"Thanks. But that's not the problem." She ducked her head as if she could dodge that arrow of kindness. "I can't sail with you today, Parker."

"Yes, you can. You're here now." Parker glanced around, waving to a friend passing by on the boards. "To hell with whatever other plans you have."

"I've already canceled all my other appointments today." She tapped the cigarette on her knee, turning it over and over in her hand. "All that's really left is to talk to you."

Squinting against the sun, she looked up into Parker's face and saw his expression shift.

"Listen," he said, "you already backed out on me once this week. Sail with me today and tell me what the hell's going on."

"Can't sail."

"I'll *listen.* I promise."

"I know you will, Park—"

"We're just going out on the Sound. It's a calm day. I won't be distracted."

"Here's the problem: I'm not a good swimmer."

Parker's brow rippled. "I know you're not. Two years in a row you flaked out on lessons with Jessica. But what does that have to do with us?"

"After I finish saying what I've got to say, we'll be in deep water."

"So?"

"You're likely to throw me off the boat."

Parker went very still. With shaky hands, she pulled out an old lighter and flicked it a few times, trying to ignite the spark. For the past week she had mulled this very moment over and over, searching for the words that would hurt this good man the least. She certainly couldn't tell him that only now did she realize that she'd spent the last seven years trying to be the woman the world expected her to be, rather than the woman she really was. Nor could she tell Parker that she didn't love him anymore. That was simply not true.

What she dreaded most was the chance that Parker would behave like Trey had yesterday, on the boat with Kelly. Audrey had given her the blow-by-blow. If Parker flew into as fierce a passion as Trey had, Wendy knew she would lose the Zen-like calm that had descended upon her. She would lose the crystal clarity of her thoughts. She would lose her sureness of heart.

Then the words tumbled out of her, loose from where her guilt festered. "I'm so sorry, Parker. I'm calling it off."

His face shuttered. He backed up a step, and then another, finally stumbling back against the opposite gunwale. She watched him as he braced himself against the far side of the boat, his shoulders slumping, his polo shirt clinging to his chest. A thought passed fleetingly through her mind: what a terribly malicious thing love was, to bring to her attention the startling beauty of the man she was giving up.

Then he crossed his arms, flexing his fingers over his biceps. "I don't want to know about it."

She stilled, tilting her head.

"I get it, Wendy." The wind picked up from the west and began to weave in his fair hair as he shifted the crossing of his arms. "I'm not an idiot. I know you had a last sowing of the oats."

Her heart made a full stop. He couldn't know. *Nobody* knew. She hadn't even divulged that secret to Marta, Kelly, or Dhara.

It wasn't possible.

"You don't think I've noticed? This crazy decision to keep me hands-off three full months before the wedding? How distant you've been?"

"Parker—"

"You're not the only one nervous about the wedding. You're not the only one wondering if you're ready for this." Parker pushed away from the gunwale to move around the boat, shifting bags, pulling out the white wine and shoving it into the ice bucket. "My father has been talking to me about life insurance, annuities. Screws with my head."

"Parker—"

"Not a word. I don't want to know anything." His arms bulged as he stowed the last of the bags into storage. "If I find out who this guy is, I'll floor him."

Her breathing hitched. Wendy weighed her next words, watching an ant work its way across the thin fissures on the weathered boards, trying so very hard not to get mired in the cracks. It was one of life's strange ironies that it might have been better if she admitted the affair with Gabriel. Then he'd have a source to blame, a solid reason for her decision.

"There's no other man, Parker."

In truth, Gabriel wasn't the real cause of this separation. Gabriel had been the catalyst, the man who showed her how foolish she'd been, trying to become her mother's version of a good Wainwright girl. Her doubts about Parker had always been there. Even when Parker had dropped to one knee on this very dock, her lips had said yes to his proposal but a little voice in her heart had whispered *no*.

Parker would never have reason to suspect otherwise. She'd ended it with Gabriel almost as soon as it began. She'd burned into her memory the sensation of his hand cradling her head. She'd preserved it like a crocus plucked from the snow and pressed between the pages of an old book. It hurt to hear Gabriel's pained voice on her voice mail, still urging her to reconsider. But she'd cheated on her fiancé. If she became Gabriel's lover, she would destroy Parker. If she became Gabriel's lover, guilt would destroy that relationship too. Infidelity was a poison that seeped both ways. No matter how long she tried to think this all through, it always ended with three broken hearts.

The least she could do was protect Parker by letting Gabriel go.

"Then it's over," Parker said. "Good." He nodded once and then held out his hand. "Now let's go sailing."

She felt a chill in her blood. She searched his face, waiting for his expression to betray some suppressed fury. He deserved to yell. He'd certainly earned the right to be incensed, just with suspicion. She told herself it must be a coping mechanism. Later, she thought, he'd go out and get drunk with Trey.

Wendy put the cigarette in her mouth. She bent her head and flicked the lighter once, twice, until it finally caught flame. She sucked the smoke in through the filter, felt the hit in her lungs. She held the smoke for a moment and closed her eyes as her senses spun with the rush of nicotine.

"It's the sailing." He yanked on one of the ropes, setting it loose from the cleat. "It's a jealous mistress."

"It's not the sailing." Though, Wendy thought, it probably helped that his attention wasn't always laser-focused on her these past years. "You never made me feel second place, Parker."

"Have you told your mother?"

"No. Not yet."

She wished she could see his eyes. She wished she could read his mind. But he was absorbed in the new knot he was winding around the cleat, pulling on it with far more force than was necessary, in a sailor's knot she didn't recognize— much more complicated than a simple clove hitch.

"Good." He pulled the knot secure and then checked the tension. "I admire your mother. But I'd rather we decided how to handle this ourselves."

"Handle this."

"There are going to be a lot of questions. It's going to be the talk of the season. Everyone is going to want to know why the wedding is off."

Wendy was very glad she was sitting down. Hearing those words out of his mouth was like a scythe to the back of her knees. Had she been standing, she would have collapsed in a heap on the dock. As it was, she felt as if the boards had just given way beneath her and sent her through the pilings to the water gurgling below.

"Blame me." Her voice was hoarse. "Just blame me."

"I'd rather blame it on the sailing."

"That would work, too."

She looked up at him, hoping that he would see in her eyes how sorry she was, how much her heart ached. She looked up at him, knowing that his expression would gut her.

Yet his face was lifted to the elements. He was searching the sky, taking note of the scuttling clouds, probing their depth for any hint of rain. He turned his face this way and that, using it as a compass to determine the direction of the wind. He looked unnervingly careless, though an engagement of nearly two years had just collapsed between them.

Then in a moment of crystalline clarity, she saw in her mind's eye a whole new view of their relationship, peppered with moments like this, passed over with unnerving detachment, ending in calm, rigid silences. The chill that had blown through her heart moments ago dropped a few thousand degrees, threatening to freeze the very marrow of her bones.

"Tell them anything," she said. "Tell them that I caught you in bed with a naked supermodel."

"I won't do that."

"It'll shut everyone up."

"Better if we keep this cordial."

"You don't have to avoid unpleasantness, not this time. You can tell any story you want. I'm beyond the pale now. I'll back you up."

"You really don't care, do you?"

"I do care. I care about *you*."

Just a flicker, a little light, in those dear blue eyes. "I mean you don't care about what people think. About Birdie, about your choice of lifestyle, your choice of friends."

"No, I don't care. Never really have. I'll tell them any story you like."

"How about the truth?" He shoved his fists in his pockets. "I'll tell them you never loved me."

"No." She hauled herself off the boards. She flicked the cigarette onto the dock. She crushed it under a foot as she swept up her purse. "That's the one thing I won't say."

"It's the truth."

"The truth is," she said, slipping the topaz ring off her finger, "this hurts all the more because I really do love you."

"Not enough to marry me."

The ring gleamed in the sunlight. She took the two steps that brought her to the edge of the dock. She held it out to him. She looked deep into his searching blue eyes as he took it into his palm. The wind played in his hair. The sun lay bright on his broad shoulders.

She searched for an answer that didn't come.

Sometimes, there were no words.

As softly as she could, she turned away from Parker Pryce-Weston and headed home.

～ that weekend

It was the longest walk Marta had ever made.

She stood up from the couch and climbed across Wendy's feet, and then sidled past the broken chair. The carpet was knobby and thin beneath her feet. She felt her friends' gazes like warm breath on the back of her neck. She trailed her fingernails along the wall as she approached the bathroom door.

In her mind came the image of Esperanza, her first babysitter. Marta had idolized the fifteen-year-old with her press-on nails and dangling gold earrings and rhinestone-studded jeans. Esperanza was full of life, always laughing on the phone. When Esperanza stopped babysitting, Marta's mother wouldn't tell her why. A year later, Marta glimpsed the sixteen-year-old in front of a five-floor walk-up not far from the school, struggling to carry an infant as she folded the stroller with one hand already laden with groceries.

Marta had always hoped she'd be smarter than this.

Just before she turned into the bathroom, she closed her eyes and tugged on the gold cross around her neck, the one she'd received on her first communion, and whispered a prayer for a single blue line.

On the edge of the sink lay the white stick.

She saw it, and the breath rushed out of her, and with it came a strange strangled sound, and then her knees hit the cool tiles of the bathroom at bruising velocity. Spots swam before her eyes.

Then they were all there, clutching at her, Dhara's hair sweeping across her face, Kelly pulling her upright. Wendy picked up the stick and the box and compared the two, the little furrow between her eyebrows deepening as she announced the news.

Marta's heart pounded as they pulled her off the bathroom floor and led her back to the living room. Her legs weren't her own, and the vaulted ceiling danced before her. They eased her onto the couch, murmuring words she could hear but didn't understand. All she could think of was that she was pregnant.

Oh, God, she was pregnant.

Kelly offered her a cup of steaming tea. Marta hesitated. "Is there caffeine in this?"

"No," Kelly said. "Just chamomile."

"I can't drink caffeine now. I can't eat seafood now. I can't drink whiskey now." Marta brought the cup to her lips with hands that wouldn't stop shaking. "I can't go to law school now."

Wendy exchanged a glance with Dhara. Marta read the unspoken communication and knew there was no avoiding the conversation.

"Oh, God, I was so stupid." Marta squeezed her eyes shut and let the tea warm the palms of her hands. "Please, scream at me. Tell me how stupid I was."

"Marta," Wendy said gently. "Nobody is going to yell at you."

"It was a condom fail. I thought the timing was all wrong. I didn't think..."

"It could have happened to me and Josef," Wendy said. "It could have happened to Kelly and Trey."

Marta looked anywhere but in those three pairs of worried eyes. This wasn't really happening. She was just having a very bad dream. She'd been so stressed, waiting on acceptance letters from law schools, finishing up her senior thesis, trying to keep up with schoolwork and summer job applications, trying to figure out why—despite the fabulous sex—her boyfriend, Chuck, had dumped her two weeks ago for that fawning mousy-haired English major. She wished someone would pinch her. She wished she could wake up and find her life all neatly planned again.

"It's still early." Wendy sat close, her bare arm pressing against hers. "Those tests aren't one hundred percent accurate. It could be a false positive."

It wasn't. Marta knew, deep down, as sure as she'd ever been about anything. Her body had already started changing in small but perceptible ways. Her breasts were tender, and there was an odd fullness across her lower abdomen. She was pregnant, and if nature followed its course, in eight months she would give birth to a daughter or son.

Oh, God.

Marta rattled the teacup onto the coffee table and stared at her shaking hands as if they didn't belong to her, as if her whole body didn't belong to her. This couldn't possibly be happening to her. It was happening to that other girl, the one with the dark tangled hair quivering in her place on the sofa.

In the tense silence, she sensed another unspoken communication passing between Wendy and Dhara. She knew they were weighing how to broach a subject they knew Marta did not want to hear. The subject was complicated by the fact that Kelly was here—adopted Kelly, the abandoned Gloucester baby—rocking on the other side of the coffee table, her eyes glazed, her pale face a mask of shock.

Marta knew what Kelly was thinking. She knew it as if Kelly were screaming it from the rafters. Kelly's biological mother had faced the same choices that Marta faced now. There was one decision that woman did *not* make, a choice that was the reason a full-grown Kelly was now here in this room. Kelly's mother had instead chosen to leave her two-day-old daughter swaddled tight on the firehouse stairs, giving Kelly life, even as she forever gave up the chance to raise the brilliant, beautiful redhead she'd brought into the world.

Marta already knew what she was going to do. She'd spent the last two and a half weeks pretending she wasn't thinking about this, every morning, every night, and every moment in between, when in truth she was burning out desk bulbs drafting flowcharts for every possible outcome.

With a sinking heart she thought of her mother's double

shifts, the lack of family vacations, the little economies her parents had practiced in order to pay Marta's way through college. With her throat tightening, Marta thought of Chuck and the quagmire of issues the two of them would need to work out. And then, for one last time, she thought of her whole Life Plan, going up in a ribbon of smoke.

"This is going to break my mother's heart," she said, as she cleared her throat and tried to collect herself, wiping the moisture from the corner of her eyes. "She had such great hopes for me. But she will help me." She took a deep, shuddering breath. "I can't raise a baby alone."

Without a word, the girls clambered onto the sofa. Dhara slung an arm around Marta's neck, pulling her close. Wendy's face dug into her shoulder. And Kelly, climbing barefoot over the coffee table, grasped Marta's cheeks in both hands as she gave her a long, solemn look. She smothered Marta in her wild hair as she pressed her lips close to her ear.

"Look around you, Marta. You are not doing this alone."

chapter seventeen

"So, basically, I met the Ghost of Christmas Future at a speed-dating event," Marta said, "and everything she predicted came true."

Marta braced her elbows against the splintered gunwales of the wooden rowboat and slumped at the stern. She scanned the shores of the Adirondack lake as Wendy pulled the oars to propel them farther away from the Wainwright family cabin. Marta felt like she'd lost about six pounds in confession and gained ten more in public failure. But it felt good to finally share the whole story. Her life was madness. Every time she came up with a hopeful new plan, fate swept in and knocked it right over.

She was tired of doing this alone.

"Girl, you have a pair of melon-size *cojones*." Wendy checked over her shoulder, aiming the bow of the boat to the center of the lake. "In that situation, I would have excused myself to the ladies' room and clawed my way out a dirty broken window."

"Rat me out." Marta ran her fingers through her hair, tangled from driving two hundred miles with an open window. "The whole coven will be here tonight. I need an intervention."

"It's my bachelorette party." Wendy pulled the oars hard. "I've got other plans."

"I've broken two rules at least. I didn't wait six months after Carlos, and I went after an ex."

"No can do. We've reached our official summer intervention quota."

Marta trailed her fingers in the water. "You know, my *abuela* used to warn me to stop casting off my boyfriends like old socks. She said one day I'd wake up, and I'd be—"

"Sockless?"

"Alone."

"You've got me and Kelly and Dhara and a hundred and fifty-two close relatives, at last count. You should be screaming for privacy."

"Wendy, you have to admit that I'm heading down a path that leads to Stouffer's single servings and an excess of goldfish."

"I like frozen dinners."

"Wendy."

"Is this some sort of Roman Catholic thing? A need to confess, pay penance, be absolved?"

Marta flicked her wet fingers at her. "Two thousand years of tradition, *chica.* It works."

"Yeah, but I'm no priest. And right now, I'm the last person you should be asking for romantic advice."

Marta disagreed. Wendy was the *best* person to ask for advice. Marta had ducked out of work on a Friday just to arrive here before any other bachelorette party guests. But as she watched Wendy spin one oar straight and then dip it back in the water, Marta suddenly noticed how thin her friend looked in a fitted T-back top and bike pants. Wendy's shoulders looked bony, her hips angular. Wendy's throat corded with each pull of the oars.

Poor girl. That wedding was really taking a toll. Marta hoped Wendy's mother would back off a bit, give Wendy some breathing space. But before Marta could make a joking comment about General Bitsy, Wendy stopped rowing.

"Marta, I want you to do something for me." Wendy twisted the oars and laid the blades inside the boat. "Turn around, put your feet up, and lay your head on this seat."

"What?"

"Trust me." She patted the wooden bench. "I'll lie next to you. It'll be snug, but we'll fit."

Marta gripped the edges of the boat. She hadn't been too keen about going out on the lake in this rickety dinghy, but she'd arrived at the cabin just as Wendy was about to take a solo row around the lake. It would have been rude to demur. "Don't you think you should row? So we know where we're going?"

"You came here for advice, right?"

She nodded with some reluctance.

"Well, my advice right now is to shut up and hit the deck."

Marta lay down upon the hard boards, suppressing a sigh. What she really craved for the weekend were mudpacks,

Swedish massages, and an IV of pomegranate Cosmos. But if this little trip out on the lake was any indicator, it looked like Wendy was going to turn this party into one of those granola-eating, bike-riding, weird communing-with-nature sort of weekends.

Above the gunwales, all Marta could see was wide-open sky. She braced the heels of her sneakers against the bow. "Tell me that there are no waterfalls nearby."

Wendy scuttled down, then swiveled to lie down beside her. "It's a little mountain lake fed by little mountain creeks."

"No nearby white-water rivers? No weird currents that are going to grip the bottom and send us swirling?"

"The most dangerous things around here are the black flies, and the season has passed." Wendy pulled her ponytail from under her head and sent it dangling over the edge of the seat. "Relax. Look at the clouds. And tell me once again why you decided to go speed-dating."

Marta flexed her feet, trying to take comfort in the solidity of the wood beneath her flats. "Do you remember what Kelly said about probabilities at the hospital that day? It hurt my brain while she was talking, but later, thinking about it, I realized that some of it actually made sense. I'm never going to find an appropriate single guy unless I start looking for one, and at that point, it's just a numbers game—the more guys I meet, the more likely it will be that I'll find someone good."

"Listen to you. It's like you're picking fruit off a conveyor belt."

"Actually, yes."

"It also means you'll likely reject a perfectly fine one because of a few superficial bruises."

Marta grew warm, thinking of how she'd criticized all the men who'd passed by her table, making instant judgments, instant rejections.

"I just don't think you can *summon* Mr. Right," Wendy said, "any more than you can ignore him once he shows up."

"I did a damn good job ignoring Tito though, didn't I?"

Marta absorbed for the thousandth time the pinch of that ugly truth. She blinked up at the sky to stop the prickling at the back of her throat. The sky was blue, so blue, and scuttled with little white clouds. Beneath the weathered boards of the boat, she could hear the gurgle of the lake water. The whole dinghy rocked gently. It should be comforting, like snoozing on a hammock strung between two trees.

It wasn't.

"Listen," Marta said, stretching her palm against the side to establish some sense of equilibrium. "You know I've never really had a problem finding a guy. The real problem is what happens after I've found him." The boat bobbed more vigorously, as if it were caught in a wake. "I always thought attraction led to great sex led to a relationship led to love, right? But no, that's not how it works. Not for me anyway. Something happens after the sex and before the love. Are you sure we're safe floating around like this?"

"Relax, Marta."

"I mean, I'm perfectly okay with sitting back up."

"Relationships," Wendy reminded her. "You were giving me the lowdown on relationships à la Sanchez."

Marta strained to hear the sound of a motor, but heard nothing but birdsong and the burble of water. She took a deep breath. She was with a Wainwright, whose distant ancestors probably played lacrosse with the Iroquois and thus had a pact with the local Native American lake deity.

"For me," Marta said, "a relationship has always been about attraction and then great sex and then *really* great sex. But except for Tito, who is, like, the most patient man on the planet, none of those guys ever hung around after the initial rush of excitement. And, honestly, here's the scary part: until Carlos dumped me, I really didn't mind letting them go."

"Okay, I'm about to say something you're not going to like. Are you going to swear at me in Spanish?"

"Possibly."

"Then I'll pretend I just don't understand the curses you taught me in Aruba." Wendy flattened her sneakers against the bow. "Marta, you're treating your reluctant singlehood like it's an IPO. A project to strategize, to be tackled, managed, bullet-pointed, and marked by discrete little steps to success."

"No kidding." Marta felt a little sheepish. Even now, her fingers itched for a legal pad and the comfort of a pen, but when Wendy had urged her onto the boat, Marta had left her briefcase behind, unwilling to risk the Italian leather. "That's just a coping device. It's the way I always tackle problems."

"Hey, do you manage our relationship like that?"

"Of course not. Oh, for goodness sake, I'm not blind. I know relationships are messy. You guys are up in my face all the time but I love you anyway. I *get* that. I know that to really know someone, it takes time, and you have to take the good with the bad. But I gave Carlos sixteen months. Sixteen months, Wendy, and still it didn't progress."

"That's because you were concentrating all your fierce Sanchez energies achieving Life Plan bullet-point sixteen."

"Yeah. Making *partner*."

The old tingling abated before it really started.

"The problem," Wendy said, "is that *husband* was bullet-point seventeen. Poor Tito was fighting all the way back at twelve."

"What you and the girls persist in ignoring is that until now, that plan has worked."

"Who's to say you wouldn't have gotten here if you hadn't been following it in the first place?"

"That's *ignoratio elenchi*, counselor, an illogical conclusion to an unrelated argument." Marta gripped the gunwale as the boat rocked. "That's it. We're going to knock into something, I just know it, and this boat of yours is going to shatter into toothpick-size splinters, and I'm going to have to put my feet on the wormy bottom."

Marta began to haul herself up but Wendy grabbed her arm.

"It's hard, isn't it?" Wendy's eyes were suspiciously bright. "Just drifting along, not knowing where you're going?"

"It's making me dizzy." She wished there were a towrope tied to the dock. Or an anchor, at least, dug into the lake mud. The fact that they were floating like a big cork was unsettling. "I'm starting to feel nauseous."

"It scares the hell out of me too."

The comment was so odd that Marta stopped worrying about the boat long enough to take a fresh look at her friend. She noticed the shadows under Wendy's cheekbones, the twitchy look on her face.

"Hey." Marta reached out to touch Wendy's arm, shocked at how close the bones felt beneath the skin. "Are you okay?"

"Drift, Marta." Wendy put her hand over Marta's. "Just for a little while."

"Please tell me that's not your advice."

"Whatever I say wouldn't matter anyway."

"Yes, it would! I came here in search of words of wisdom and some concrete suggestions. You know, like something about the importance of compromise or an online Web site for exotic aphrodisiacs."

"It's not fun watching a friend in pain. I really wish I could make a difference." Wendy shrugged against the boards. "You, me, Kelly, and Dhara, we try to help each other. Sometimes we try *too* hard. But I think when it comes to this—to men, to relationships—we're all deaf to one another's advice."

"I'm not deaf."

"But if I sit here and tell you that ever since that weekend—and all the difficult months after—that you've had some serious issues with emotional intimacy, you're going to disagree with me, right?"

Marta sputtered. She wanted to argue that Wendy was wrong. She wanted to tell her that what happened that weekend had absolutely no bearing on her later relationships with men. But truth had a way of cutting through bullshit, and she flinched at the wound.

"Listen," Wendy said. "I'll always be here when you want to talk. I can take you out for mojitos when a relationship tanks. I can bring you tea while you're sobbing in your room. But when it comes to making the big risky decisions...well, you know this better than all of us, Marta. We've got to figure out our *own* hearts."

"Not all of us."

"Yes, all of us."

"No. You're a seven-year survivor. You got it right. That's why I pulled an all-nighter finishing papers so I could make it here before anyone else. I need to talk to a pro. You and Parker, *chica*—you're the golden couple."

Wendy went very still. The boat bobbed more vigorously. Wendy turned her face back to the sky. A breeze picked up and skittered the dinghy across the surface, and, watching Wendy's pained expression, Marta became aware of another shift, a far deeper one, a sliding sense of vertigo.

"There's something I have to tell you, Marta. I'm afraid you're not going to like it."

Hours later, Marta followed the girls away from the farmhouse table into the vaulted living room of the cabin. Dhara sat cross-legged on the rug. Wendy curled into a ball on the end of the couch closest to the huge stone fireplace. Kelly sprawled on the facing couch. Marta chose a little spot on the floor where she could lean against the arm of a sofa.

She'd had hours to process Wendy's mind-bending news, far longer than the other girls, who'd just been informed over a dinner of roast pheasant, risotto, and French beans. The girls had taken the news with shock that had already warmed into compassion. But Marta was still reeling. She felt like she was walking beside herself, bundled in some invisible insulation so that even the sound of their voices was dulled.

On a lacquered cross section of a giant white pine lay boas, bachelorette-party card games, noisemakers, and three nicely wrapped presents, all the trappings of a party whose nature had been fundamentally altered by Wendy's announcement that the wedding was canceled. Under the girls' urging, Wendy opened the presents anyway. Marta watched, lifting the fine red wine to her mouth, not tasting the liquid that wet her lips.

Dhara's present was a bronze statue of a dancing half-elephant. Dhara explained that it was a statue of Ganesh, the Hindu deity for—among other things—domestic bliss. Marta tried to muster an attentive smile while Wendy unwrapped the leather bustier that Marta had found in an East Village fetish store, much to the grim amusement of the girls. Amusement dissolved swiftly as Wendy opened Kelly's gift and out tumbled a length of airy chiffon.

With a wistful smile, Wendy crushed the wedding negligee in her lap. "Domestic bliss, romance, and hot sex. I'm glad I canceled all the other guests this weekend. I knew I could count on you three to bring me everything I need."

In the silence came the crackle of the fire and the buzz of the cicadas in the dark woods. Maybe it was the effects of her second glass of wine, but Marta was struck with déjà vu. The four of them had been together like this before, sprawled on the floor of their Terrace apartment. That time, the table had been littered with take-out Chinese. She remembered Wendy reaching for a pack of cigarettes sitting on the table. She remembered Kelly and her solemn eyes. She remembered the way it felt, to have her entire world turned upside down.

"Here we are again."

Marta didn't realize that it was her own voice that had broken the silence until she became aware of all the girls looking at her.

"We're here again," she said, waving to the vaulted ceiling with its striking pine beams. "Different place, maybe, but it's the same situation as that weekend in college. The whole world is turned upside down, all over again."

"Oh, I don't know," Kelly said, hesitating. "It was pretty bad then, Marta."

"Aren't you still hurting, because of the exact same guy?"

"Well, yeah, but it's different. Back then, I didn't understand what had happened. This time, I'm the one who made a decision. And I don't regret going back to Trey at all."

Marta took a feigned interest in the depths of her wine. Of all the revelations of this day, at least the one about Kelly's breakup with Trey made sense. Marta just wished she could be half as certain about anything right now.

Wendy knocked a cigarette out of a pack. "Trey would love to have you back, Kelly. You know that, right? He'd return to you in a heartbeat."

Marta started. The stem of the wineglass slipped between her fingers.

"Last week on the tennis court, my brother knocked James on his butt." Wendy pulled a long, slim wooden skewer from the canister by the hearth and stuck the end in the fire. "And it happened right after James made some nasty comment about you."

Marta cast a glance Kelly's way. Kelly drew her feet up under her floral skirt and folded herself tight into the corner of the couch.

"And now Trey is running. I mean *running*. Miles and miles and miles, every day. Like he's training to carry the Olympic torch." Wendy held the flaming tip of the stick to the end of her cigarette. "I've always wondered what kind of girl it would take to knock sense into my wastrel brother. Turns out it's one of my best friends."

Marta clinked her glass on the table as the room swam before her eyes. "Wendy, what are you doing?"

"I'm stating an unnerving fact. And I agree with Kelly, by the way. Broken engagement and all, this weekend doesn't feel as unbelievably confusing as that one. For a lot of reasons." Wendy gave Marta a raised brow, then tossed the stick into the flames and watched the fire consume the sliver of wood. "For me, Josef blindsided me that weekend. But I saw Gabriel coming. Just being around him made me realize what a fool I'd been. After Soho, I took the job my mother tossed in my lap. And then I got involved with a great guy I knew would never hurt me. And that was my biggest mistake."

"God, we were so young then." Dhara rolled a can of soda between her hands. "We were all so scared, trying to order the world in a way that would save us pain. I'm wondering if that's possible, really." She paused, for one long moment. "After everything that happened back then, Marta, I would think you would agree the most."

Marta closed her eyes, wishing the memory away. "Dhara, tell me you're not joining the chorus."

"Sorry, I am. I feel different now than I felt then. I dread seeing Cole on Monday, but whatever happens, I won't change my mind. I've chosen my husband. And yes," she added, a smile teasing the corners of her lips, "I am looking forward to the wedding night."

A length of white chiffon unfurled through the air and landed like a cloud in Dhara's lap. "I'm sure Kelly won't mind if I regift," Wendy said. "You can use this more than me."

Marta felt the earth shift beneath her feet, as if a great fissure split the pine boards of the cabin and sent her reeling away from her friends. She didn't understand any of this. Dhara was marrying a stranger. The perfect couple was split. Wendy was encouraging the most unlikely twosome. And they were all sure they were right. Yet here she was, Marta Sanchez, hurt and confused and mentally staggering. She, who had thought everything out, right down to the very last detail.

Oh yes, she'd thought of everything back then, too. She'd avoided shellfish and caffeine and alcohol. Dhara had accompanied Marta to the local clinic to get prenatal vitamins and to confirm what she already knew. Marta had bought the book, the one whose chapters terrified her, and tried to read a little every day. With Kelly's help, she'd made it through the torment of finals. She kept the news from her beaming mother all through the graduation celebrations, allowing her parents their well-earned moment of joy as she paraded in her cap and gown through the daisy chain to receive her diploma.

She'd made new lists, too, after the law school acceptances came in. Fordham Law would allow her a one-year deferment. She considered open adoption, but knew in her heart that her mother would never give up this grandchild. Her mother would move mountains, change shifts, and work out childcare among aunts, so that Marta could still attend classes in Manhattan. For the year off, Marta was determined to work at her uncle's store to save money for baby formula, diapers, and all the pink or blue things that she couldn't beg or borrow from her relatives. Kelly had already tossed her job applications to start-up tech companies in Silicon Valley in favor of a position in Manhattan, to be nearby to help. Wendy had offered the second bedroom in the Soho loft she intended to rent in the fall. The plans grew stronger in her mind every day—the list more solid. Plans that took into account a child who hadn't asked to be conceived—a child growing ever more real inside her. A boy she would call Diego, she decided. A girl, Catalina.

And on the very day she sat at the kitchen table and told her mother that she was pregnant, those plans collapsed.

Eleven weeks.

She remembered staring at the ceiling tiles in the doctor's office while the gynecologist ruled out polycystic ovary syndrome and hypothyroidism and various autoimmune diseases and instead discussed progesterone deficiency and chromosomal abnormalities. Her mother, the nurse, squeezed her hand and assured Marta that medically this was not so uncommon, that someday—when she was ready, when the timing was better—Marta would again conceive.

Now, in the safety of Wendy's cabin, Marta's breath still came short and fast. The memory was raw. She didn't like to think about it. She'd been such a bundle of contradicting emotions. She'd made plans for her whole life, and they'd been destroyed. Then she made new plans for the baby, and those plans had been destroyed too.

Wendy was the one who'd urged her out of bed two weeks after she'd lost that baby and swept her away to her home. Wendy was the one who'd gently reminded her of the original Life Plan. Marta could go to law school in the fall now. She could return to those old dreams, and do them in the right order, in the right way, in her own good time.

This time, Marta had vowed, she would not drift from the plan. This time, she would remain in complete control.

Marta stood up abruptly. She strode toward the stairs, startling the girls. She knew what she had to do. The grim knowledge expanded inside her, like a thin rubber balloon filling with air. She took the stairs two at a time. At the top, she pushed a door open to a small bedroom. Her briefcase lay upon a quilt. She slipped her hand into a zippered pocket and tugged out a piece of paper.

She kept a version of this with her always. Through high school, through Vassar, even when she thought she'd have to cross off half the goals for the sake of a baby. She'd kept it close, to remind her where she came from, to mark the places she'd been, and to point her to where she was going.

But life was unpredictable.

Maybe it was supposed to be that way.

She padded downstairs much more slowly, feeling as nauseous and jittery as if she'd drunk a whole pot of coffee. She came upon the girls in quiet conversation, a conversation they stopped as she approached.

Marta unfolded the yellowed paper. She glanced upon the loopy, hopeful handwriting. She scanned it one last time, marking each hard-earned success. Then, with a pounding heart, she ripped it straight down the middle.

In the room rose a collective gasp.

"Marta," Dhara said, "is that—"

"Yes." She ripped the paper again, taking shaky pleasure in the sound. "Yes, it is."

She tossed the remnants in the fire. She watched as the flames blackened the edges. She felt chilled and light-headed as the flames flared. She had the strange sensation that one gust of wind would knock her flat upon her face.

Then her friends were there, holding her.

Reminding her that she wasn't alone.

chapter eighteen

Dhara walked out the rear door of the North Woods Renewal Center and caught sight of Cole immediately. He was sitting on a stone bench in the well-manicured garden with his back toward her. He wore a T-shirt from the Portland Bluegrass Festival, the one that used to be navy but had been faded to a stonewashed blue by multiple washings. His hair had grown long, and now it lay combed against his head, curling at the ends.

His neck looked pale and vulnerable.

She took a deep, shuddering breath and headed down the path. Her flats scuffed against the paving stones. She rounded a bend and noticed that Cole was not alone. He was deep in conversation with two other people sitting on benches, shielded from sight by low hedges. As Dhara approached, the woman in the group glanced up, caught sight of her, and leaned forward to say something. Cole started and shot to his feet.

Her heart did a painful little roll. An arrhythmia, she noted, probably caused by a premature ventricular contraction overriding the sinoatrial node and compensated for by a powerful subsequent contraction. Probably caused by the sight of a vibrant Cole, unfolding to his full height and striding through the sunshine with a smile stretched across his face.

She thrust out her hands to forestall what she, in a panic, perceived as a lean into a kiss. His step hitched for a moment, but he recovered quickly. He reached for her hands and squeezed them tightly.

"I'm glad you came."

She couldn't look away from him. Her doctor's eye noticed the clear whites of his eyes, the flush to his skin, and the respectable portion of weight in muscle he had gained, enough to put some stress on the shoulder seams of his T-shirt.

"I know. Miraculous." He gave her a sideways smile and a quirk of a brow. "It's amazing what a steady diet of clean living can do for a guy."

"You look good, Cole."

"Right back at you."

She'd worn a *shalwar kameez* of Rajasthani cotton, a soft, sky-blue tunic over loose pants. It was the sort of thing she always wore when she traveled long distances in the car, for the comfort of the drawstring waistline. Under his gaze, the choice took on multiple shades of meaning.

He glanced over her shoulder, searching the path behind her. "You came alone?"

"No, Kelly and I came together. We just left Wendy's cabin this morning." Dhara gestured vaguely to the grand lodge with its lovely wraparound porch. "Kelly's curled up on a wicker chair somewhere reading *People* magazine. She said she'd join us later."

"Let's take a walk then. There'll be a discussion group meeting out here in a few minutes. They'll be smoking like fiends. And I don't think you want to hear about Mr. Blowhard's obsession with Internet porn."

"No, no, definitely not."

"There's a path through the woods." He turned down one of the winding stone lanes. "It's officially called the Pine Promenade. But the rest of us call it the Boozer's Byway."

"Ah." Dhara fell into step beside him. "A little black humor."

"Yeah." He made a strange little sound, half laugh, half snort. "That goes a long way in here."

She hesitated, debating for a moment whether to wade in to the minefield. "I suppose, despite all the lovely landscaping, that there are a dozen Nurse Ratcheds in there, reeling you in with curfews and rules."

"Well, the Swedish masseuse can be a little rough," he admitted, "and just the other night some reality-TV-show guy was complaining about how the roast lamb screamed for a good merlot."

Dhara didn't know whether to laugh or cringe, so she settled for covering her mouth.

"Oh, I'm not complaining. This place is incredible, a weird mix of luxury and distress. Like a live version of *Celebrity Rehab*." He shoved his fingers into the pockets of his low-slung jeans, striding with great energy. "The thing is, my golf game is improving. And who can complain about having nothing to do but sleep, eat, and talk?"

"Sounds like college."

"Yeah." He laughed. "Except with better food and no beer. And no freshman orientation. The first week here was hell. Still now, every day, some serious shit comes out in the morning meetings."

His honesty was unnerving. She resisted the urge to take his arm or press her cheek against his biceps. It wasn't her place anymore.

"And guess what?" he said, with a gravelly little laugh. "It turns out that it's not normal for a father meeting his son for the first time in twelve years to shove him on the first bus leaving town."

Her breath hitched.

"And it turns out," he continued, "that it's not normal for a twelve-year-old to be drying cannabis on the back porch, or smoking it at fourteen."

She couldn't help herself. She brushed his shoulder briefly, before veering away. He noticed. His step slowed as they plunged into the cool shadow of the pinewoods. Paint on the trees marked a confluence of three different trails, and without looking up, Cole led the way down the one designated white.

"Thanks," he murmured, "for not saying 'I told you so.'"

"Cole, I didn't even know what was wrong." She'd always been fascinated by his upbringing, and had even envied his no-structure-no-rules lifestyle, too blinded at first to notice the destruction that kind of freedom had wreaked upon him. "I flailed about, looking for reasons for the vodka bottles under the bed, and then brought up the very things you didn't want to talk about."

"Yeah, well, you figured it out. Long before I did."

He gave her a rueful little smile. Oh, there he was suddenly, the warm guy she'd had a terrible crush on in college, the lanky, long-haired hippie with the easy ways that seemed to coax her—*come close, come near, I won't hurt you.*

Dhara focused on the path before her to steady herself from a sense of dizziness. Fresh from Wendy's bachelorette party—and a little woozy from lack of sleep—she thought she'd be better prepared to face Cole today. She'd spent a good part of the weekend quizzing her friends for advice. Only Wendy had any to give, and it wasn't something she didn't know already: there was no easy way to break a man's heart.

And yet, she had to. While Cole had been a patient in her hospital, he'd had the grace not to ask for any promises. But among old lovers and even older friends, some promises were made without speaking, and some expectations grew out of a simple request for a game of online poker.

Layers of brown needles crinkled under her feet, and Dhara breathed in the scent of resin. "I can't tell you how happy I am to see you're doing well, Cole. I've always wished the best for you—"

"Don't."

His voice was low and sure. All his humor was gone. He'd hooked his hands behind his back, as if forcibly holding them still.

"I know that speech." A muscle danced near his jaw. "I don't want—I don't need—" He stopped. Then he craned his neck as if seeking a nest up the straight trunks of the white pines. "Dhara, I already know that I've lost you."

Dhara stumbled, one foot catching on a stone hidden under the pine needles. She righted herself as Cole continued forward, rounding a curve to a little wooden bench. He flung himself on it. He gazed through the thinning trees to a narrow valley and, beyond, the slate blue outline of the mountains.

Dhara slipped onto the other end of the bench feeling unmoored. Around them, the cicadas sang, their buzzing music rising in the trees.

"It's the clothes." He crossed his arms, tucking his fingers beneath his biceps. "I knew the minute I saw you coming down the path in your *shalwar kameez* that you'd chosen the Hindu way."

She choked down the urge to object. She could say she'd worn the outfit for comfort, but it really didn't matter. It had been so long since she'd dealt with the sober Cole that she'd forgotten how perceptive he could be.

She found herself remembering all the years she'd resisted him, before they became lovers. In college, she'd convinced herself it was impossible. During medical school, they were physically apart but kept in contact. Even after she returned to New York for her residency and certifications, she'd told herself that it wouldn't work. All those years, she'd gently discouraged him. Yet he always came around, just when she wanted to see him most. Just when she was most susceptible. He understood on some deep level her reticence. He kept her close—but not too close.

Now, more than ever, she understood his behavior. Ironically, the very freedom of spirit that she admired in him was the one thing that drove them apart. And the very strong sense of loyalty and family that he admired in her was the one part of her he couldn't handle.

"There's this thing," he said. "It's one of the twelve steps to recovery, they tell me. I have to apologize for all the damage I've done."

"You don't have to apologize to me."

"Yes, I do. You more than anyone. It's why I wanted to see you today. Why I was glad you actually showed up."

"Of course I—"

"No," he interrupted. "No, Dhara. There's no 'of course.' Not after some of the things I said to you. You put up with more crap than any human should. You stuck with me years longer than any sane person would have. Had you not left me, who knows how long it would have continued? We might still be caught in that same cycle of dysfunction."

She closed off the memories. She tried not to think of the terrible words he'd said to her in his drunkenness. She didn't want to remember his unpredictable anger, the slurs he made against her family, and the hateful words he used denying his addiction.

"That's the worst part, you know." His knee started to bob, and then he slapped his hand on it to keep it still. "All the apologies in the world aren't going to erase those bad memories. I can't…make it good. Good like it used to be, even when we were just friends. What I did, in the end, will always taint what we had."

"You're already forgiven."

He made a half laugh, a sound of easy disbelief, as he shook his head. "You're making it too easy."

"This is easy?"

He looked at her with a face full of regret. The light fell on his cheek, and she saw the constellation of freckles there, a faint cluster of Pleiades. She used to trace them beneath his wispy sideburns.

Dhara reached for his hand. His palm was cold, his muscles stiff, and it took a few minutes before he let his fingers relax.

"Do you remember," she whispered, "the first night we spent in Cape May?"

His pulse jumped. She squeezed his hand harder.

"Do you remember," she continued, "that first moment, after we arrived at our room, and you closed the door behind us?"

Dhara could still hear the crash of the sea and the cries of sea birds through the open window. A breeze billowed the sheer curtains and washed over the bed that filled the room. It was a four-poster with a blue spread, looking to her innocent eyes impossibly decadent. The door had clicked shut, and she'd turned to see the man she loved standing before it. Bathed in the late afternoon light. Looking tall and dangerous.

Her heart had leaped in her breast.

He said softly, "I remember."

It had been their first time. They'd talked about it, planned it, and anticipated it for so very long. Twelve years of friendship fueled the moment, and, during the car ride down, they'd spent three aching hours holding hands and imagining.

"I was so nervous." She laughed. "I couldn't manage the buttons on your shirt. They kept slipping out of my hands like little peas."

"Lost two of them," he said. "Never bothered looking for them after."

She could still summon the creaking sound of Cole's footfalls on the old boards as he crossed the space that separated them. She could still summon the feel of his hands as he seized her waist, as he dragged her shirt up over her ribs. She remembered how he'd pulled the band out of her ponytail to let her hair tumble down her naked back. He'd sifted his fingers through it, over and over, as she struggled to shimmy out of her jeans. Her whole body had ached, and her skin was fevered, as bits of medical knowledge about respiratory rates and racing pulses and human physiological responses skittered through her mind.

Now, with the cicadas singing around them in the pinewoods, Dhara buried herself in the memory—in *all* of it, from the silly way he'd tripped as he dragged her, laughing, toward the bed, to the sudden shyness she'd felt, exposed under his hungry eyes, to the sublime sensation of his fingers touching her where no man had ever touched her before.

This is how a bride feels, she remembered thinking, *when the goddess Rati stirs within her.*

Then, as now, she looked up into Cole's flushed face and saw him blinking, his hazel eyes suspiciously bright.

"Someday, I'll be as shriveled and gray as Auntie Bhuvi, Cole. But I can promise you this." She pressed his hand against her cheek. "Whenever I think of you, what I'll remember is that night we shared in Cape May."

chapter nineteen

Kelly hunched down in the passenger seat of Dhara's rental car as Dhara took a right turn onto Fifty-sixth Street and drove up between the rows of parked cars toward Kelly's apartment building.

"Tell me he's not sitting there anymore." Kelly crushed her knees against the dashboard. "Tell me he gave up and left."

Dhara's expression told her the bad news before she even spoke. "This is the third time around the block. He's going to recognize either me or the fact that this car has come around three times, Kelly. You need to make a decision."

Kelly closed her eyes and groaned. She was exhausted from lack of sleep and from overindulgence in socializing. The weekend at Wendy's cabin had felt like a time slip to their college days, but that amount of intimate interaction, even with her best friends, tended to overload her social processing system. After that, and all those weeks with Cole on her couch, she'd been looking forward to an evening alone, preferably with a bowl of cereal on her lap and a Bollywood movie on TV.

"You might as well pull over." Kelly pushed herself up to a sitting position, jerking her floral skirt from under her. "Wendy must have told Trey about when we were going to arrive. I'm going to have a few words with her for that."

"Go easy on the girl, she's reeling." Dhara glanced in the rearview mirror and pulled the car as close to the side as she could without clipping any mirrors. "Anyway, Wendy probably thought she was doing a good karmic deed."

"But why did he have to come here at all? It's so *over*. I couldn't have made it any clearer on the yacht." It didn't help that it was so typical for him to arrive like this—with no call, no text, no warning. It made her hackles rise. Kelly yanked her messenger bag onto her lap, swinging the strap over her head. "I'm trying so very hard to just let it go, to preserve the *good* memories, you know?"

"Oh, yes," Dhara said quietly. "Yes, I get that."

Kelly slung an arm around Dhara's neck. Her body folded into her as Kelly tightened her grip.

Kelly murmured, "You take care, okay?"

"Sure you don't want me to circle the block a few more times, just in case?"

"No, I'll be fine." She squeezed out the door while Dhara pulled her overstuffed weekend tote out of the backseat and handed it to her across the passenger seat. "I'll tell you all about it tomorrow."

As Dhara drove away, Kelly strode through the parked cars to face the man on her front stoop. Trey had the grace to look sheepish. Sheepish in the way of a puppy dog, facing his owner knowing he'd made a doo-doo on the living room carpet. That was quite a feat for a man six foot three, who'd apparently been jogging, dressed as he was in a loose T-shirt and running pants, his sweaty hair clinging to his temples.

"I know." He avoided her eye as he rolled his thumb around his iPod. "I should have called."

"I'm tired, Trey." She dropped her bags on the sidewalk and flipped open the flap of her messenger bag to search for her apartment keys. "All I want to do is go inside, change into my pajamas, and go to sleep."

"Must have been a good weekend." He clipped the iPod back onto the strap around his biceps. "Is Wendy okay?"

She paused, wondering how much Wendy had told him.

"I found out through Parker." He planted his elbows on his knees and then clasped his hands in between. "Parker's a mess, but he didn't want to talk about it. When I called Wendy, she didn't want to talk about it either. Meanwhile, at the club, everyone is talking about it."

Kelly searched blindly among her wallet, cell phone, pens, and sanitizer for the familiar shape of her *Starship Enterprise* key chain. She didn't quite know what to say. She had never liked being caught between Wendy and Trey, even when she was indulging in an affair, and this felt . . . well, she couldn't say anything. Wendy deserved her privacy.

"That's a real problem in my family," Trey said, "that reluctance to really talk about things."

"Clearly."

"I remember a time when my uncle Tad had an accident a few days before Christmas. It was his second DUI. So my aunt arrives at my house. 'So sorry Tad can't be here,' she says. 'He's taking some time upstate.' And without missing a beat my mother says, 'Terribly sorry to hear that, Boop. Would you like your scotch straight, or on the rocks?'"

Kelly searched Trey's face, downcast, taking a deep interest in his own intertwined fingers.

"You see," he said, his voice deep, "in my family, it doesn't matter what's *really* going on. As long as you avoid an awkward social moment."

"Trey, I think you're trying to say something, but my powers of interpreting subtext are sorely depleted."

"I'm telling you I should have decked James on the yacht." He shuffled his sneakers on the stoop. "I didn't, because I was working off muscle memory. I was trying to avoid an ugly public argument."

Kelly had a sudden image of her father one summer during a good fishing season, screaming with all the salty language a sailing man could muster at two greenhorns he'd hired to help on the boat. Her father ripped them up—right in front of her—when they tangled the ropes. Yet a week later, when her father finally gave one of those greenhorns a faint nod of approval, that boy puffed up like a rooster. A single nod from her dad became the equivalent to clanging bells of praise.

Sometimes it astonished her, the fundamentally different ways she and Trey had been raised.

"You disappointed me, Trey."

"Join the club. In fact, if you were to put all the people I've disappointed into a room, their sheer mass would probably warp space-time."

She paused, giving him a grudging nod, as she lifted her weekend bag from the ground. "That's pretty good."

"See? There's more to me than just dumb good looks."

"So, do you ever think you should stop disappointing people?"

"All the fucking time. I'd like to start by not disappointing you."

Too late.

She tightened her grip on her keys. She'd flushed her system of Trey on the yacht. She'd let him know in one magnificently awkward moment that she didn't want anything to do with him anymore. And then she'd moved on. On Tuesday, she was seeing the premier of an independent sci-fi movie with Lee Zhao.

Yet looking at Trey now, in all his sweaty glory, she couldn't deny she was still attracted to him. She didn't think she'd ever forget the knee-melting thrill she'd had when she'd first seen him standing outside her building in the rain, that reckless smile spreading across his face. She missed walking with him through the streets of New York City, her heart in her chest like a warm toaster. And the sex—*oh,* she missed the *sex*—digging her fingers into those strong shoulders while his breathing kept pace with hers.

But Good Lord, how she'd built him up as some sort of golden prince. When she looked at him now, she saw only the shadow of that imaginary royalty. Trey was handsome; Trey was charming; Trey was deeply flawed.

Trey was, in effect, an ordinary man.

A man she could no longer trust with her heart.

"It's starting to rain." Drops splattered on the sidewalk around her. She rattled the keys in her hand and looked pointedly at him, sitting on the stoop blocking access to her building.

He placed his hands on his knees and pushed off, lumbering to his full height. He jogged the three steps to the sidewalk, giving her a wide berth. She was up the stairs with the key in the door when he called her name.

"I want you to know that I'm training right now." He stood by a signpost, shaking out one leg, then another. "I'm planning on running a marathon."

"That's really great, Trey."

She turned the bolt and then searched for the key for the second lock, anxious for this confrontation to be over.

"It's the New York City Marathon. I've got only four months to prepare. But hell, I've never done a marathon before. Never completed one, anyway. I thought I'd set my mind on it. See if I could finally see something through, beginning to end."

She paused, pushing the front door open, sensing more to this confession than an awkward way to say good-bye. "Isn't a marathon more than twenty-six miles?"

"Yeah."

"You do, what, six miles a day now?"

"Yeah, it's a reach." He shrugged. "But running is one of the few things I actually *like* to do. You once told me to find a passion. Maybe this is it."

Kelly thought of the fifteen-hour days she had spent in the summers, her fingers numb with cold as she sorted fish, her mother dulling the edge of her high school anxiety by saying she smelled like a mermaid. She remembered the day she'd fallen asleep on a test in graduate school in bleary-eyed exhaustion from working at a greasy spoon so she could pay the rent, split four ways, for a two-bedroom, roach-infested apartment.

And for the first time, Kelly began to appreciate the many unsung benefits that came along with a hardscrabble, working-class upbringing—all the intangibles that came along with being the famous Gloucester baby, found on the firehouse steps.

"Good luck, Trey." Kelly shouldered the front door wide. "Really, I wish you all the best."

chapter twenty

Wendy waved as Birdie, sporting a white bathing cap and goggles, took a leap into an Olympic-size swimming pool. Birdie's personal swimming instructor caught her underwater and hauled her up, allowing Birdie to kick up enough spray to splatter the Plexiglas window that separated Wendy from the pool area. Wendy pantomimed shaking off the water as Birdie squealed.

Wendy smiled as she settled back in the cushioned seat of the viewing room of the Wyndom-Dell Assisted Living Home. Her sister had taken the news of the broken engagement in her usual way, focusing less on what had happened than what Wendy now *felt*. Birdie had quickly overpowered her with hugs and kisses until those hugs and kisses turned into a giggling game of gotcha-last. Now Wendy nursed the bruises, determined to enjoy these last moments of tranquility before she returned home to the spreading consequences of a broken engagement.

She heard the door to the viewing room squeal open. Over the tinge of chlorine, she caught the grassy scent of a familiar perfume.

Her body went cold.

"There you are, darling." Her mother, dressed in a creamy silk shell and wide-legged linen pants, airily planted a kiss on her head before slinging her white bag on the floor between them. "I was beginning to wonder if you'd ever emerge from that dusty old cabin."

Wendy let the muted barb pass. She took a deep breath and let it out slowly, in the hopes of summoning the serenity, patience, and fortitude she'd cultivated during the weekend with her friends. "I thought we were meeting later this afternoon, Mom. For dinner at home."

"That was the plan. But then I called here yesterday to tell the concierge that I'd be visiting Birdie later today. He happened to let slip that you'd be here in the morning."

"So you rearranged your schedule."

"We have much to talk about, and the sooner we talk, the better."

Wendy took a sip of her coffee but it slipped tasteless down her throat. Before she'd left for the cabin, she'd told her mother only the basics. That she'd broken it off with Parker, that the break was permanent, and that when she got back, she'd call the wedding planner to cancel whatever arrangements she could. Her mother had been amazingly composed. She'd responded as if Wendy were canceling a birthday party and not a wedding she'd dedicated a year and a half of her life to arranging.

But Wendy knew that had been only an act. The fact that her mother had driven two hours just to talk suggested that Wendy was about to be subjected to a much more personal agenda.

She closed her eyes and wished for palm trees, tropical breezes, and a really strong piña colada.

"Terry and I have been working quite diligently these past few days." Her mother folded herself in the chair beside her. "You'll be happy to know that the caterer has been generous with the cancellation, as has the florist. Except for the South American orchids, of course. I've decided to give them to the church when they come in. They'll look lovely upon the altar, don't you think?"

"I'm sure they will."

"The only real problem I've encountered is with the jeweler. He won't take back those slides for the pearl necklaces, engraved as they are, for your friends."

"I'll pay the balance." The girls deserved them. Dhara, Marta, and Kelly were the only people in the world right now who had, with touching loyalty, absolved her of all blame. "I'll give them as Christmas presents."

"That's a lovely idea." Her mother absently curled her pearls around her fingers. "Pity about the gown, though. I've asked Stella's advice. She thought you might want to keep the dress—"

"No." Wendy shook her head sharply. "Give it to Aunt Boop. An anonymous donation for her next charity fashion show."

"My dear, it was *designed* for you—"

"I couldn't possibly keep it. That dress was meant for Parker's eyes."

His name hung in the air between them. She sensed, in her mother's stillness, the quivering restraint of a hundred thousand questions. Wendy ignored the expectant silence.

If she told her mother the truth, there would be no hugs or kisses or games of gotcha-last. Long ago, she gave up sharing the details of her life with the woman she always disappointed.

"You do know," her mother said, leaning forward to wave at Birdie through the window, "that Parker made a discreet announcement at the club Saturday afternoon?"

Wendy stared at her leopard-print ballet flats, trying hard to be stone-faced. "I figured he'd say something over the weekend. Fortunately, cell phone service at the cabin is spotty. So no, I didn't know."

"The way the news spread, you'd think the club manager was caught pants down with that blowsy coat-check girl."

Sharp prickles of shame made their way up Wendy's chest. She could just imagine the tennis ladies leaning across the tables and the clusters of golfers in the entrance hall, their avid speculation echoing off the dome.

"I surmise," her mother murmured, "there's no chance of a reconciliation?"

"None."

"Darling, it can't be so permanent as that." Her mother shifted on the chair, straightening her back. "You've been together for so many years. Practically married in all but name. Whatever has happened, surely there must be a way—"

"That ship," Wendy interrupted, "has sailed."

"It's all so very sudden. And after the discussion we had at Stella's studio, I can't help feel that I'm part of this rupture."

"Oh, for goodness sake."

"If it's the wedding plans that are causing so much trouble, we can cut back. You must know that the only reason I got involved at all was because you seemed so overwhelmed by the process—"

"Stop." Wendy held up her hand. "The wedding plans had nothing to do with it. Stop martyring yourself."

"But—"

"I know this will seem crazy to you, but I chose to end this engagement. It was wholly my choice."

"That doesn't surprise me. You are perpetually making strange choices. For once, I'd like to understand *why*."

Wendy considered, for one rebellious moment, telling her mother that she'd slept with a Brazilian artist, framing the whole affair in such a way that her mother would think, yes, once again, Wendy had been playing the tart with another supposedly inappropriate man.

But it wasn't true. The words wouldn't leave her tongue. What she'd shared with Gabriel wasn't tawdry. It was sweet and wonderful and overwhelming and badly timed.

"Anything I say will disappoint you."

"You two are the perfect couple. Of course I'll be disappointed."

"It's always something. My multiple piercings. My disgracefully tasteless shoes. My utterly unsuitable boyfriends." Wendy glanced about the empty room, with its wall paintings of seascapes, casting for one of a thousand details. "A piece of modern art that I adore but you simply can't understand. And now, it's the fact that I'm ending an engagement to a perfect man."

"All questionable decisions, wouldn't you agree?"

"I am who I am. I can't change that, any more than Birdie could change."

"Birdie was born this way."

"Do you accept Birdie just the way she is?"

"Of *course* I do."

"Then maybe it's time you accepted me, just the way I am."

In the awkward silence that followed, Wendy sensed her mother's subtle withdrawal, the slowly growing tension in the room, and the palpable depths of her offense. The expression on her mother's face shuttered, and then, in degrees, melted into a look Wendy couldn't quite read. Before she could decipher it, her mother turned her face away, the tendons in her neck taut.

Wendy gazed at her mother's deft French twist, wearily remembering a million other times she'd been granted the view of the back of her mother's finely coiffed head. When Wendy was in her teens, their interactions had always been volatile, usually ending with Wendy seething and her mother stoically striding out of the room. As adults, their relationship had morphed into an uneasy détente, aided by the fact that they'd hardly spoken to each other while she worked in the Soho art gallery. And once in the museum—her mother's most fervent wish fulfilled—Wendy had considered her mother's growing warmth as a sign that their charged silences, unspoken hurts, and fundamental disagreements would fade. But the stresses of the wedding had ripped the veneer off that rapprochement.

Wendy was just so tired of fighting.

"Wendy, I know you don't believe this, but I never wanted to change you. But I can't deny that I was happy when you left that life of yours in Soho. I won't deny that I was thrilled when you took your position at the museum. And I won't deny that I was over the moon when I first saw you on the arm of Parker Pryce-Weston."

Wendy ached for a cigarette.

"I thought you'd finally got past a phase, that everything would be normal now." Her mother made an odd hiccup that she swiftly covered by clearing her throat. "It's just so difficult to know what's best for one's children. I know you disagree with me about Birdie, but at least she's settled here, and happy. I've all but given up on Trey."

Wendy thought about Kelly, about Trey's sudden passion for running, about the look in his eye when he decked James. "Don't give up on Trey. He's a screwup, but I suspect he's redeemable."

"I would *never* give up on any of you." Her mother turned to grab her purse from the floor between them. "Even now—most especially now—I won't give up on *you*."

Wendy blinked at the sight of her mother's profile. Her mother's cheeks were wet. But it couldn't be from tears. Her mother didn't cry. Not when Wendy, at thirteen years of age, went off to Miss Porter's Boarding School for Girls. Certainly not when Wendy went off to college. Her mother hadn't cried when Grandma died. Vulgar, she'd said once, after seeing a friend collapse in sobs at her husband's funeral. Even the sudden death of her mother's favorite King Charles spaniel brought nothing more than a quiver to her lips.

Yet here her mother was, blotchy-faced, fumbling with the clasp of her purse. Those were tears on her mother's cheeks, tears welling in her mother's blue eyes, tears that her mother was making no effort to wipe away.

"You're right, you know." Her mother's voice was raw. "I'm always meddling. Your relationship with Parker is none of my damn business."

Wendy waited for her to stand up from the chair, slip her purse over her shoulder, swivel on one foot, and show Wendy the back of her head again. That's how conversations like this usually ended.

But her mother stayed seated, as tense as a high wire in the wind. "This isn't going at *all* as I planned it. Why is it, my dear, that we're always at loggerheads?"

"Because I'm an alley cat born into a family of purebred dogs." Wendy looked down at her hands, wondering why they were shaking. "If I didn't look so much like a Wainwright, I'd be asking you about the milkman."

"Oh, but you are a Wainwright. You are more Wainwright than you know. Your great-great aunt, Violet Wainwright, was one of the wilder eccentrics in a long, long line of them. She bobbed her hair in 1921."

Wendy clasped her hands together to stop them from shaking. "An unrepentant rebel."

"Sounds tame now." Her mother dabbed at her nose with a tissue. "But that was, I believe, the generational equivalent of a belly button piercing. It was also an indicator of future horrors. She eventually ran off with a Canadian rum-running gangster."

Wendy paused. "I thought that was just one of Uncle Tad's fish tales."

"I'm afraid not. They had difficult lives, those unconventional ancestors of yours. It didn't always end well."

"Yes, but here you are, still telling the stories."

"I had hoped you'd take the more traditional path. I hoped your eccentricity would end at a tragus piercing." She let out a long, slow sigh. "I was trying to protect you. Someday you'll understand. That's what mothers do."

Wendy turned away. She thought of Audrey and her utter devotion to her children. She thought of Kelly's biological mother, swaddling her daughter tightly before leaving her on the firehouse stairs. She thought of Marta, giving up caffeine minutes after she'd discovered she was pregnant, when the little soul within her was no more than a bundle of cells.

Wendy glanced through the glass at Birdie's bright face. Wendy would always believe that her sister, considering their family's resources, would have been better served at home. But she supposed there was no denying that her mother just as strongly believed that this place—with its staff of nurses and its weight room and pool and Jacuzzi and art, bingo, sculpture, and exercise classes—was infinitely better.

Then Wendy thought of Trey and the series of jobs that her father had arranged for him. She thought of the way her mother couched Trey's foibles in romantic terms when she spoke of him to her friends. His screwups and job losses always sounded like the inevitable result of a young man too smart, too great-thinking, to be contained in some windowless office.

"Grant me a mulligan, Wendy." Her mother snapped her purse closed and set it on her lap. "I'd like to put my golf ball back at the starting tee, if you don't mind."

Wendy looked anywhere but at her mother, unsure of how to respond.

"What I came here to tell you today was how truly, truly sorry I am about you and Parker. If you're very sure this is the right thing for both of you . . . well, I'll do my very best to do what a mother *should* do, what I'm very good at, and that is smooth troubled waters."

Wendy bowed her head, strangely moved. She noticed her mother's hands. Normally, her mother's fingernails were finished with the subtle rosy hues of a French manicure, refreshed every Monday morning. Now, those white tips were ragged with chips, the cuticles bitten into little bloody strips.

And it came to her that while she was at the cabin, licking her wounds and seeking comfort among her friends, her mother had remained at the club, skipping all her appointments, facing the swarm of gossips with no information at all.

Wendy reached out and took her mother's hand. Across her mother's face passed a spastic little smile that threatened to quiver into a sob.

"Maybe, Mom," Wendy murmured, "it's time you started treating me less like a daughter and more like a friend."

"Oh, Wendy." Her mother laughed, a little laugh that was half relief and half despair. "How in God's name am I ever going to do that, when I can so clearly see disaster coming?"

"Just hold your breath and cover your eyes." Wendy thought of the weekend she'd just spent with Dhara, Marta, and Kelly, thinking of what true friends do for one another. "If it all goes badly, well . . . I could always use help picking up the pieces."

chapter twenty-one

They say there's nothing like April in Paris, but Marta was convinced the City of Lights couldn't hold a candle to September in New York City. This month was a crystal blue calm between the hordes of summer tourists and the crush of the Christmas season. To her, the air smelled of pencil shavings and the warm-linen perfume of new note-books. Even if she had no other reason, the fine weather alone was a good excuse to take a Sunday stroll through Central Park.

She wandered into a maze of white tents that marked a craft fair. She paused at one pavilion to peruse a vendor's collection of painted wooden bracelets. She breathed in the scent of fried dough and promised herself some for lunch. She bought a straw hat tied with a coral scarf that matched the sundress she was wearing. No reason to hurry. Scurrying to get things done was an old habit she was trying hard to change.

Two-thirds down the second row, she came upon Gabriel

Teixeira's booth. She slowed her approach, scanning the paintings hooked on the flaps. Yesterday, in the popcorn-scented shadows of a seedy Asbury Park bar, Wendy had finally cracked enough to give some details about the man and his work. Marta figured the three watered-down drinks had a lot to do with the loosening of Wendy's tongue, but it didn't hurt that the four of them had spent the day amid the rough-edged pleasures of the Jersey boardwalk. Riding a fifties-era wooden roller coaster seemed like a fitting way to blot out the fact that yesterday would have been Wendy's wedding day.

Marta saw the man's feet first. His black sneakers were hiked up on the table. He tilted back on a folding chair, his face buried in a tattered book. With a quiver of worry, Marta looked away. This man had torn apart an engagement and unhinged a steady woman. So she sent up a Hail Mary hoping he wasn't an unkempt jerk of a hipster, a newer version of Wendy's former weakness.

Hiding her face with the brim of her new hat, she wandered to a pile of large framed paintings leaning against the tent pole. She thumbed through them, becoming more convinced with every click of the frames that she'd found the right Gabriel. Each new canvas illuminated what Wendy had been trying so hard to describe: the fragility of everyday things, and the hopefulness of pure light.

Then she found it.

"Can I help you?"

Marta startled. She glanced up. *Up.* She found herself face-to-face with a dark-eyed, dark-haired hunk. Clean-shaven. His hair a crisp temptation for a woman's fingers. His features, utterly arresting.

She considered a moment, searching his face for the unknowable. Character. Integrity. Kindness.

Physically, at least, she approved.

"Yes, actually, you can help me." She tipped the frames against her legs to better reveal the painting that Wendy had so lovingly described. It was a collection of four bottles of different shapes and sizes, clustered together in the light pouring through an old window. "How much for this one?"

His expression shifted, lightning-quick, from polite curiosity to surprise. "That isn't for sale." He hefted the painting and then carried it around the table. "Apologies. That wasn't supposed to be there."

"Please don't disappoint me." She followed as he leaned the frame gingerly against the back tent post. "A friend of mine saw that painting about a month ago, and she can't stop thinking about it. She wanted to buy it then, but the circumstances weren't right."

"I have others that are similar." He walked to the other end of the tent and started flicking through a different set. "Let me show you—"

"Sorry. My friend fell in love with that one the moment she saw it. She has very particular taste." Marta pulled off her sunglasses. "She works in the Haight-Livingston Museum."

Marta was sure Dhara could name those long muscles in a man's back, the strong swooping ones that go from the shoulder to the hollow of the lower spine. They flexed as Gabriel stilled.

"She'd probably kill me if she knew I was here today, spilling her story to a stranger. But I felt compelled." She softened her voice, not for privacy's sake, for around them buzzed skateboarders and strollers and weekend joggers, but because she sensed the tension emanating from Gabriel. "It's a heartbreaking story. About the same time she fell in love with this painting, she broke an engagement. She has been in pieces since."

He turned to her with eyes full of emotions she couldn't begin to name. Except for pain. Yes, she recognized that kind of pain.

Marta's heart did a little lurch.

Oh, Wendy. Now I see.

And she felt a certainty come over her, as if she had just seized the ball during a championship game and could envision the path through centers and forwards to the opposite end of the court. She hadn't been sure how she'd handle this today, willing, for once in her life, not to make a set of bullet points to guide the conversation. All she knew was that once-bookish little Marta had shot up through the world like a rocket and—because of bad timing and single-minded stupidity—she'd lost one of the best guys the world had to offer.

She didn't want that to happen to Wendy.

"It's a strange thing," she said. "With everything my friend has been going through, she can't get this painting off her mind."

Gabriel crossed his arms and swayed a little. "Better not buy it for her then. It'll just remind her of bad times."

"On the contrary. It'll remind her that she made the right decision."

Moods shifted across his face. He searched some horizon beyond her, some point much farther than the opposite booth. "You're Marta, aren't you?"

She flinched.

"I guessed right."

"Honestly," she sputtered, "I can neither confirm nor deny—"

"She used to talk about her friends. Kelly, the computer genius. And the doctor, Diana—"

"Dhara."

"Yes, Dhara." He changed focus, fixing on her. "Wasn't hard to figure. The only one of you likely to risk getting into the middle of this was the high-powered Manhattan attorney."

She dropped her gaze as she felt for the first time in a while an honest little thrill for being pinned as both a successful lawyer and a good friend. "You're mistaken. This girl, Martha, whoever she is, should know better than to stick her nose into her best friend's business."

"Dangerous, that."

"There may be an exception, though. Like, if she's hoping to stop one painful decision from turning into two."

He made a little grunt and tightened his grip on his arms. "Frankly, I'm not convinced selling this painting to you will do any good."

He crouched down before the painting again. He rubbed his bare neck as his head sank between his shoulders. For a long time he just stared, as close to the painting as a man would come to the face of the woman he wanted very much to kiss.

Lucky, lucky Wendy.

"You know, you're right." She took a step away from the table into the bright September sunshine. "I'm not buying it today. It shouldn't be me who gives her that painting."

"She won't take it from me."

"Maybe not now."

"I want her to have it."

"Why don't you hold it for her until she's ready to see it again?"

He granted her his profile, tight and infinitely sad. "You really think that time will ever come?"

Marta slipped on her sunglasses, thinking about how long it took to heal a battered heart.

"Give it six months," she murmured. "Yeah, six months ought to do it."

⌒⌒

These days, Marta's heart felt like a helium balloon drifting loose in her chest. The experience of Dhara's wedding ceremony swelled it to an exquisite fullness.

Desh had arrived midday amid a raucous entourage of family and friends. He greeted Dhara's mother at the entrance to the hall where she blessed him by marking his forehead in red. (Vermillion and turmeric powder, Kelly whispered later, as they stood on the bridal side of the wedding canopy watching the achingly gorgeous couple circle the sacred fires.) Dhara's father welcomed Desh at the wedding canopy, offering presents before escorting his daughter down the aisle. At the end of the Vedic rituals, the grandparents—stooped and smiling—shuffled down the flowerstrewn aisle so the bride and the bridegroom could touch their feet in reverence.

And now, the ceremony over, the photos taken, and the whole reception waiting in the hall for the married couple to make their official appearance, Marta stood by a tall terrace window blinking into the sunlight. She gripped the folds of her organza sari, determined not to use the fabric to dab at the tears that kept threatening the kohl around her eyes.

A tissue appeared in the blurry range of her vision. Marta grasped it and then glanced beyond to Kelly's teasing wink.

"You wouldn't know that I've been to dozens of weddings." Marta patted under her eyes. "I mean, I had like eighteen bridesmaid's dresses. I gave them all to a niece last year."

"There's nothing like a Hindu wedding." Kelly's jewel-blue sari set off her piled red hair to striking effect. "And this one, particularly so."

Marta nodded her agreement. This three-day series of ceremonies and parties, the chanting of the Sanskrit, and the whole ritual joining of the families had revealed to her so much that she had never understood. Dhara and Cole's long, cautious courtship suddenly made sense. Dhara's battle with Cole's addiction seemed, in Marta's estimation, one step closer to heroism. Marta wasn't about to set her own aunt Fidelia on a hunt for an appropriate bridegroom, but right now, crumpling her soggy tissue, she was filled with new appreciation for Dhara's leap of faith.

"Desh really is a hottie, isn't he?" Marta flicked open the latch of her clutch and shoved the soggy tissue within. "In a scholarly, owlish sort of way."

"He adores her."

"He's star-struck. She looks like a goddess."

"I think that's the point. Oh God, I want a wedding just like this."

"Here's your chance." Marta caught sight of a young man by a small café table glancing their way. "Ravi is eyeballing you for about the fifteenth time today."

Kelly scanned the room until she caught Ravi's eye. She sent him an awkward little wave. "He doesn't recognize me. I keep looking at my reflection and not recognizing my-self."

"Don't be silly. He remembers you from the engagement party."

"He is sort of cute, isn't he?"

"Yes, he is. Now stop grinning and turn around, *chica*. Give the guy a chance to chase."

"I don't know." Kelly moved to the opposite side of the window, leaning against the frame, so Ravi could see only her back. "Ravi might be a complication right now."

"What, three guys chasing you is too much for Kelly Palazzo to handle?"

"What's this about Kelly and three guys?" Wendy joined them. She looked as fragile as a harem slave, the kohl she must have freshened in the ladies' room making her brown eyes look enormous. "Don't disappoint me, Kell. I have my heart set on you and Trey."

"Up in the air." Kelly furrowed her brow. "Possible but unlikely."

"My money's on Lee Zhao." Marta jerked her chin in Ravi's direction. "But I wouldn't mind another Hindu wedding."

As Wendy riffled through her purse for what Marta suspected was a cigarette, Marta exchanged a glance with Kelly. Dhara had specifically tasked Marta and Kelly to watch over Wendy during the three days of ceremonies. A wedding so close after the date of Wendy's own broken plans couldn't help but bring up difficult emotions. Now Marta searched her heart-weary friend's fine features for some subtle sign of distress.

"Please, you two." Wendy rolled her eyes as she pulled out a pack of mints. "Practice a little subtlety, huh?"

"We're just worried about you."

"Did you see Dhara? Did you see how she was beaming? You think I would have been beaming at my own wedding?" She ripped open the end of the roll and offered them a mint. "No way. I'd have been vomiting in the planters."

"Just checking, *chica*."

"This is the way a wedding should be. Every day, I'm more sure of that."

A noise at the other end of the hall caught their attention. The doors swung open to reveal Desh and Dhara, striding in to cheers and congratulations. They'd changed clothes from their gilded reds, and now both Dhara's gloriously beaded sari and Desh's long tunic were a pure white. The couple was soon lost in a crowd of well-wishers.

Only when the music filled the room with swirling lights and a rocking beat did the crowd around the couple disperse to rush the dance floor. Through the activity, Marta glimpsed a radiant Dhara ducking as she wove through the dancers toward the three of them clustered by the window. Behind her trailed a tall, grinning Desh, clasping her hand tightly.

"A happy bride," Wendy stated, "should look like that."

And she, Kelly, and Wendy—all three of them, all at once—threw their arms wide in welcome.

acknowledgments

Novelists are thought to live solitary lives. That's pure fiction. Like most of my colleagues, I live in a house full of children, on a street full of good neighbors, and in a working community teeming with fascinating people. My stories could never be written without help and guidance from these dear friends.

The first tip of the hat goes to the Sunday Evening Ladies, my darling critique group, whose insightful opinions are given with a dose of laughter and always make the book better. Thanks, too, to Shobhan Bantwal, a fabulous novelist who reviewed this manuscript with an eye toward Indian culture; to Carol Higgins, former volunteer EMT and current cardiothoracic nurse, who guided me through the thorny thicket of medical issues; and to Tom Donatelli, bon vivant, for nautical advice and raucous dinnertime conversation. Everything I did right is due to them; anything I did wrong is purely my own fault.

I'd also like to raise a huge huzzah to the folks at Grand Central Publishing. The foreign rights staff continues to do a mighty job selling my stories to far shores (and, yes, I'm sure we'll convince those Frenchmen to stop laughing at my last name, eventually). I marvel at the creativity of the art department, the hard work of the marketing folks, and the energy of the sales staff. Thanks for doing such a wonderful job screaming from the rooftops.

Most of all, I'd like to express my gratitude to Alex Logan, strong advocate and editor extraordinaire. Thanks for adding this filly to your stable.

reading group guide

one good friend deserves another

1. What's your opinion of these women's rules for relationships? How many of them have you followed? How many have you broken?
    a. Choose Your Own Man.
    b. Make Sure Your Friends Approve.
    c. No One-Night Stands.
    d. Trust Your Instincts.
    e. Never Make the Same Mistake Twice.
    f. After a Break-up, Wait Six Months Before Dating Again.

2. If you were to write five rules of your own for romantic relationships, what would they be? Do you think these rules are universal, or purely applicable to your own personal experiences? How do they compare with the rules written by others in your reading group?

3. During the course of this story each woman makes a huge leap of faith. Kelly, when she decides to let Trey back into her life; Dhara, when she decides on an arranged marriage; Wendy, when she determines to end her engagement to Parker; and, finally, Marta, when she decides to stop bullet-pointing her way through life. In your own life, have you ever decided not to follow what would be considered the logical path, and instead "embraced the chaos"? If so, what were the consequences, for better or worse?

4. All four of these women could be called "straddlers"— that is, they straddle two different worlds, ethnically, culturally, or socioeconomically. Is there anything in your background that can relate to this sense of dislocation?

5. In the beginning, Kelly is in awe of the privileges and possibilities that growing up in a wealthy family could provide, and only toward the end does she begin to realize the many intangible benefits she received growing up in a hard-working, blue-collar family. Think about your own particularly individual upbringings. What sort of intangible benefits—or detriments—came from your early formative experiences?

6. Which of the four characters do you relate to most, and why?

7. Dhara makes, by American standards, a very drastic

choice when she allows her parents to arrange a marriage for her. How do you feel about her choice? Do you think it is possible to find happiness in such a union?

8. If your parents were arranging a marriage for you—or if you were to go speed-dating in search of a date—what sort of easy-to-determine qualities would you look for in a potential mate? How long is your list? What qualities would make your "absolutely not" list?

9. Kelly makes an enormous leap of faith when she decides to become involved with the man who treated her so terribly, years ago. How do you feel about her decision? Was she right to keep it from her friends? Do you think the relationship between Kelly and Trey could mature into something more lasting?

10. Marta struggles with issues of emotional intimacy, using sex as the primary vehicle to express her feelings. The pregnancy and subsequent miscarriage have left deep emotional scars. Do you think it is possible that Marta will find someone with whom she'll feel comfortable enough to finally fall in love? Or could Marta be happier, ultimately, as a single woman?

11. Wendy arguably has the most difficult breakup in this novel. Does she handle it well? Would you have handled it differently? Is there any gentle way, really, to end a long-term relationship?

12. Wendy falls for Gabriel quite quickly, and the feelings

appear mutual. Is she right to destroy a long-term, well-tested relationship for a sudden, unexpected surge of feeling for a relative stranger? Do you think, considering their disparate backgrounds, that Gabriel and Wendy could have a successful relationship?

13. Marta wants so very much to be accepted for who she is, but it seems every arena in which she arrives—at home, in high school, in law school, and at a large law firm—she's the oddball. What is it about her three good friends from college that makes her relax her hypervigilant sense of oddity to finally enjoy some emotional intimacy?

14. During the time period of this novel, Cole struggles with some very serious demons. Do you feel that Dhara should have postponed the wedding to care for the man who'd been such a huge part of her life for so many years? Or did she make the right decision, making a clean break? If she had stayed with Cole, do you think, ultimately, they would have had a successful marriage?

15. Trey has some fundamental character flaws that are thwarting his ability to live successfully, both in his romantic and professional life. Do you think, at his age, he will be capable of recognizing these flaws and taking the necessary steps to change his life for the better?

author's note

I am a mother of three teenage daughters. They are smart, lovely young women who are the source of all joy—and chaos!—in my life. I didn't write *One Good Friend Deserves Another* because I'm considering arranged marriages for them. But I'll sheepishly confess that the thought has crossed my mind.

I can't help myself. Like any mother, I feel the possibility of their future pain keenly. I wish I could protect them from heartbreak in the same the way I once protected them from scraped knees, burned fingers, and broken glass. I know that's impossible. There isn't a salve in the world that can mend a broken heart.

And I've yet to meet a woman who hasn't experienced one.

Here's the paradox: When I'm out to dinner with new friends, one of the first questions I ask is how the couple met. We all have our tales. Strange are the circumstances that can lead a German sailor to fall in love with an American college student while they both happen to be abroad in

Spain. Or how an engaged woman could abruptly end her wedding plans after bumping into an old boyfriend at a high school reunion. Or how a rugby player could surrender his plans to enter a New York City law school just to follow his girl to the opposite coast. A moment of madness for which this now married woman is profoundly grateful.

All these tenuous connections, odd circumstances, and life-altering risks are precisely what led—improbably, impossibly—to the solid relationships many of my friends and I now cherish. Hearts thrive on chaos, in fiction as in life. What kind of existence would any of us lead, without that glorious unpredictability?

So this mother braces herself for the inevitable. I know my future sons-in-law are out there. I know my girls will eventually find them. Until then, I will do what any mother, and any friend, should do. I will breathe very slowly, keep my counsel until asked, and hope the fates are kind.

For what I really want for my daughters is a chance to experience wonder, joy, love…and to gather some breathtaking stories of their own.